THE FRONTIERS SAGA
PART 2: ROGUE CASTES
EPISODE 1

ESCALATION
RYK BROWN

CHAPTER ONE

The young man's head snapped to the right as the woman's open hand made contact with his left cheek. By now, he had grown accustomed to such reactions. "I'll take that as a no, then," he said to himself as she stormed off in a huff. He flexed his jaw from side to side, then picked up his drink from the bar and tossed it down his throat. "Another, please," he told the bartender, sliding his empty glass toward him.

"This ain't that kind of place," the bartender warned as he filled the empty shot glass.

The young man looked to either side. The bar was full of scantily clad women, some in groups, some alone, but all of them trying their best to look appealing to the young men prowling the dingy, poorly lit establishment, looking for the same thing he was. "Right," he replied, picking up his refilled glass and emptying it in one smooth motion.

"Maybe it's your style, Josh."

It was a woman's voice, older, and one that Josh knew all too well. "Go away, Neli, you'll scare away all the respectable young women."

"Don't you think you're doing that on your own, already?" Neli signaled the bartender. "Palean rum, one ice."

"What are you doing here?" Josh asked, still not looking at her.

"You might try talking to them a bit...you know, *before* you ask them to perform some deviant sexual act." Neli picked up her drink and took a sip. "You might not get your face slapped as often."

"I don't like to waste time," Josh replied, only half-joking. He finally turned and looked at her. "Does Marcus know you're here?" he asked, one eyebrow raised.

"Marcus sent me."

"You mean, he finally came to his senses and sent you packing?"

Neli sneered at him. "We got another run. Departure in two hours."

"But I just got here," Josh protested.

Neli examined Josh's face. "Not by the looks of it," she retorted as she picked up her drink again. "You should try to alternate between right-handed and left-handed women...maybe it'll even out the redness."

Josh flashed a fake smile at her as he put his credits on the counter to pay for his drinks. He looked at Neli as she tossed back the rest of her drink.

"Thanks for the drink," she told him as she turned to leave. "See you back at the ship."

Josh rolled his eyes and placed another credit on the counter. "Keep it."

"See ya next time, Josh," the bartender replied.

Josh made his way to the door, then turned back and scanned the crowd. He flipped his jacket collar up and sighed, then continued through the door.

Josh hated Arikar this time of year. It rained nearly every evening, like clockwork. And it wasn't a pleasant, refreshing rain. It was a dreary, cold downpour that soaked you to the bone if you stayed out for too long.

At least they would be getting off this world in a couple hours.

* * *

Jessica maintained a steady pace as she followed the group of men about twenty meters ahead of her.

There were five of them, four younger men in black suits, all surrounding a much older one carrying a metal briefcase attached to his wrist with a silver chain. The group couldn't have been more obvious if they tried. It was another one of the stupid traditions commonly found on fringe worlds, to proudly display one's wealth and power at all times, especially in public. Stupid, yes, but it did guarantee a steady stream of opportunities for some easy credits, and jobs like this generally paid quite well.

She had been tailing them for only a few blocks before she spotted another tail. A couple on the opposite side of the street, dressed inappropriately for warmer weather on Jixbo. "Male and female, opposite side of the street," she mumbled, as if talking to herself.

"*I have them,*" a voice replied in her earpiece.

"*Another pair, fifty meters ahead of the target,*" another voice reported. "*Two men, business suits, one brown, one blue. Opposite direction... They're both carrying.*"

"What about the couple?" Jessica wondered. "They carrying?"

"*Negative.*"

"*Two behind you, Jess,*" a third voice reported anxiously. "*Casual dress. White shirt and red shirt. Both are carrying.*"

"That's six," Jessica realized. "You think they're all on the same team, or is there more than one interested party here?"

"*Weapons are all the same,*" the first voice reported. "*Jixian stunners. The low-power kind that don't set off the cheap detectors most of these building owners use.*"

"How much is this guy carrying?" Jessica

3

wondered aloud.

"*I don't know, but I think we should be charging more,*" the first voice replied.

"Three, keep on the couple across the street," Jessica instructed over her hidden comm-set. "Two, on the ones in the suits. One, stay on the target group."

"*What about the two behind you?*" the first voice inquired.

"I'll handle them. You just keep on the target, in case one of his men is in on this. If that case gets away from us, we don't get paid."

"*Copy.*"

Jessica slowed her pace, taking a less-efficient path between pedestrians moving in the opposite direction, so as not to appear obvious to the two men approaching from behind.

"*Target is approaching the intersection,*" the first voice warned. "*He should be turning to the right.*"

The two men in casual attire passed Jessica to her right, neither of them paying her any undue attention as they picked up their pace. "My two have picked up speed," Jessica warned in a barely audible voice. She moved to her right, falling in behind the two men in casual attire, then adjusted her pace to keep up with them.

"*Target has stopped,*" the first voice reported in a concerned tone.

"*Suits are crossing the intersection,*" the second voice announced. "*They're drawing!*"

"Take them out," Jessica whispered, her eyes fixed on the two men in front of her. The man on the right, the one wearing the red shirt, pulled a stunner from his right pocket.

Two bright blue, needle-like beams of energy

struck the two men in suits who were advancing confidently across the intersection as they pulled their weapons. The beams struck each man in the middle of their heads, burning through their skulls in an instant and dropping them in the middle of the street.

Tires screeched as vehicles slammed on their brakes. People screamed, and pedestrians scattered in all directions as two more beams of blue struck the couple charging in from the opposite side of the street.

Jessica ran forward. After three steps, she tucked forward, placing both hands on the ground, and flipped over, popping up into the air. Her feet struck the men in front of her, both red and white shirts, in the sides of their heads, knocking them sideways.

The black-suited guard standing to the back right of the old man carrying the metal briefcase had pulled his weapon, but instead of turning to defend, he shot the similarly dressed guard in front of him. His partner to his left did the same, dropping the guard in front of him.

Jessica landed on both feet, then spun around to face the red-shirted man to her left who had not fallen all the way to the ground. His stunner still in hand, he brought it around and fired. Jessica anticipated his move and dropped to the ground, spinning around to her left as she fell. Her left leg shot out and caught the red-shirted man's leg, taking him down. She rolled, came back up to her knees, and then slammed down with her right elbow, driving it into the fallen man's nose.

As a needle beam of blue struck the rear right guard in the back of the head, the rear left guard pulled a laser knife, and in a single, smooth motion, chopped off the old man's forearm. The old man screamed out in pain as he fell to his knees.

Jessica rolled, pulling the body of the stunned, bleeding, red-shirted man over her as his white-shirted partner fired his stunner in her direction. The yellow flash struck the red-shirted man on top of her, instantly rendering him unconscious.

"*I've got it!*" a man's voice cried out a few meters ahead of her.

"*The case is on the move!*" the first voice reported over Jessica's comm-set.

Another blue needle beam struck the white-shirted man square in his chest as he was about to fire his stunner again. The white-shirted man's eyes doubled in size as he gasped for air, a sizzling hole now in his chest. Before he could look down at the wound, a second blue beam pierced his forehead with a crackling sound. The white-shirted man's head snapped back, and he dropped to his knees, falling backwards to the pavement.

"*The case is moving west! Crossing the street! Anyone got a shot?*"

"*Negative!*"

"*Too many bystanders! I've got nothing.*"

"Three! Move to the other side of the building and see if you can pick him up on the other side!" Jessica instructed as she pushed the unconscious, red-shirted man off of her and quickly scrambled to her feet.

"*Three is moving!*"

"One, scan for secondaries!" Jessica ordered as she ran in pursuit of the black-suited man who had hacked off the arm of the man he had supposedly been protecting, making off with the metal briefcase still attached to the old man's forearm. "I'm on him!"

"Two more coming from behind you!" the second voice warned. *"Hit the deck, Jess!"*

Jessica didn't question her instructions, and immediately dove to the pavement as two balls of yellow light streaked over her head, slamming into innocent bystanders desperately trying to get away from the commotion, knocking them to the pavement.

Two more beams of blue rained down from above, striking the two men who had just fired stunners at Jessica, killing them both.

"You're clear!" the second voice reported.

Jessica jumped to her feet to continue her pursuit, but had lost sight of her target. "Which way?"

"Straight ahead, down the street to your left," the first voice instructed. *"Three, he should be coming out your side in five seconds."*

"Three is in position!"

Jessica charged off in the direction given, skirting around the people trying to help the stunned bystanders who were lying unconscious in the street. She could hear sirens in the distance as the Jixian authorities responded to the incident. She had minutes to catch the man with the briefcase and take possession, or things would get a lot more complicated.

"I've got him!" the third voice reported.

Jessica heard the unmistakable sound of energy beams blowing apart the pavement as she rounded the corner of the building and headed to her left down the cross street.

"Damn! He's still moving!" the third voice reported. *"He knows I'm up here! He's using the traffic as cover!"*

A man stepped out of the building without warning, directly in Jessica's path. Jessica ran into

7

him, and he grabbed her as if to keep her from falling.

"Sorry, miss," the man said. He smiled, revealing a gold tooth. But for some reason, the man wasn't letting her go.

Jessica squinted, noticing something sinister in the man's smile.

"*Runner is turning right, heading up Twenty-First!*" the third voice reported.

The man still hadn't released her. Jessica drove her knee into his groin. As he bent over in pain, she broke his grip, wrapping her arm around his neck, and walked up the building wall to her left. She pushed off, and came over the top of him. The man twisted to his left in well-practiced fashion, to prevent her from snapping his neck as she rolled over his back. He was left with no choice but to fall onto his back. As he hit the sidewalk, he continued to roll, utilizing the momentum she had imparted onto him.

Jessica landed less than a meter to the right, but was taken down as the gold-toothed man rolled into her legs. A moment later, he was on his feet and trying to drive his boot heel into her face. Jessica rolled to avoid the blow as a blue beam of energy struck the gold-toothed man's shoulder.

The gold-toothed man roared in pain. It wasn't a cry of pain, but rather a pain-fueled howl of fury. Jessica's foot came up and struck him in the side, and another needle-like, blue beam struck him in the neck. His growl was replaced with a gurgling sound as blood spewed from his open, sizzling wound. The gold-toothed man grasped his neck, but still stood... until a third needle beam pierced his skull and took him down for good.

"Thanks," Jessica said as she scrambled to her

feet and resumed her pursuit.

"*You're leaving my view,*" the first voice warned. "*Three, cover her as she comes around to your right.*"

Jessica reached the end of the street and headed left.

"*I've got her,*" the third voice acknowledged.

"*Two is almost to street level,*" the second voice reported. "*I'll be a block behind you when you turn up Twenty-First, so I should catch you by the time you cross Alder.*"

"In your dreams," Jessica retorted as she ran up the street and turned right onto Twenty-First Avenue. She made the next intersection in seconds, slowing just enough to scan both directions for the intruder. She heard screams directly ahead and continued up Twenty-First Avenue, sure that the commotion was caused by the man she was pursuing. "He's still headed east on Twenty-First!" she announced. "OUT OF THE WAY!" she ordered pedestrians in front of her.

"*Authorities are three out,*" the first voice warned over her comm-set. "*Jumper is standing off ten clicks south.*"

Ahead, the crowd of bystanders parted, staring at something on the ground. As Jessica charged through the gaping hole in the crowd, she spotted what they were all looking at...the old man's severed forearm lying on the sidewalk. At least she was headed in the right direction.

The sound of screeching tires and the crunch of metal and breaking glass to her left told Jessica which way to turn at the next intersection. She veered left, darting out into the middle of the street, not wanting to lose time by weaving her way through panicked bystanders. By now, most of the traffic had stopped, halted by the sudden commotion in the distance.

"I've got eyes on!" Jessica exclaimed, finally spotting her fleeing prey. "He's headed down Baron Street! Southbound! I'll have him by Nineteenth!"

"*Are you sure?*" the first voice asked.

"Just call in the jumper to pick everyone up!" she ordered as she closed on the target. "Then meet me at Nineteenth and Baron!"

"*Copy that!*" the first voice replied. "*Three, stay put, I'm coming to you!*"

"*I've got her crossing Twentieth!*" the second voice reported. "*I'll head up the alley and converge with her!*"

"*Jumper One! Eagle One! Move to position three for pickup!*"

He was only three meters ahead of her now, sprinting between two lanes of stopped traffic. Every time he looked back at Jessica, the distance between them closed a few more centimeters.

"*Jumper One moving to position three, in five.*"

The target began to slow as he approached the intersection, wanting to avoid running out into the moving cross traffic. Jessica was one lane to his left. She made a running jump up onto the back of the last car before the intersection, ran onto its roof and leapt into the air just as a flash of blue-white light came from behind her. As the sound of the jump-flash followed, she flew through the air, landing on the fleeing man with the metal briefcase, bringing him to the ground. They both rolled across the street as vehicles in either direction screeched to a stop. The man lost his grip on the metal briefcase, sending it skidding across the pavement. He rolled to his right, Jessica to her left. The metal briefcase struck the tire of a parked vehicle and bounced back nearly a meter into the street.

Both Jessica and the target rose to their feet at the same time. The man looked at Jessica, then the metal briefcase, and then back at Jessica again. The sirens were getting closer, and there was a roar of shuttle engines only a few blocks away. A sinister smile formed on the man's face as he pulled a long-bladed knife from its sheath under his jacket. "Wanna dance, bitch?" he snarled.

The man charged at Jessica. She waited for him to close in, then spun to her right and moved her left foot out slightly to catch his. He stumbled, and Jessica spun around to drive her closed right fist into the back of his head. The man rolled forward, coming back to his feet, knife still in hand as he turned to face her once again.

Jessica moved first this time, stepping into him, knowing that he would react by lunging forward with his knife hand. She reacted with practiced precision, swiftly and strongly grabbing his knife hand as she twisted and drove her knee up into his forearm. It gave with an audible snap, eliciting a bloodcurdling cry of pain from her would-be dance partner. She crouched low and used his forward momentum, causing him to fall over the top of her with only the slightest of tugs. As he did so, she pulled the weapon from his hand as the break in his forearm forced his knife hand open. She followed him over, flipping over herself, feet coming up from behind. He hit the ground, landing on his back, the air knocked from his lungs. A split-second later, she was on one knee beside him, plunging his own knife deep into his heart.

Jessica gave the knife a twist, opening up the wound to ensure a rapid death. She paused a moment, then released her grip on the knife and stood. She turned and looked down at the man. "I don't dance, asshole."

Sergeant Todd came running up to her as the sound of the jump shuttle's engines grew closer. "Damn, Jess. That was a nice move."

"Grab the case," she instructed as she reached down and pulled the knife out of the dead man's chest. "Thanks for the knife," she told his corpse as she wiped the blade off on his sleeve.

Sergeant Todd picked up the case as the jump shuttle descended into a hover over the intersection and dropped its rescue line. He moved over to Jessica as she slipped one of the two rescue harnesses over her head and under her arms. The sergeant did the same, and seconds later they were hauled inside the open door of the combat jump shuttle by the smiling face of its crew chief, Sergeant Torwell.

Jessica took her seat as Sergeant Todd handed the briefcase to her. Jessica pulled the electronic key card out of her pocket and inserted it into the locking mechanism of the case as the shuttle began to climb out. A small, orange status light on the key card flashed several times, then turned green, and the latches on the metal briefcase popped open. She waited for a moment while Sergeant Torwell closed the side door, then opened the case. Inside were several title documents. "Stocks, bonds, titles, letters of authenticity... It's all here." Jessica smiled broadly. "Let's go get paid, boys."

* * *

"You are using the close personal friendship between your late father and the owner of the Glendanon to force this deal upon us," Mister Angus argued.

Deliza sat quietly for a moment, pretending to ponder the elder businessman's charges. "And if I am?"

"You know very well that the Pentaurus Trade Commission does not care for such arrangements," Mister Angus reminded her, growing more furious at the young woman's failure to acquiesce to his position and level of respect within the interstellar trade community.

"Except when such arrangements work in their favor," Deliza continued calmly. "Or when it is between well-established businessmen such as yourself."

"You have..."

"Did you not use nepotism to steal a competing contract out from under us in the Devi system two years ago?" Deliza wondered aloud. "And then again last year to land the contract with the Hawson Company? And wasn't the Allen deal the result of your relationship with their transportation director, Paulo Asadin?"

"In business, young lady, it's often about who you know. It's about people preferring to do business with those whom they know, and trust..."

"As I am quickly learning, Mister Angus. Hence my desire to maintain my working relationship with the owners of the Glendanon. However, if you believe that it is fair for you to use your connections to land contracts, but it is unfair when I do the same, then feel free to file a complaint with the commission." Deliza smiled politely. "In the meantime, our offer stands. You can either accept it now and enjoy a fair and equitable arrangement for both our companies, or you can stew on it for a few days, at which point you will have no choice but to accept my offer. Of course, by that time, since you will be stuck, I will most likely raise our per-pound shipping rates."

"You would do that, just to spite me?"

Deliza continued smiling. "Wouldn't you?"

Mister Angus stared at her for a moment. "Yes, I suppose I would." He sighed. "How old are you?"

"Twenty-seven Earth years, thirty-two by Haven's calendar, twenty-six on Corinair, and I believe twenty-five and a half by your world's standards. Is that important?"

Mister Angus sighed again. "Send the contracts to my attorney," he agreed as he rose. "I'll have them back to you by the next comm-drone."

Deliza sat quietly as Mister Angus and his staff left the conference room. Biarra, her new assistant, quickly packed up the briefcase and prepared to leave. Finally, once they were alone in the room, she could no longer control herself. "That was incredible," Biarra gushed, barely able to contain her excitement. "You had him backed into a corner with no way out. How did you do that?"

"He put himself into that corner," Deliza replied simply. "I just let him do it and then made sure he was aware that he had done so, once I was sure he had no way out."

"Did you see the look on his face, though?" Biarra continued. She stopped a moment, a realization dawning on her. "Is that why you had me look up all his old contracts?"

"It's all about the research," Deliza said as she rose. "Call Loki and tell him we will be departing in thirty minutes. I'd like to get back to Corinair before dinner."

"Yes ma'am."

* * *

"Where are we going, Cap?" Josh asked as he walked up the Seiiki's aft cargo ramp.

"Paradar, Rama, and back here again," Marcus told him as he lashed down the last stack of cargo pods.

"I thought we were done for the day," Josh wondered. He looked around. "Where's our wheels?"

"Dalen took them into town to get some provisions," Marcus said.

"I thought provisions were Neli's job," Josh pointed out to the captain, who still hadn't spoken.

"She was busy hunting you down," Captain Tuplo explained, casting a disapproving glance at his copilot.

"You said we were done for the day, Captain," Josh defended. "Otherwise, I would've stayed in port."

"Relax, Josh," Captain Tuplo replied. "I'm kidding. The Borabay went down with a bad thruster, so we got tossed this run at the last minute."

Josh moved over to help the captain lash down some loose gear. "I thought we weren't taking runs so close to Takara?"

"That's what I told Marcus," Captain Tuplo agreed.

"I'm just trying to keep up good relations with the port officer," Marcus explained. "Besides, it's a cake run, Captain. All the cargo is legit, and the passengers all have proper ID and travel papers. I checked them myself."

"You know I don't like going into ports controlled by nobles," Captain Tuplo reminded him. "They charge way too much for port fees, and we've been on a tight budget ever since our thousand-jump overhaul."

"Which we're not going to recover from if we don't

take every run offered to us," Marcus argued. "I ran the numbers on this one, Connor. We'll still make a profit on the run. Not much, but still a profit."

"Did you factor in the overhaul cost of each jump?" Captain Tuplo wondered as he finished stowing the last of the loose gear.

"Yes, sir, I did it just like you showed me," Marcus grumbled as he climbed down off the stack of cargo pods. "How many times are you going to rake me about that one, Captain?"

"Until I'm sure you'll never forget," Captain Tuplo replied. "Josh, go forward and check the passenger cabins are ready."

"But that's Neli's job," Josh complained.

"Everyone does what they can, when they can," Captain Tuplo said sternly. "Besides, Neli's changing out of her wet clothes after tracking you down. Now go."

Josh rolled his eyes and headed up the ladder at the front of the cargo deck, disappearing through the hatch a moment later.

"When are those two going to make peace?" Captain Tuplo asked Marcus.

"She's tryin', Cap, honest she is," Marcus promised. "He just doesn't like her."

Captain Tuplo paused a moment, stroking his thick beard as he examined the state of their cargo bay. "See if you can find some more pods going to Rama or Paradar. Some strays that got left behind, or something."

"Where are we going to put them?" Marcus wondered. "There's barely enough room for the vehicle as it is."

"We'll be back here in a few hours, right? Leave it behind. Pay the cargo captain to store it for us until we get back. We'll make more than enough to cover the storage fee by hauling the extra pods."

"And if we don't get back as scheduled?" Marcus asked.

"That only happened the one time," Captain Tuplo said. "How many times are you going to rake *me* over *that* one?"

"You're not the one who had to carry rations for five kilometers," Marcus replied.

"Go and rustle up some more cargo," Captain Tuplo suggested. "We start loading passengers in one hour."

* * *

Jessica and Sergeant Todd walked into the client's office and up to his desk. "Here's your case," she said, placing the metal briefcase in front of him on the desk. "Pay up."

The client opened the case and pulled out the documents, carefully inspecting each one. "Was it really necessary to kill all those people?" the client asked as he examined the documents. "They were only carrying stunners, after all."

"Tell that to the one who wanted me to dance with his knife," Jessica replied flatly. "Now pay us, so we can get off this crummy rock of yours."

"Yes, I imagine that you would like to jump out before the authorities catch up to you, wouldn't you?"

"Or, I could go to them directly, and show them the contents there, and let them sort it all out," Jessica suggested. "It should only take them a few months, right? That won't interfere with your client's plans, will it? Wait, those are transfer documents, right? Don't they expire in less than a day?"

The man on the other side of the desk looked up

from the documents. "Everything appears to be in order. See my assistant in the outer office, the one you so rudely ignored on your way in here, and she will transfer the agreed-upon funds to your credit chip. You did bring your credit chip with you?"

Jessica held up her credit chip. "Tell me, Beekman, are all you insurance guys such assholes, or is it just you?"

"Nature of the business, I'm afraid." The agent shrugged and turned his attention back to the documents. "Until next time, Miss Nash. Safe travels."

Jessica rolled her eyes, then turned and headed back out into the outer office. "We've got to stop taking these bullshit security gigs," she mumbled to Sergeant Todd on their way out of the office.

"They pay well," the sergeant reminded her. "And we need the extra funds to repair the boxcar."

"I'd much rather be in a straight-up shooting war," Jessica said, "with someone worth killing."

"I hear you, Lieutenant," the sergeant agreed.

Jessica handed the credit chip to the girl in the outer office.

"Preferred currency?" the girl asked as she inserted the credit chip into the reader on her desk.

"PEUs, please," Jessica replied.

"Yes, ma'am."

Jessica tapped her comm-set. "We'll be out in a few minutes," she called. "How long do you need?"

"*We'll be topped off in five,*" Sergeant Torwell replied. "*We'll be there to pick you up in ten minutes.*"

"Here you are," the girl said as she handed the credit chip back to Jessica.

Jessica pressed the chip between her thumb and forefinger. The chip recognized her prints and displayed a balance sheet in the air directly in front of her. Jessica smiled. "Pleasure doing business with you." She placed the chip back in her pocket and headed out the door, with Sergeant Todd close behind.

"It's still not enough," the sergeant mentioned as they left the office and headed down the hallway.

"It's a start," Jessica said.

"Hey, I saw a glopsy cart on the corner when we came in. Can we stop and get something to eat? I'm starving."

"You like that shit?"

"Are you kidding? Have you tried it with the sweet and sour sauce?"

"Fine, as long as we're off this world and jumping our way back to Sherma in ten minutes."

* * *

The limousine rolled across the tarmac, passing by several private shuttles before finally arriving at its destination. It pulled up next to a shuttle that was not the largest on the line at the spaceport, but was impressive nonetheless. It had clean lines, a black hull with gold trim, and the logo for Ranni Enterprises next to the boarding hatch. Unlike most of the other corporate shuttles, this ship was not a conversion. She was built from the ground up as a corporate jump shuttle.

Loki stood proudly at the boarding hatch. He had been serving as the sole pilot for this shuttle since it began its service life five years ago, and he loved every minute of it. The ship was a joy to operate, with more automation and safety features than one could imagine. For something to go wrong with this ship, you had to *make* it go wrong.

The ship was small, with a passenger capacity of

only four, plus the two seats in the cockpit. Although it was comfortable, it was still cramped inside. However, their trips were always short, lasting no more than thirty minutes to an hour at the most. All in all, it was an easy, low-stress job that paid well, and allowed him to be home every night with his wife and daughter. It wasn't exciting by any stretch of the imagination, but it *was* safe. And he was doing what he loved to do. He was a pilot.

The limousine door opened, and Deliza and her assistant, Biarra, stepped out.

"Miss Ta'Akar," Loki greeted.

Deliza smiled. After all these years, Loki still insisted on playing the role of a polite, corporate shuttle pilot. She had told him time and again that he didn't need to be so formal, as they had been friends for nearly a decade, ever since Loki and Josh had rescued her and her family from Haven. But Loki insisted on the formalities, at least in public. "Everything ready to go?" she asked as she approached.

"Yes, ma'am. We already have our departure clearance, and can be wheels up in five minutes."

"Excellent. I'm starving."

"We should be on the ground at Aitkenna in thirty minutes," Loki assured her. "I trust your negotiations went well?"

"Well enough," Deliza replied as she stepped up into the shuttle, and disappeared through the hatch.

"She was amazing," Biarra whispered as she followed Deliza.

Loki smiled as he followed them inside and closed the hatch. Biarra had only been serving as Deliza's personal assistant for a few months now, and this was her fourth business trip with her. Yet she was still amazed by everything Deliza Ta'Akar did.

Loki turned aft to make sure that the ladies were in their seats, then stepped forward between the seats, and slid down into the pilot's seat on the left of the cockpit. He tapped the auto-start button and watched the primary display screen on his console as the ship's computers cycled through all the pre-start checks. Thirty seconds later, the shuttle's engines began to spin up, and thirty seconds after that, the ship's flight control computer showed they were ready for departure.

"Dobson Control, Ranni One," Loki called over his comm-set. "At pad one four, with India. Ready for departure."

"Ranni One, Dobson Control. Cleared for liftoff. On wheels up, fly heading one four five to one zero thousand, then proceed as filed and jump at two zero thousand to transition Alpha Sierra Seven Four."

"Cleared for liftoff on one four, heading one four five to one zero thousand, as filed, and jump to Alpha Sierra Seven Four at two zero thousand, for Ranni One."

"Ranni One, read-back correct. Safe flight."

Loki pressed the intercom button. "Prepare for liftoff," he announced. He double-checked the flight profile in the auto-flight computer one last time, and then pressed the execute button. The whine of the shuttle's engines increased in pitch and intensity, and a few seconds later, the shuttle rose smoothly from the pad, climbing at a slow, yet constant rate as its nose rotated around to its first course heading.

The landing gear lights switched from green to red, then went out as the gear door lights lit up green. The ship began to accelerate forward, and its climb rate increased as its engines went to full power. In a few minutes, they would reach their assigned jump point, and the ship would auto-jump to the assigned transition zone well beyond the standard orbits of Dobson. All Loki had to do was sit back and monitor the shuttle's progress.

Yup, Josh would hate this, Loki mused.

* * *

Captain Tuplo walked across the tarmac toward his ship, only protected from the pouring Palean rain by his long, black trench coat and its oversized hood.

Marcus stood at the top of the ramp, just inside the Seiiki's cargo bay, watching as his employer approached. Most people ran from cover to cover when it was raining this hard, but not his captain. Connor Tuplo walked, unaffected by the downpour. Marcus had often wondered if there was some special tech installed in the captain's jacket, something that reduced or negated the bitter cold that the storms of this world carried. In the five years that Marcus and Josh had been in Captain Tuplo's employ, he could not remember ever seeing the captain leave the Seiiki without that coat. And when he wasn't wearing it, it was locked away in his cabin.

"Captain," Marcus greeted as Captain Tuplo walked up the boarding ramp.

Captain Tuplo pushed back his hood and looked around the tightly packed cargo bay. "Looks like you squeezed in everything you could. Nicely done, Marcus."

"Thank you, sir."

"I trust we're about ready?" the captain asked as he continued forward, making his way to the aft, portside ladder.

"Last of the passengers are boarding now, Cap'n."

"Let's close her up then," the captain instructed as he climbed the ladder. "Tell Josh to start the departure prep. I'll be up after I dry off and change."

"Yes, sir," Marcus replied, twisting the cargo ramp control lever to retract the ramp and close the cargo bay doors.

Captain Tuplo ascended the short ladder, stepped onto the port landing, and moved through the hatch into the corridor.

"Captain," Dalen called from the forward end of the corridor. "He did it again."

"Did what again, Voss?" the captain asked as he headed toward him down the narrow corridor.

"Marcus packed so much shit into the cargo hold that I couldn't get to the engineering crawl spaces if I wanted to. How the fuck am I supposed to fix something if it breaks in flight?"

"I thought your job was to make sure things *didn't* break in flight," Captain Tuplo remarked as he reached the door to his cabin.

"Of course, but..."

"I'll make sure Marcus shifts the load around to keep the crawl space hatches clear once we off-load some of the cargo on Paradar."

"Thank you, Captain, but can you tell him not to..."

"You know, Dalen, you are an adult. You can tell him yourself."

"He doesn't listen to me, Cap'n. He only listens to you."

Captain Tuplo sighed. Dalen Voss was a gifted mechanic, but he *was* a kid, barely old enough to leave home. Because of that, Dalen felt uncomfortable standing up to Marcus, who was old enough to be his father. And Marcus saw little reason to listen to anything Dalen had to say, regardless of how skilled the young man was at keeping the ship's systems in proper working order. "I'll speak to Marcus," he promised as he disappeared into his cabin.

Captain Tuplo closed the door, removed his overcoat and hung it up on a hook on the wall next to his gun belt. Although runs in the more prosperous regions of the Pentaurus sector did not pay as well, especially after the higher port fees and propellant costs, at least he didn't have to carry a weapon at all times.

He slipped off his foul-weather boots and heavy trousers, replacing them with black pants, deck shoes, and his captain's shirt. They were carrying passengers on this trip, and he would have to pass through the forward cabin to get to the flight deck. If the good side of plying the inner Pentaurus sector was not having to carry a gun, the bad side was always having to play the part of captain in front of passengers.

Captain Tuplo quickly shook the water from his thick beard and smoothed it down with his hand. He then placed the traditional captain's hat on his head and exited his cabin.

A few steps forward and Captain Tuplo was through the forward hatch and in the forward passenger cabin. Between this cabin and the one above the cargo bay, the Seiiki could comfortably carry fifty paying passengers. It had been a big financial gamble for the captain to invest in the conversion of those spaces to carry passengers, but it had increased their earning potential significantly, especially after the idea of traveling by jump drive became more commonplace. Whenever possible, Captain Tuplo had chosen to sell the seats directly, and at a lower price than the passenger-only carriers, hoping to attract people who normally could not afford the high cost of interstellar travel. It had worked, at least for a while. But eventually, other carriers had realized the potential of that same market, trading higher per-seat prices for volume instead. These days, the only advantage the Seiiki had was the fact that they had not tried to cram too many seats into too small a space.

As usual, the captain earned more than a few worried glances from passengers. With his thick beard and wavy brown hair sticking out at odd angles from under his cap, Connor Tuplo did not exactly engender confidence in those who laid eyes on him, at least not at first. It usually took a few minutes of conversation with the rather quiet captain, and a bit of solid eye contact, to overcome the initial negative reaction to his appearance. But sooner or later, his blue eyes and his polite manner would win a person over.

However, today he was running late, and he avoided the passengers by moving quickly forward. Moments later, he was passing Neli, who was securing the forward hatch.

"Full load?" the captain asked.

"Yes, sir," Neli replied. "Both cabins."

"That's what I like to hear," he replied as turned the corner and ascended the steps up onto the flight deck.

The cockpit of the Seiiki was where Captain Tuplo felt most at home. She was not the newest, nor the most modern of ships. Like most other jump ships navigating the Pentaurus sector, her jump drive had been added on shortly after the Karuzari and their leader, posing as the mythical savior Na-Tan from the ancient Legend of Origins, liberated the Pentaurus cluster. But unlike many converted FTL ships, she still had her FTL drives. For some reason, the previous owners had opted for both systems, which had cut into their cargo space. When the decision to carry passengers had been made, all plans to remove the old FTL systems and regain that lost cargo space were abandoned. That had been a decision that Marcus vehemently opposed. 'Passengers just complicate everything' had been his primary argument. Of course, he had been correct to some extent. But financially speaking, it had gotten them a lot more paying runs and was rapidly approaching the point where it would finally pay for itself.

"How are we looking?" Captain Tuplo asked Josh as he climbed into the left seat.

"Pressure on the starboard propellant pump is bouncing around again," Josh replied. "I'm running the backup just to be safe."

"I thought Dalen fixed that."

"I keep telling everyone that Dalen isn't as great as you all think he is, Cap'n."

"It's not Dalen's fault, Josh," Captain Tuplo defended. "He asked for a new pump, and I told him to keep the old one going for a few more hops. The budget is tight enough as it is."

"Why don't you just have him swap the primary with the backup, then?"

"The secondary takes twice as long to remove," the captain explained. "We'd be down for a couple days. Primary only takes a day to swap out."

"We gonna make enough from this run to replace it?"

"If we don't get shafted on fees again," the captain

replied. "Did you file?"

"Yup. Got our departure clearance a few minutes ago. It's good until twenty-two twenty local, which gives us about four minutes to get off the ground."

"Then let's get going," the captain said as he donned his comm-set. "Palee Ground, Seiiki, ready for rollback."

"*Seiiki, Palee Ground. Cleared for rollback. Once clear, taxi via bravo delta foxtrot to departure pad six left and contact tower.*"

"Seiiki cleared for rollback," Captain Tuplo replied over the comms. "Bravo delta foxtrot to d-pad six left and go to tower." Captain Tuplo nodded at Josh, who activated the Seiiki's four independently-powered main gear, sending the ship rolling slowly away from the terminal building. The captain watched the various exterior camera views on the display screens, while keeping an eye on the proximity alert system. Although there was plenty of room for them to maneuver, even in the crowded spaceport complex, one never knew when some idiot in a ground vehicle was going to suddenly dart across your path, mistakenly believing he could make it across safely.

Once clear, the Seiiki stopped, its landing gear rotated, and the ship pivoted to port until its nose was pointed toward the entrance to Bravo taxiway. In a few minutes, they would be on the departure pad and would lift off into the rainy night skies of Palee, climbing to their jump altitude.

* * *

Yanni Hiller sat in his office, studying a set of technical drawings he had copied from the Corinairan version of the Earth's Data Ark. There were still so many technologies from Earth's past, before the bio-digital plague, that had yet to be developed. At times, he felt guilty for the unrestricted access he had to the Ark's data files. The people of the Darvano and Savoy systems, the last two systems in the cluster that were still active members of the Sol-Pentaurus Alliance, were still being fed the technologies contained within the data files at a measured pace, so as not to upset the economies of the sector. Although most of the technologies contained within were inferior to their own, there were still many areas of study, and many ideas that they had not yet explored. A few of those had been exploited by Ranni Enterprises, as well as Deliza's late father, Prince Casimir Ta'Akar, in order to not only fund the Alliance's defense against the Jung Empire back in the Sol sector, but also to give Ranni Enterprises a running start. It was a decision that had not sat well with her. But at the time, Deliza had nearly exhausted her late father's fortune funding the Alliance's efforts back in the Sol sector, as well as helping with the recovery of the Earth itself.

And so, Yanni found himself studying the files, looking for technologies that they could bid on to develop, if given permission by the Corinairan Ark committee. It was the best way to kill time while Deliza was away.

Yanni couldn't help but worry whenever Deliza was away on business. In the beginning, he traveled everywhere with her, but as the years went by, and his own responsibilities at Ranni Enterprises became more demanding of his time, he was more often than not forced to stay behind. At least he was comforted in the knowledge that their trusted friend, Loki, was her pilot, and that wherever she traveled, their security chief had always hired protective services to keep her safe. Although tensions between Corinair and the Takaran nobles had eased over the years, there were still a few powerful noblemen on Takara who would prefer her dead and gone. For as long as the last surviving heir to house Ta'Akar breathed air, those who led the revolution that resulted in her father's untimely demise had no choice but to constantly look over their shoulders.

Yanni would not admit it to anyone, but he often took satisfaction at the thought of those so-called noblemen, in fear of the retribution of Deliza Ta'Akar. To Yanni, she was the sweetest, most gentle woman he had ever known. And although she had gained a reputation as a ruthless businesswoman in recent years, he could not imagine her seeking revenge against those who killed not only her father, but her younger sister as well.

"Are you busy?" a familiar female voice asked from the door.

"Lael," Yanni greeted as he rose from his chair. He immediately noticed the blanketed bundle in her arms. "Oh, my...is this... Is this Ailsa?"

"Yes," Lael replied as she entered Yanni's office. "I wanted to meet Loki when he returned, and I know how much you wanted to meet Ailsa."

"I'm so sorry that I couldn't be there when she was born."

"It's quite all right," Lael assured him. "I know how busy you have been lately. You don't even accompany Deliza anymore."

"I'm starting to realize how difficult it has been for you the last few months," Yanni said as he reached out to peek at baby Ailsa. "Oh, she is so tiny."

"According to my mother, all the women in our family have tiny babies."

"You wouldn't know it by the size of your brothers,"

Yanni joked.

"Would you like to hold her?"

"I don't know," Yanni said, suddenly becoming apprehensive. "Do you think it's all right? I mean, I don't want to hurt her."

"Just support her head like this," Lael explained, demonstrating for him.

Yanni accepted the infant from Lael, taking great care to be as gentle as possible. "She is amazing, Lael. You and Loki must be so happy."

"Yes, we are. I'll be even happier when they return, though. I don't get a moment's rest while Loki is away. He is so good with her. When he is home, if it weren't for the fact that I'm the one with the breasts, I'd never get to hold her," Lael commented with a giggle. She took advantage of the brief respite and sat down. "Any idea when they will arrive?"

"Doran called just before you arrived. He said they should be jumping into the system at any moment now, so about ten minutes or so."

"Good," Lael replied. "It's getting late, and I'm starved."

"Deliza and I are having food delivered to the office tonight. You and Loki are more than welcome to join us."

"Thank you, no. If I know Deliza, it's a working dinner, and I don't think I can handle watching Biarra doing my job."

"Don't worry, it will still be your job when you're ready to return. You know that."

Lael sat watching Yanni bounce baby Ailsa gently in his arms, cooing to her softly. "When are you two going to start having kids?"

"We talked about it, but you know how Deliza is. She wants to make sure the company is completely secure, financially speaking, before we start a family."

"Yes, I do know how she is," Lael agreed. "I don't suppose she's ever given you an estimate?"

"Let's just say it's going to be a few more years and leave it at that." Yanni looked down at baby Ailsa as the infant grasped his pinky. "Although, if she spends any time with you, little one, it may happen much sooner than she thinks... Yes."

* * *

Six jump flashes appeared in orbit above Takara, each of them occurring within seconds of one another. From the flashes, massive ships with black hulls trimmed in crimson appeared. Without any provocation or warning, the six ships opened fire on the Takaran warships in orbit.

The Takaran warships returned fire without hesitation, each of them targeting a different ship. But in that first moment of battle, they were already equally matched in number. Even worse, they appeared to be outgunned.

The Takaran ships began to maneuver, breaking ranks and making for open space in differing directions, making it difficult for the invading ships to concentrate their fire on any one of them. Two Takaran cruisers jumped away, reappearing only a few million kilometers away in order to turn and attack from a more advantageous angle without taking fire. As they turned, another black and crimson ship, this one a battleship, jumped in to ambush them. Within seconds, both cruisers' shields were overwhelmed, and a few seconds later, they were destroyed.

The remaining four ships in orbit over Takara fought bravely. Left with no alternative, they came about sharply to bring their plasma torpedo tubes to bear on the unknown intruders once they cleared the planet. One ship took rounds from a dozen rail guns, as well as plasma weapons. Her shields failed, and the enemy fire soon cut her in half, devastating explosions tearing through her as she came apart. The second ship, a destroyer, was more maneuverable and had already opened up on one of the smaller attacking ships with its forward plasma torpedo cannons. Firing in rapid succession to the point of overheating her plasma generators, the Takaran destroyer scored the first enemy kill of the sudden and unexpected engagement, tearing apart one of the black and crimson frigates. But the battleship that had ambushed the previous two Takaran cruisers appeared behind the destroyer without warning, cutting her victory short with its massive rail guns. Seconds later, the destroyer became the fourth Takaran warship to fall to the attack.

The remaining two frigates were no match for the enemy fleet, and although they chose to die defending their world, their efforts were in vain. Within five minutes of the initial jump flashes, the once mighty Takaran Empire had fallen.

The question was, to whom?

CHAPTER TWO

Commander Golan sat behind the captain's desk in his ready room, studying the supply requests from the ship's various department heads. As the Avendahl's executive officer, supplies were not his responsibility. However, his new quartermaster had only a few months on the job, and a little oversight was necessary.

"*XO, Communications,*" the call came over the intercom.

Commander Golan pressed the intercom button. "XO."

"*Message from Captain Navarro, sir,*" the communications officer reported. "*He is going to be delayed another day. A mechanical problem with his private shuttle has him temporarily grounded on Getzten.*"

Commander Golan sighed in resignation. "Very well," he replied, as he switched off the intercom. His own shore leave would be delayed. It was not an uncommon occurrence for the captain's return to be postponed a day or two. He was, after all, the captain, and the owner of the Avendahl. Relations between the Darvano system and the noble houses of Takara had remained peaceful since the Takaran revolution seven years ago. Thus, both Captain Navarro and Commander Golan had been spending much more time on the surface of Corinair with their families. So much so, in fact, that Commander Golan's family had nearly doubled in size. And in a few days, yet another son would be added to House Golan on Corinair.

"*XO, Watch!*" another voice called urgently over

the intercom.

"XO," the commander replied.

Over the ready room's door, the ship's status light turned red, and an audible alert sounded. *"General quarters!"*

"Four ships just jumped in! They're firing!"

"Raise shields!" Commander Golan ordered as he rose from his seat and moved quickly toward the door.

It took the commander only seconds to exit the ready room and walk onto the bridge. "Report!" he bellowed.

Suddenly, the bridge shook, and all the view screens on the forward bulkhead flickered.

"Two battleships, and two heavy cruisers!" Commander Hyam replied. "They jumped in at close range and opened fire without warning!"

"Did you get our shields up?"

"Yes, sir!" Commander Hyam assured him. "The moment they fired."

"We've lost shields two through seven, port side!" the officer in charge of the Avendahl's defensive systems reported.

"Where are they?" Commander Golan demanded as he stepped up onto the command platform.

"Two groups now!" Lieutenant Cahnis reported from the sensor station. "A battleship and cruiser in each! One group is still coming dead-on, the second is turning to our port! Second group is jumping away!"

"Ship is at general quarters!" Lieutenant Permon reported from the communications station.

"Weapons free, Mister Rogal," Commander Golan ordered as he sat down in the command chair. "Fire at will!"

"Weapons free! Fire at will, aye!" the lieutenant acknowledged. "Targeting all forward weapons onto the two ships directly ahead."

"Helm, take us higher and turn to port. Don't let them get a shot at our unprotected areas!"

"Aye, sir!"

"Comms, notify Captain Navarro that the Avendahl is under attack. And alert Darvano Defense Command."

"New jump flashes!" the sensor officer announced. "Directly astern!"

"Is it the same group that..."

"Negative!" the sensor officer replied, cutting the commander short. "New targets! Smaller, more heavily armed! They look like destroyers, sir! They're firing missiles... Multiple flashes! They're jump missiles!"

"All hands! Brace for..."

The bridge shook violently as eight jump missiles suddenly appeared less than a kilometer away from the Avendahl, immediately slamming into her shields and detonating.

"We've lost all port shields!" Lieutenant Rogal warned.

"Have you got a firing solution on the forward targets?" Commander Golan demanded.

"Aye, sir!"

"Fire all forward tubes! Lock jump missiles on all available targets and launch! Helm! Jump us two light minutes out as soon as those missiles are away!"

"More flashes!" the sensor officer exclaimed. "More missiles!"

"Laying down a point-defense wall to port!" Lieutenant Rogal announced. "Firing all forward plasma torpedoes! Locking jump missiles on all targets!"

The Avendahl shook again, more violently than before. Along the forward bulkhead, a console overloaded, erupting in a shower of sparks and throwing its operator backward. Another explosion to the port side sent pieces of bulkhead and consoles shooting into the bridge, sending more bodies flying.

"*Direct hits to our port hull!*" the damage control officer called over the intercom. "*Decks seven through twenty-eight, sections A though C are open to space! Fires in the...*"

Commander Golan punched the mute button. He already knew his ship was in trouble. He didn't need the details at this moment. He needed to get his ship out of the enemy's firing solutions.

"Launching all jump missiles!"

"Stand by to jump!" Commander Golan ordered.

"Captain! The port side took a direct hit," Commander Hyam warned. "The emitter array may..."

"No choice," Commander Golan insisted.

"Jump missiles away!" the weapons officer reported.

Commander Golan took a deep breath, clenching the arms of his command chair. "Jump."

Doran Montrose burst into Yanni's office without warning, followed by several of his security officers. "Mister Hiller, Miss Sheehan. You must come with me."

"What's going on here?" Yanni asked, shocked by the sudden arrival of the security chief.

"The Avendahl is under attack," Doran explained.

"By who?"

"We do not know. But it does not matter. We must move you to a safer location. All of you."

"Are you in contact with the Avendahl?" Yanni asked.

"Yes, but they have jumped out of comms range."

"They left?" Yanni's eyes widened.

"For the moment," Doran replied. "They are undoubtedly maneuvering for a counterattack."

"Then they will return."

"Of course," Doran said. "They have stood as Corinair's defense for seven years now. They will not run at the first sign of trouble. Not Captain Navarro."

"Of course, of course."

"Please, if you'll all follow me," Doran insisted.

"To where?" Yanni asked, as he followed Mister Montrose out the door and into the corridor.

"To the shuttle pad outside. We must be prepared to evacuate the three of you, as well as Doctors Sato and Megel, to a secure location."

"How?" Yanni asked. "The shuttle has not returned."

"The Avendahl will send a shuttle for us," Doran promised.

"Are you sure about that?" Yanni wondered. "Deliza has not communicated directly with Captain Navarro for years..."

Doran stopped in the middle of the corridor, turning to look at Yanni. "The captain made a promise to Deliza's father. He will not ignore that promise. It is not in his nature."

———

"Jump complete!" the Avendahl's helmsman reported.

"Locking second wave of jump missiles on targets now!" Lieutenant Rogal announced.

"Helm, turn us into the nearest battleship."

"Turning onto target now."

"Firing jump missiles!"

"Missile launches!" the sensor officer warned. "Jump missiles!"

Eight more jump flashes appeared on the starboard view screen, momentarily filling the Avendahl's bridge with their blue-white light. A moment later, the ship shuddered again, and the view screen went black.

"Starboard midship shields are down to twenty percent!"

"We're lined up on the battleship," the helmsman reported.

"Locking all forward tubes on the battleship," the weapons officer announced.

"Two ships moving in to attack our port side," Lieutenant Cahnis warned. "The destroyers."

"Weapons, launch a mine spreader in front of those destroyers," Commander Golan ordered. "I don't want them to be able to get into firing position so easily."

"Aye, sir!" the lieutenant replied. "Firing forward torpedo tubes! Loading four mine spreaders!"

"Direct hits on the battleship, sir!" the sensor officer reported. "Her forward shields are down to forty percent!"

"Helm, hold her steady. Weapons, keep firing all forward tubes."

"Launching mine spreaders," Lieutenant Rogal responded. "Firing all forward tubes."

High above the planet Corinair, two black-hulled destroyers, both trimmed with crimson stripes, charged toward the Avendahl. Four jump flashes, spread apart equally to form the four points of a square, appeared in the path of the onrushing warships. Seconds later, several dozen flashes in the same positions as the first four, followed by more than a hundred, spread out in a precise pattern across the path of the approaching destroyers.

The destroyers opened fire on the field of mines deployed before them, in the hopes of clearing a safe path through the wall of explosive devices. One by one, the devices were blown apart by the enemy destroyers' point-defenses, but as the warships drew nearer, the devices sensed the enemy vessels and detonated.

Brilliant flashes from tiny antimatter warheads formed together to create a wall of white light. The charging destroyers struck the blinding barrier, causing their forward shields to overload. Shield emitters all over the bows of both ships exploded, unable to accommodate the tremendous amount of energy.

But when the antimatter flash faded a few seconds later, the two destroyers were still advancing toward the Avendahl.

———

"Both destroyers have lost their forward shields," the Avendahl's sensor officer reported.

"Another round of jump missiles on those destroyers," Commander Golan ordered. "Where are those other three ships?"

"I don't have them on my screens," the weapons officer replied.

"They must have jumped away just after we did," Commander Hyam realized.

"They'll be back," the commander grumbled. "Cahnis, any ID on them yet?"

"Negative, sir," the sensor officer replied.

"Are you sure they're not Takaran?"

"Yes, sir," the sensor officer assured him.

"Firing jump missiles," the weapons officer announced. "Continuing fire on the battleship directly ahead of us."

"I've checked them against all known ships from the Pentaurus sector," the sensor officer continued.

"Direct hits!" the weapons officer exclaimed.

"Confirmed!" the sensor officer added. "Both destroyers have taken multiple hits. One of them has lost main power and maneuvering, the other is turning away."

"Another round, Mister Rogal," the commander ordered.

"Aye, sir!"

"Captain, the battleship has lost her forward shields as well."

"Forward torpedo tubes are near critical heat!" the systems officer warned.

"Main rail guns on the battleship, Mister Rogal," the commander ordered. "Tear that bastard apart!"

"Locking jump missiles on the destroyers, bringing main rail guns on the battleship," the weapons officer responded.

"Captain," Lieutenant Permon called. "Corinairan defense reports enemy troop ships and fighter escorts jumping into lower atmosphere all over the planet!"

"Scramble all fighters," Commander Golan ordered. "Comms, contact Ranni Enterprises and tell them to evacuate all key personnel."

"Jump missiles away," the weapons officer reported.

"Battleship is taking heavy damage from our rail guns," Lieutenant Cahnis reported from the sensor station. "She's turning to starboard and powering up her jump emitters."

"Forward torpedoes!" Commander Golan shouted. "Don't let her get away!"

"Direct hits on the destroyers," the sensor operator reported.

"The forward torpedoes are at critical..."

"I said fire!"

"Firing!"

Commander Golan watched the forward view screen as eight mark five plasma torpedoes left his ship, headed for the enemy battleship. Just as the enemy ship's jump fields solidified over her hull and began to build into a jump flash, all eight balls of red-orange plasma slammed into her unprotected forward sections. The battleship's nose blew apart, sending a wave of internal explosions deeper into her hull. When the wave reached the battleship's midsection, the rest of the ship blew apart in one massive, yellow-white explosion, sending debris spreading out in all directions.

"The battleship is destroyed!" the sensor officer reported.

"What about those destroyers?" the commander asked.

"They have been defeated as well."

"I've lost plasma torpedo generators three and five," the systems officer reported.

"Incoming message from Ranni Enterprises," the comms officer announced. "It's Doran Montrose, their chief of security. He is requesting an evac shuttle for Mister Hiller, and Doctors Sato and Megel."

"Hiller?" Commander Hyam asked, unfamiliar with the name.

"Deliza Ta'Akar's husband," Commander Golan

reminded him. "I thought they had their own shuttle."

"Mister Montrose says that Miss Ta'Akar has the shuttle and is overdue to return," the comms officer explained.

"Launch a rescue shuttle," the commander ordered. "And tell Mister Montrose to be ready."

"Where did those fighters come from?" Commander Hyam asked. He turned to the sensor officer. "Did that battleship launch any fighters or troop shuttles?"

"No, sir."

"I think I know where they came from," Commander Golan said. "Helm, jump us around to the far side of Corinair. Maximum orbit."

"They wanted us on this side of Corinair," Commander Hyam realized. His brow furrowed as he continued to think. "Whose ships are these?"

"I don't know," Commander Golan admitted, "but they knew enough about us to keep us on the opposite side of their invasion force."

The shuttle's windows turned opaque as the tiny ship completed its last jump.

Deliza looked up from her data pad, noticing that the window had cleared and was not turning opaque again. "I guess we're home. Time to call in our order. I want to start eating the moment we hit the conference room."

"You and me both," Biarra agreed.

The shuttle veered sharply to port. Although the ship had inertial dampeners that were capable of protecting the occupants of the shuttle from most maneuvers, they could still feel the force of the extremely abrupt turn.

Deliza grabbed her armrests to steady herself. "What is it?" she called to Loki in the cockpit. It wasn't the first time they had been forced to make a sudden maneuver just after jumping into a heavily-populated system, despite the use of standard arrival zones used by most of the populated systems of the Pentaurus cluster.

"Get secure!" Loki demanded.

Deliza immediately rose from her seat and moved forward toward the cockpit.

"I told you to get secure," Loki said impatiently, noticing Deliza entering the cockpit.

"I am," Deliza insisted as she squeezed between Loki and the copilot's seat and sat down in the right seat. "I'm just doing it in here. What's going on?"

"Look," Loki said, pointing at the screen in the middle of the console.

Deliza studied the screen, her eyes narrowing. "Why are all those ship icons red?"

"Red means hostile," Loki replied.

"Isn't that one the Avendahl?" Deliza said, pointing at the large blue icon.

"Avendahl, Avendahl. This is Ranni One, holding two million kilometers from Corinair. We show multiple unidentified hostiles. Are you engaged?"

"Ranni One, Avendahl. We are under attack by at least six ships. Three have been destroyed. Corinair is being invaded."

"Oh, my God!" Deliza exclaimed.

"Suggest you remain clear."

"We have to get to the office," Deliza insisted. "Yanni... Your wife and baby... Michi and Tori..."

"Avendahl, Ranni One, negative. We have primaries on the surface that must be evacuated. Requesting safe approach recommendations."

"Negative, Ranni One. Stay clear. We have a rescue shuttle on its way to your offices now."

———————

Doran, Yanni, and the others all crouched down behind the blast wall that protected passersby from the thrust of landing and departing shuttles. Flashes appeared all over the sky in groups of three to six every other minute or so.

"Are they ours?" Yanni wondered as he stared at the flashes of light in the evening skies over Aitkenna.

"Some of them," Doran replied, "but not many."

Yanni watched as an enemy fighter dove toward them, with two of the Avendahl's fighters in close pursuit. The lead Takaran fighter opened fire, sending red, needle-like beams toward the diving enemy fighter. As it did so, two more enemy fighters appeared behind flashes of blue-white light, and quickly opened fire. The two fighters of Takaran design came apart, and what was left fell to the surface.

Yanni and Doran ducked as the diving enemy fighter pulled level and flew directly over them at a low altitude. Yanni looked at Doran with his eyes wide. "Wasn't that...?"

"A Jung fighter." Doran finished for him. "It sure as hell looked like one."

"But I thought the Jung didn't have jump technology."

"Last I heard, they didn't."

Another flash occurred nearby, followed by the familiar thunderous tearing sound. Doran turned and spotted one of the Avendahl's jump shuttles on a rapid approach to their position. Then three more flashes appeared above and behind the descending shuttle.

"*Montrose, Rescue One Five,*" the pilot's voice crackled over Doran's comm-set. "*Inbound for Ranni pad. Wheels down in two. Stand by for extraction.*"

Doran stared at the three new arrivals, trying to discern their shapes in the darkness. One of them passed directly in front of the rising moon, casting a perfect silhouette. His expression changed, and he tapped his comm-set. "Rescue One Five, Montrose! Three bandits, five high! Suggest you..."

It was too late. Streaks of reddish-orange lashed out from two of the three enemy fighters, striking the descending jump shuttle high on the starboard side. The shuttle's aft engine pod exploded, taking a portion of the shuttle's hull with it. With the lift suddenly removed from the back corner of the ship, the shuttle's back-right corner dropped rapidly, and the shuttle rolled to its right as it entered a sharp, uncoordinated right turn. The shuttle spiraled down, smoke pouring from its aft end, then clipped a building and fell the last twenty meters to the street below, exploding on impact.

Yanni stared in horror, frozen in fear.

"We've got to get out of here!" Doran insisted, as more troop ships appeared behind flashes of blue-white light.

"They'll send another shuttle, right?" Lael asked nervously. "Shouldn't we be here when..."

"When it gets shot down?" Doran said. "Those are troop ships," he said, pointing at the flashes of light in the sky. "We have to get someplace safe!"

"Where?" Doctor Sato wondered.

"Someplace outside of the city!" Doran said. "Someplace that the Jung are not likely to be!"

———————

"Jump complete," the Avendahl's helmsman reported.

Commander Golan discreetly breathed a sigh of

relief. Jumping a heavily-damaged ship was a risky move.

"Multiple contacts," the sensor officer announced. "Very large, but only point-defenses."

"Troop ships," Commander Hyam surmised. "You were right."

"Lieutenant Rogal, target those troop ships," Commander Golan ordered.

"Flight reports Rescue One Five is down," the communications officer reported.

"Targets acquired," the weapons officer announced. "Firing!"

Commander Golan glanced at one of the many view screens on the overhead in front of him, quickly picking out the view from one of their main rail gun's cameras. Brilliant balls of red-orange plasma slammed into the target's shields, turning them an opaque amber. As more plasma charges impacted their shields, the amber color intensified, until finally the shields failed. Pieces of the enemy troop ship began to break off as the slugs from the Avendahl's massive rail guns slammed into her hull. Debris spread out on the opposite side of the target, as the kinetic energy of the slug impacts sent debris flying away and downrange. After a few seconds, the rail gun slugs found sensitive elements deeper inside the troop ship's hull, and secondary explosions ignited. The target came apart, and a wave of satisfaction swept over the commander.

The satisfaction was short-lived.

"Jump flashes!" Lieutenant Cahnis reported from the sensor station. "Three contacts! The battleship and the cruisers! They're launching missiles! More flashes! Oh, my God! Jump missiles! Dozens of them!"

"Helm! Snap jump! Now! Now! Now!"

———

Pale-blue waves of energy poured out of the Avendahl's jump field emitters. In the blink of an eye, the energy spread across her hull, joining with the other expanding pools of energy. In a fraction of a second, the Avendahl's entire hull was covered with the jump field, its pale-blue light hugging the ship's surface. Once formed, the blue field grew in its intensity, building rapidly toward a brilliant white as the ship began its jump.

But the process was interrupted as several dozen enemy jump missiles appeared only a few hundred meters away from the Avendahl, behind their own flashes of blue-white light. The missiles slammed into the Avendahl's hull and detonated. Brilliant flashes of yellow, followed by orange and black clouds of fire and debris, ended the once-proud capital ship owned by the last truly noble house of Takara. The blue-white glow instantly disappeared behind the detonations. The orange and black clouds of fire died away in seconds, as whatever oxidizers had fed them were quickly consumed. Large sections of the hull scattered off in all directions, followed by sections of the mighty ship's interior, as well as her crew. In only a few seconds, several thousand men, who had spent the last seven years standing guard over the people of the Darvano and Savoy systems, lost their lives.

Corinair had lost its freedom once again.

———

"Oh, my God!" Deliza exclaimed as she stared at the shuttle's sensor screen in disbelief.

"What?" Loki wondered, turning his head toward the screen as well.

"The icon for the Avendahl..."

Loki looked at the sensor screen. The blue triangle that represented the Avendahl had changed to a circular field of blue dots, and the diameter of that field was growing.

"Is it...?" Deliza couldn't bring herself to say the words.

Loki did not reply. "Avendahl, Avendahl," he began after keying his mic. "This is Ranni One. Do you copy?" Loki paused for a moment, waiting for a response before continuing. "Avendahl, Avendahl. This is Ranni One. We've lost your track. Do you copy?" Loki closed his eyes. His mind was racing. He keyed his mic again. "Avendahl Rescue Shuttle inbound to Ranni Enterprises. This is Ranni One. Do you copy?" Loki sighed. "This is Ranni One. Does anyone copy?"

"*Ranni One, Jaker Two Seven!*" The caller's voice was frantic and stressed. Loki could hear the familiar sound of a weapons lock warning alarm in the background, along with the sound of engines screaming at full power. "*Rescue One Five is down!*"

"Jaker Two Seven, Ranni One," Loki replied urgently. "Did Rescue One Five make their evac?"

"*Negative! Nega...*" the transmission was cut short by the screech of a jump flash, another familiar sound to Loki after spending two years in the backseat of a Falcon jump interceptor. "*...need to get the hell out of here!*" the fighter pilot continued. "*The Avendahl is gone, and there are enemy fighters all over the fucking place!*"

Loki heard the sound of the Takaran fighter's plasma cannons in the background. "Jaker Two Seven, Ranni One. Who are they? Who is attacking Corinair?"

"It's the fucking Ju..."

Loki looked at Deliza. Both their mouths were hanging open, and their eyes wide. "Jaker Two Seven! Did you say the attackers are Jung?" Loki waited for a moment, but got no response. "Jaker Two Seven, Ranni One! Do you copy?"

"Ranni One, Jaker Four Five! Two Seven is down! Strongly suggest you leave the system! Corinair is lost!"

"Jaker Four Five, Glendanon," an older, male voice responded. The transmission was garbled, with lots of static. *"How many friendlies do you have left?"*

"Glendanon, Jaker Four Five! Maybe twenty or thirty! But there are hundreds of bandits! They're jumping us in packs of six or eight! We can't..."

"Glendanon to all Avendahl fighters. The Avendahl is down. I say again, the Avendahl is destroyed. Corinair has fallen. Takara has fallen..."

Loki felt a cold shiver go down his spine. He glanced at Deliza. Tears were streaking down her cheeks. He looked over his shoulder at Biarra. She was sitting in her seat, staring forward at him, dumbfounded and terrified.

"...Suggest all Avendahl fighters rendezvous with us at position two five seven by one eight two, Corinair relative. We have room to recover all of you. But make it quick, it won't take long for the Jung to figure out where you're going. And my finger is on the jump button, gentlemen."

"Jaker One Eight to all Jakers!" another pilot called. *"Rendezvous with the Glendanon now, or get left behind!"*

"Ranni One, Glendanon. Is Deliza on board?"

"Glendanon, Ranni One, affirmative."

"Then I suggest you jump the hell out of here,

49

immediately, Loki."

"Negative," Loki replied. "We have people on the surface. We're going after them." Loki looked at Deliza. "Right?"

"Damn right," Deliza replied.

"*Ranni One, Jaker One Eight! You'll never even get close! Aitkenna is crawling with Jung! In the air and on the ground!*"

"Jaker One Eight, thanks," Loki replied, "but we've got to try."

"*Ranni One, Jaker Three Five! A few of us can cover you. Just let us know where you'll be jumping in at.*"

"Negative," Loki insisted. "Get to the Glendanon. We can handle it ourselves."

"*It's a suicide run!*"

"I'll keep my finger on the escape jump trigger at all times," Loki assured him, using lingo he was sure the other pilot would understand.

"*Good luck, then. Three Five, jumping to rally point.*"

Loki concentrated a moment, as fighter after fighter reported that they were jumping out of the skies of Corinair to rendezvous with the nearby cargo ship. The jump fighters had extremely limited amounts of jump energy stored on board, and once it was depleted, they would be easy targets for Jung fighters. The Glendanon was their last hope of survival, now that the Avendahl was gone and the Darvano system was about to fall to the Jung.

Loki took a deep breath, changed communication frequencies, and keyed his comm-set mic again. "Ranni Base, Ranni One. Do you copy?"

The streets of Aitkenna were thrown into a panic.

Jung fighters streaked low over the buildings, and troop ships were landing in the larger intersections. Corinairans were running in all directions. They all had one common goal: to escape.

Doran led Yanni, Lael and her baby, and Doctors Sato and Megel quickly down the sides of the buildings and away from the city center. The security chief, ex-Alliance master chief, and ex-Corinari knew that the initial invasion would focus on the government and financial districts of the city, as well as the spaceport and major infrastructure sites. The residential areas should be the safest place at the moment. But he didn't know how long it would last.

They turned the corner and found themselves face-to-face with a squad of four Jung soldiers, each of them clad in black body armor trimmed in crimson and gold.

"Halt!" one of the soldiers commanded, raising his weapon to fire at the sight of Doran and the two security officers carrying energy pistols.

Doran opened fire without hesitation, dropping one of the Jung soldiers with a well-placed series of shots across his chest, tearing into the seam under the soldier's right arm. As his two officers also opened fire, Doran dropped to his left knee, continuing to fire, then rolled to his left to get out of the immediate firing line. After a single roll, he came up to one knee again, still firing. The last Jung soldier took an energy bolt to his knee, melting the kneecap armor and severing his leg in a sickening sizzle of flesh and bone. The soldier fell to the street, screaming in pain.

Red bolts of energy burst from the fallen soldier's weapon and streaked past Doran's head, slamming into the building behind him. Doran fired three more times, finally finding an opening just below the soldier's faceplate. The shot burned a hole in the soldier's neck, spewing blood onto the ground. The soldier fell onto his back, grasping at his neck as he quickly bled out.

"Doran!" Michi yelled from behind.

Doran turned his head, spotting the Nifelmian doctor kneeling beside one of his wounded security guards. Doran scrambled back to his feet and ran over to them. He looked over at Michi's partner, Doctor Megel, who was kneeling next to the body of his other officer. Doctor Megel looked at Doran and shook his head.

Doran looked back at Doctor Sato. "How bad?"

The wounded officer spoke first. "I can... I can..." He swallowed hard, trying to breathe through the pain. There was an open wound in his abdomen, the edges of which were still smoldering, and his left arm was severed just below the elbow. "Give me... my weapon. I can... still..."

Doran watched the young man take his last breath, then reached down and picked up the dead officer's energy pistol from the pavement. "Take this," he told Doctor Sato as he handed her the weapon. "Shoot anyone dressed in black and red."

"I've never..."

"Just point and shoot," Doran instructed, "and don't stop until the person you're shooting is dead." He turned to Doctor Megel. "Tori, take that man's weapon, and do the same. Understood?"

Doctor Megel nodded, then pulled the energy pistol from the dead officer's hand.

Doran turned toward Lael. "This one is yours. Use it if you must."

"What are you going to use?" Lael asked.

"Theirs," Doran replied, as he started walking across the street toward the dead Jung soldiers.

"Maybe I should take it?" Yanni suggested, noticing Lael's trepidation at holding a weapon.

"You get one of these," Doran said as he picked up the first Jung energy rifle and tossed it to Yanni.

Yanni caught the weapon, nearly dropping it in the process. It was lighter than it looked, with a folding stock and a long black barrel with a surprisingly large diameter. Yanni looked at the trigger mechanism, and the various dials and switches on the side of the weapon's main body. The writing was familiar; however, he had never learned to read Jung. Not seven years ago, nor since.

Doran slung a Jung rifle over his shoulder and picked up two more before returning. "We need to keep moving. Someone will notice that these men are down, if they haven't already."

"I'm not sure if I know how to use this," Yanni admitted.

Doran walked up to Yanni. "Hold it like this," he explained, bringing his own rifle's stock up against his shoulder. He took aim at one of the dead soldiers across the street, then pressed the firing button and held it for a few seconds. A series of red bolts of energy leapt from his barrel with a screeching zing. It sounded like the air was on fire. "Now you try."

Yanni raised his rifle in similar fashion, took aim, and pressed the trigger, releasing it immediately. Three bolts of energy left his rifle's barrel, slamming into one of the dead soldier's bodies.

"Tap once for a single shot, hold down for one second for a triplet, or keep holding it down for continuous fire," Doran explained. "But not for more than ten seconds straight. These things can get hot, fast."

Yanni looked surprised. "How do you know all this?"

"Telles told me, a long time ago." Doran handed him another rifle. "Sling this one over your shoulder, just in case."

"*Ranni Base, Ranni One,*" Doran's headset crackled.

"Sheehan! Is that you?"

"Loki!" Lael exclaimed.

"*Chief!*" Loki called over Doran's comm-set. "*Where are you? Are Lael and Ailsa with you?*"

"Yes! They are with me! We're at Brighton and Mickleson, just south of the Wesley Amphitheater! I've got Yanni, Sato, and Megel with me as well. There are Jung everywhere. The Avendahl sent a rescue shuttle, but it was shot down on approach. Are you in contact with the Avendahl?"

"*The Avendahl is gone,*" Loki replied solemnly.

"She jumped away?"

"*No, she was destroyed! We're coming to pick you up!*"

"That ship won't hold all of us!"

"*The hell it won't,*" Loki said.

"It's too dangerous," Doran insisted, as more Jung fighters streaked overhead. "There are enemy fighters everywhere! They'll tear you apart!"

"*We weren't asking your permission, Chief,*" Deliza commented over the comm-set.

"*Head for the amphitheater!*" Loki instructed. "*We'll set down on the foreyard, in front of the east entrance, in three.*"

"Shit," Doran muttered. "Copy that." He looked at Yanni. "Your wife is one stubborn young lady."

"Tell me about it," Yanni replied with a sigh.

Doran took a deep breath. "All right then. Everyone, stay tight on my six, stay against the buildings, move quickly, and never stay out in the open for more than a few seconds, if at all. If anything looks like a threat, shoot it. Understood?" Doran scanned their faces. They were not the most confident-looking bunch. He closed his eyes a moment and sighed. "Remind me to ask your wife for a raise later," he said as he turned and headed down the street.

"How are we going to fit six people back there?" Deliza asked.

"We don't have to," Loki told her, as he punched in the first jump coordinates. "If I know Doran, he's not planning on going. He won't leave his family behind."

"That still leaves five people, for three seats."

"Lael in one holding Ailsa, Sato and Megel in the other two. Yanni can sit on the floor."

"Can this ship get that many people off the ground?"

"If it can take six people with full fuel and luggage, it can take seven and a baby, with..." Loki glanced at his propellant indicators. "Shit."

"What is it now?"

"We're down to twenty-three percent."

"Twenty-three percent of what? Propellant?" Deliza's expression turned fearful. "Is that going to be enough?"

"We're only going to get one chance at this," Loki warned, "if we still want to have enough fuel left to land somewhere else." Loki activated the jump sequencer. "Hold on, we jump in five..."

Doran took aim with his Jung energy rifle and

pressed the trigger. A bolt of red energy streaked from his barrel, blasting through one of the amphitheater's gates, blowing it apart. "Through here," he instructed the others. "Watch the edges. They're still hot."

Yanni helped Lael through the opening in the twisted metal gate, steadying her to make sure that neither she, nor the infant she was carrying, came close to the still-glowing ends of the sheared metal. "Michi," he called, after Lael was safely through.

Doctor Sato was next through the gate, stepping through carefully, then followed by Doctor Megel, Yanni, and finally Chief Montrose.

"*Doran, we're about to jump in!*" Loki called over Doran's comm-set. "*Are you at the amphitheater?*"

"Yes!" Doran replied. "We're entering the foregrounds now!"

"*Is the landing zone secure?*"

"There are no ground forces following us, if that's what you mean."

"*Ranni One, Jaker Six!*" another voice called. "*Ground troops moving toward the amphitheater!*"

"Giortone, is that you?" Loki asked.

"*Affirmative!*" Lieutenant Giortone replied over comms. "*Riordan and Masa are with me!*"

"You were supposed to bug out to the Glendanon!" Loki said in surprise.

"*If the daughter of Casimir Ta'Akar is going to put herself in harm's way, then we're going to cover her!*"

"How many, and how far?" Loki asked as he punched the next jump coordinates into the shuttle's jump-nav computer.

"*Three groups, maybe twenty men total!*" Lieutenant Giortone replied. "*Two minutes, max!*"

"You copy that, Doran?"

"Copy that. We're ready here. Suggest you jump in right on top of us."

"I can't do that," Loki insisted. "The shape of that amphitheater will concentrate the shock wave and would most likely kill you. I'll jump in outside the amphitheater, then slide in overhead and set down. I suggest you find cover, because there's going to be a lot of thrust wash."

"Get to the sides, behind the concession counters," Doran instructed, pointing to the long counters along the edges of the grassy foregrounds.

"Suggest you jump in low, over Brighton between Andowl and Forrester. Might slow some of them down a bit," Lieutenant Giortone told Loki over the comms.

"Copy that," Loki replied. *"Jumping in five seconds."*

Chief Montrose moved in beside Yanni, Lael, and baby Ailsa, crouching down behind the concession counter. He helped to shield the infant in her mother's arms from the upcoming thrust wash.

"We'll be there in ten!" Lieutenant Giortone added.

"Be ready on that hatch!" Loki called to Biarra in the back of the shuttle.

The cockpit windows turned opaque for a moment, as the shuttle jumped from high orbit over Corinair down to the city of Aitkenna below. When the windows cleared a second later, the view of the planet was replaced with the view of the tops of buildings rushing toward them.

Loki pushed the lift thruster throttles full forward. All four engines screamed at full power as they fought against the sudden effects of the planet's gravity trying to pull them to their deaths. Despite their modest inertial dampening systems, the shuttle shook violently from both the sudden resistance of the atmosphere, and the force of deceleration. It had been a long time since Loki jumped into any world's atmosphere at such low altitudes. Such maneuvers were forbidden on inhabited worlds, and their tiny shuttle wasn't designed for such stresses.

The buildings shot up on either side of them as the shuttle settled into level flight a mere ten meters above Brighton Avenue. Loki glanced at the external camera screen, which showed the street directly below them. He could see the bodies of four men, all of them clad in black and red armor, lying motionless in the street.

Loki fired the deceleration thrusters at full power as the shuttle raced toward the amphitheater two blocks ahead of them. Several jump flashes appeared in the twilight above him, as the last of the Avendahl's fighters jumped in to provide cover for their rescue.

"*Jaker Six! On station! Attacking forces to the south!*" Lieutenant Giortone announced as his fighter jumped in overhead.

"*Jaker Two Two, attacking the guys to the west!*"

"*Jaker Four Six! New bandits! Six of them to the north, ten kilometers! Closing fast! Turning to intercept!*"

Deliza's eyes grew wide, pushing back in her seat as if to brace herself for collision as the amphitheater rushed toward them.

"*Mas! Join up with Rio on the intercept,*" Lieutenant Giortone ordered. "*I'll deal with the ground targets!*"

Loki's eyes danced back and forth between his console and the forward window, waiting and calculating, betting that full lift thrust would eventually raise them up a few more meters to clear the top of the amphitheater's hillsides.

"*Copy that, Gio,*" Ensign Masa replied.

"*Glendanon to all Rakers!*" the Glendanon's captain called over the comms. "*We've got company coming. Two gunships! We bug out in two!*"

"*Rakers, Rakers, Rakers! This is Jaker One Six! I'll keep the gunships off the Glendanon to buy everyone a few more minutes! Just move your asses, damn it!*"

"*Just buy us three minutes, Sissy!*" Lieutenant Riordan replied.

"*One Six, Eight Five!*" another pilot called. "*I'm fifty clicks to your starboard, joining up to attack the gunships!*"

Loki watched as the shuttle climbed up just enough for the amphitheater's hillsides to slide under them. A wave of relief washed over him as he prepared to descend into the middle of the amphitheater's grassy foregrounds.

"*Ground forces approaching from the south are destroyed,*" Lieutenant Giortone reported.

"*New bandits!*" Ensign Masa exclaimed over the comms. "*Six more just jumped in! Two clicks to my... They're firing!*"

Loki glanced to his left, just in time to see six Jung fighters speeding toward him, two of them firing at Jaker Two Two. A small explosion appeared in Ensign Masa's right wing, and it began to trail smoke as it lost altitude.

"*I'm hit! I'm hit!*" Ensign Masa shouted. "*Two Two is going down!*"

"*Punch out, Mas!*" Lieutenant Giortone ordered.

"*No time! I'll try to put it into the...*"

Loki's eyes were fixed on his console as he reduced his lift thrust and started his descent into the middle of the amphitheater.

"Mas is down!" Lieutenant Riordan exclaimed. *"He dove and put his ship right into their ground forces!"*

"Ranni One! Climb, climb, climb!" Lieutenant Giortone ordered urgently.

Loki didn't question it. He pushed his lift thrusters to full power again, causing the tiny shuttle to leap upward. The shuttle suddenly jerked hard to starboard, as if something had slammed into them and knocked them into a spin. Warning alarms went off in the cockpit, and the hatch that separated the cockpit from the passenger compartment suddenly closed.

"We're hit!" Loki announced as he struggled to regain control of the damaged shuttle. "We've got a hull breach, and we've lost the number four lift thruster!"

Deliza twisted to her left, looking aft through the window in the hatch that had just closed automatically behind them. There was a gaping hole in the port side of the shuttle, exposing the passenger compartment to the outside. Debris flew around, and there were loose wires and pieces of the cabin's interior flailing about. Then she spotted Biarra, still strapped in her seat, half of her body seemingly ripped away. "Biarra!"

More shots streaked past their windows as Loki fought to keep the shuttle from falling to the ground.

"Get out of here!" Doran ordered over the comms.

"Find Dumar!" Deliza ordered. "Find Dumar!"

"Stretch! Jump now!" Lieutenant Giortone ordered. *"Montrose! You're clear to the east! Forces approaching from the north, one minute out! I'll try to slow them down while you make your escape!"*

"I copy all!" Doran replied from the amphitheater below. *"Moving east."*

"I'm sorry," Loki said as he pressed the escape jump button.

* * *

The combat jump shuttle began to shake as it came out of its jump, and its windows cleared again. Jessica peered out at the landscape below as they approached the spaceport outside of Lawrence. Burgess had been her home since she left Earth seven years ago. It was nowhere near as industrialized as most worlds in and around the Pentaurus sector, but it had enough to provide for its measly population of two million people, most of which preferred to live without the trappings of modern society.

There were only a dozen cities on the entire planet, and even those were relatively small. A large portion of Burgess's population preferred to live away from the busy areas, traveling into town only when they needed supplies.

Burgess was the perfect world for the Ghatazhak. Their leaders had welcomed them with open arms. The Sherma system, although far more accessible since the spread of jump drive technology in recent years, was still well removed from normal routes. They still had occasional problems with raiders, but the presence of Ghatazhak on their world had proven an effective deterrent. Especially with their base of operations being located right next to the planet's capital city.

Jessica continued gazing at the ground below as they passed over the farms surrounding the city. Agriculture was one of Burgess's major exports, as it had fair weather and regular rains year round. Since much of the planet was mountainous, wherever there was relatively flat land, there were farms. Even her parents had taken up farming after migrating to

Burgess, along with her brothers and their families.

It was a difficult adjustment for Jessica, however. But it had been worth it. Ania loved it here, and Jessica's training with the Ghatazhak had helped to get her post-incident stress disorder under control.

All in all, Burgess was more home to Jessica than Earth had ever been. It was a place that she cared about, full of people whom she respected and felt at home around. She had grown to know the Ghatazhak, and found them to be surprisingly warm and friendly people, once you got them to take off their combat gear, which wasn't an easy task.

The shuttle descended smoothly through the broken cloud layer, passed over the outer perimeter, then settled down onto the tarmac and began rolling toward the Ghatazhak hangar. Sergeant Torwell activated the controls, causing both the starboard and port side doors to slide open. The aroma of sweaty Ghatazhak was suddenly replaced with the warm, moist air of Burgess, along with the faint aroma of burnt propellant from the shuttle's engines.

"Fuck," Sergeant Torwell exclaimed as they rolled past a seriously damaged shuttle. "What the hell happened to them?"

Sergeant Todd looked at the burned shuttle as they rolled past, then glanced over at Jessica. "Notice the scorch marks on the side?"

"Energy weapons fire," Jessica replied.

"That ship was shot down," Sergeant Todd concluded.

"They were damned lucky to get down," Jessica added.

The shuttle rolled to a stop in front of the Ghatazhak hangar, and Jessica climbed down out of the ship. She spotted Telles walking toward her.

"General," she greeted, offering a casual but proper salute.

"The mission went well, I trust?" General Telles inquired.

"No casualties, and we got paid in full, so, yeah, I'd say it went well."

"*No* casualties?" the general said, one eyebrow raised. "That's not what I heard."

"Well, *we* didn't have any casualties," Jessica defended. "And there were no civilian casualties. At least none that I know of. Only bad guys got hurt, I swear."

"Relax, Lieutenant," the general said as he turned to escort her and the rest of her team inside. "We've got bigger problems."

"Something to do with that shot-up shuttle on pad seven?" Jessica assumed.

"Indeed," the general replied. "The occupants of that shuttle are inside, and they wish to see you."

Jessica stopped in her tracks. "Me?"

General Telles gestured toward the door, indicating she should continue inside.

Jessica cast him a suspicious look, then went through the doorway. When she stepped into the office, her jaw dropped open. "Loki!" she exclaimed in disbelief. She reached out and embraced him warmly. "How long has it been?"

"Five years, I believe." Loki turned to reveal Deliza standing behind him.

"Deliza!" Jessica cried, giving her a warm hug as well. A realization came over her. "Is that *your* shuttle outside?"

"I'm afraid it is, Jess," Loki replied.

"What the hell happened? Who fired on you?"

"You're not going to believe this," Loki warned. "It

63

was the Jung."

"What? That's impossible," Jessica said, a look of disbelief on her face. "Are you sure?"

"I've seen my fair share of Jung fighters, Jess," Loki replied. "I'm quite sure."

"Where?" Jessica asked. "Where were you when this happened?"

"Corinair."

It was not the answer she had expected, nor hoped for. "Corinair." There was a pause. "Where was the Avendahl?"

Loki looked down for a moment, then stared into Jessica's eyes again. "The Avendahl is gone, Jess. Destroyed by a Jung battle group. They've taken the entire Darvano system."

"What?" Jessica was in complete shock. "The Avendahl? But, she was the biggest... I mean... Jesus, she was almost as big as a battle platform." Jessica's mind was racing. "How many ships?"

"I don't know," Loki admitted. "Six or seven at least. And they all had jump drives."

"Jump drives," Jessica repeated. "The Jung have jump drives?"

"That's why we're here, Jessica," Deliza said. "We need your help."

CHAPTER THREE

"*Nyet*, you do not need to eat again," Vladimir insisted. "You are getting fat. All you do is lie around here all day long, sleeping and eating."

Cosmos looked at Vladimir and meowed again, in the same screeching tone he used whenever he wanted something.

"Things are going to change when we get to Earth," he told the cat. "You're going to go outside, climb trees, hunt birds...like a real cat."

The door chime sounded. Vladimir left his bedroom and headed across the living area toward the door, Cosmos following at his heels. Vladimir bent over and scooped up the cat with one hand, pulling him into his side as he opened the door.

"Commander," Cameron greeted him as the door opened.

"Captain." Vladimir dropped his cat gently to the floor as Captain Taylor entered and closed the door behind her. "Go, be useful," he instructed his cat. "Go shed on my clean clothes or something."

Cameron looked around the messy quarters skeptically. "I assume your cabin isn't always this disorganized," she commented as she entered.

"Are you kidding? This is clean for me."

"And you wonder why you're still single," Cameron said dryly. "I take it you haven't changed your mind, then?"

"No, Captain, I have not."

"Vlad, it's me. Enough with the captain crap, okay?"

"Sorry, but isn't that why you're here? To try to talk me into staying?"

"Yes, but not as your captain, as your friend. You'll get bored on Earth. You know that."

"No, I won't," Vladimir protested as he continued packing his belongings.

"You love to fix things, keep them running, make them better..."

"Which I will still be doing," Vladimir remarked. "Only I'll be doing it on the surface, in a nice, controlled environment, with all the resources I need."

"R and D isn't for you," Cameron insisted. "You belong here, on the Aurora."

"I've been *here*, on the Aurora, for nearly a decade, Cameron, just like you. It's time for a change. And now that they're finally getting around to a major overhaul on this ship, it's time for me to go."

"Who's going to get everything working properly once the overhaul is finished?" Cameron asked.

"Not me," Vladimir responded. "I won't be qualified, and we both know it."

"You'll learn the new systems, Vlad, you know you will. The refit will take *six months*. That's more than enough time for you to learn everything."

Vladimir stopped packing. "No, it's not," he said with a sigh. "They are replacing everything. The engines, the jump drive, the reactor plants...even the data and communication systems. All the stuff that I have been holding together for the last nine and a half years, Cameron." Vladimir returned to his packing. "I will learn my way around all those new systems, but I will do so in a research lab, on Earth. And I will sleep in my own dacha at night. I will eat real food. Breathe real air, feel real sunshine on my face, *every day*." Vladimir sighed again. "Ten years in space is enough for me."

"Galiardi won't be in command of the Sol sector forever, Vlad," Cameron reminded him. "He's getting up there in age, you know."

"It's not just Galiardi," Vladimir told her, "it's the life. It's the tedium. The drills, the meetings, the patrols... It's just not the same..."

"As when Nathan was in command?"

Vladimir looked at Cameron. "It's not you, Cam. You're a fine captain, and a close friend. You know that. It's just..."

"I know," Cameron sighed. "I miss him too."

"When Nathan was alive, this all felt like a grand adventure. Each day was exciting, with new challenges to face. And we faced them together. Now..." Vladimir paused again, as he remembered his long-lost friend. "Like I said, it's just not the same anymore."

Cameron had nothing to say. She knew exactly how he felt. She remembered her time as Nathan Scott's executive officer, and the grand adventures they had all shared in the Pentaurus cluster. "You know," she said as she sat down, "I despised Nathan when I first met him."

"Yes, I know."

Cameron looked at him, her brow furrowed at his quick answer.

"He complained about you a lot in the beginning," Vladimir explained.

"He did?"

"Yes, but I think you made him try harder. Even if it was only to beat you."

"I see."

"But, later, he admitted that you made him think more before making decisions," Vladimir added.

"It was always his biggest fault, acting

67

impulsively," Cameron remembered.

"It wasn't impulse," Vladimir corrected, "it was instinct. And it was also one of his greatest strengths."

"It also got him killed," Cameron pointed out.

"And saved us all," Vladimir quickly corrected her. "It all depends on your point of view."

"You're right." Cameron sat silently, watching Vladimir pack. Finally, she spoke again. "Did you ever believe it?"

"Believe what?" Vladimir replied without looking up.

"That he was Na-Tan?"

"He was," Vladimir said without missing a beat. "At least he was for those who needed him to be. That's all that mattered."

"I suppose," Cameron said, a pensive look on her face. She took in a deep breath, letting it out in a long sigh. "What time are you leaving?"

"I'm catching the afternoon shuttle out."

"Are you sure you don't want to stay for dinner? My treat?"

"What, salad?" Vladimir laughed. "No thank you... Unless, of course, you would like to give your old friend a goodbye romp in the sack?" he added with a lascivious sneer.

"Seriously? You're hitting on your captain?" Cameron laughed, rising to her feet to give her friend a heartfelt embrace.

"This could very well be your last chance..."

"In your dreams," she told him as they hugged. She pulled away from him suddenly, sneezing. "You are taking the cat, right?"

"Of course."

* * *

"After you finish shutting down, go and help Neli

prep the passenger cabin for the next boarding," Captain Tuplo instructed Josh.

"Come on, Cap, Neli can handle that herself," Josh complained.

"Everyone helps with everything," the captain said firmly as he climbed up out of his seat in the Seiiki's cockpit. "It's either help Neli, or help Marcus in the cargo hold," Captain Tuplo said. He looked at Josh, waiting for a reply. "Well?"

"I'm thinking."

"Not your strong suit," the captain said, patting Josh on the shoulder, then turning to exit.

"Where are you going?" Josh asked.

"To see if I can rustle up some extra paying cargo for the run to Rama. We're going to have some extra room in the hold after we offload the cargo bound for this port."

"I thought I was a pilot, not a steward," Josh grumbled as he finished shutting down the Seiiki's systems.

"And I thought I was a ship owner, not a salesman," Captain Tuplo said, exiting the cockpit. He descended the few steps from the cockpit to the main deck, just as Neli was coming out of the galley. "I'll be at the cargo agent's office if anyone needs me."

"Yes, sir."

"Josh will help you turn the cabin around before the next boarding. I want to get under way as soon as possible," he added as he opened the main boarding hatch. "This damn port charges by the hour."

"I'll get everyone on board and ready to go quick as I can, Cap'n," Neli assured him.

"And do me a favor, Neli," the captain added as he deployed the boarding gangway. "Make sure Marcus doesn't block access to the engineering crawl spaces. I know he's just doing it to piss off Dalen."

"I'll make sure," Neli promised.

Captain Tuplo stepped out of the hatch and made his way down the gangway to the tarmac. The skies were clear, and it was midmorning at the Ladila Spaceport. As usual, the port was bustling with activity. Unlike Palee's spaceport, this one was the definition of efficiency, with flights arriving and departing every few minutes. Ladila had always been a popular world, with temperate climates throughout most of the planet, and very stable and predictable weather patterns. The Paradar system was further away from the Pentaurus cluster compared to others; hence its slow development. However, since the proliferation of jump technology, many had migrated to work in the numerous resorts that had sprouted up all over the planet, and Ladila had become one of the more popular vacation destinations in the Pentaurus sector.

Unfortunately, the owners of her spaceport were well aware of that fact, and charged more for landing at their facility than nearly anywhere else in the sector. Ship captains had little recourse, since a run to the Paradar system always meant a full load of passengers, each willing to pay a premium for the convenience of jumping to paradise in an instant. There were even plans to set up a dedicated jump shuttle service between some of the primary Pentaurus worlds and Ladila, providing hourly flights, thus allowing people within the Pentaurus cluster to simply jump over for dinner and a show, rather than booking an entire vacation.

Of course, such a contract would not go to the likes of Connor Tuplo and the Seiiki. Those services would require dedicated passenger jump shuttles, designed for that one task. But that was fine with Captain Tuplo, as the idea of constantly jumping back and forth between the same two destinations, day in and day out, did not appeal to him. He preferred being in control of his destiny. He liked being able to pick and choose his runs as he saw fit. His dream was to someday take his ship further out into the galaxy, and provide his services to worlds that had not yet been connected by jump-capable ships. Perhaps find a group of heavily populated worlds that were just far enough apart to make interstellar commerce logistically difficult, yet still within his single jump range. He had heard rumors that there were likely hundreds, perhaps even thousands, of human-inhabited worlds out there. Considering there were at least a dozen such worlds in the Pentaurus sector alone, and they had all stemmed from a single, colonization mission that had left Earth nearly a millennium ago, it was a believable scenario indeed.

The Ladila Spaceport was a series of rings, all of which were connected to a central terminal. Each ring had its own cargo agent, and each cargo agent was linked to one another. It was not uncommon for ship captains to book more cargo than they could safely carry, just in case. They all operated with very slim profit margins, and no one ever wanted to lift off even a single kilogram under their gross takeoff weight. It was a game the cargo agents knew well, and they played it to their own advantage whenever possible. Captain Tuplo had gotten into the habit of understating his gross takeoff weight. It gave him the ability to seemingly take a risk, and help out a cargo agent looking to get goods left behind off his schedule. It was slightly less than honest, but it hurt no one and gave the captain an extra margin of safety. Of course, it also meant that, on occasion, the Seiiki *was* leaving profit behind by taking off under her gross weight. More often than not, the additional bonuses for taking stale cargo off the cargo agent's hands made up for the loss.

Connor walked into the cargo processing center and headed straight for the cargo agent's office. Although he could have simply transmitted the amount of space and weight available to the cargo agent's office without ever leaving his ship, he liked getting out and walking around, even if it was only within the spaceport complex. It also helped to make personal connections, from time to time, with the people who could send paying cargo his way. It was normally a job for Marcus, as he had a way with such men. However, Ladila was a special case for Captain Tuplo, as it was one of the few worlds where everyone seemed to be courteous and friendly. It was also one of the few worlds where he actually felt comfortable leaving the safety of his little ship. If it weren't for the exorbitant hourly port fees, he would try to make his layovers on Ladila. Unfortunately, a single overnight stay would take him a week's worth of runs to make up.

"Marl Joson," Captain Tuplo said as he entered the cargo agent's office. "Since when did you start working the day shift?"

"Since old man Aberlon got transferred to terminal four," Marl replied, offering his hand in greeting. "How are you doing, Connor?"

"Keeping ahead of the curve...barely."

"Just like the rest of us. What can I do for you?"

"I was hoping you had some stale cargo that needed to go to Rama," Connor said.

"How much are we talking about?" Marl wondered.

Captain Tuplo pulled his data pad out of his pocket and set it on the counter. He turned it on, called up the current load plan on the Seiiki, then turned the data pad around and slid it across the counter to the cargo agent.

"Not much, I see," Marl commented as he studied the data pad. He looked at his display screen. "I can give you a few pods full of *pora* beans. It won't get you to max weight, but it's better than nothing."

"Don't you have anything heavier?" Captain Tuplo asked.

"I've got some thruster cores shipping out for overhaul. But you'll have to shift things around a bit to make them fit. Still won't get you to max weight, though."

"Give me the cores *and* the *pora* beans, then," Connor suggested.

The cargo agent entered the data into his system. "That will put you over gross, Connor."

"I just won't take on any additional propellant then," Captain Tuplo said. "The prices are too damned high here anyway."

"As you wish," Marl replied. "Just give me a minute."

Captain Tuplo turned and looked up at the flight status displays, noticing that the view screen showing the flights scheduled from both the Takar and Darvano systems were not displaying any information. "Hey, what's up with the flights?"

"I don't know," Marl replied. "They've been like that for nearly an hour."

"The last jump comm-drone didn't show up," one of the other workers in the cargo office commented. "They haven't updated since nine."

"That's odd," Captain Tuplo said. "Aren't those drones usually on time?"

"It happens every once in a while," Marl assured him. "I'm sure it's just a malfunctioning drone. The next one will get here in a few minutes, and the board will update." Marl handed the data pad back to Captain Tuplo. "You're all set. I even transmitted the added cargo specs to your ship for you."

"I can hear Marcus swearing already," Captain Tuplo chuckled. "Thanks."

* * *

"If they've taken Corinair, then they must have taken Takara as well," Jessica surmised.

"Simultaneously, I would expect," General Telles said. He stood, leaning against the counter in the hangar's outer office. They had been debriefing Loki for several minutes, trying to garner every bit of information possible from him while it was all still fresh in his memory. "And you're sure the Avendahl was destroyed? She didn't just jump away at the last second?"

"No, sir. I double-checked," Loki insisted. "She was trying to jump, but she was hit by at least a dozen jump missiles as she was attempting to escape. She never flashed... She just came apart."

"Do you remember how many of her jump fighters made it to the Glendanon?" Jessica pressed.

"I heard Jaker Four Five say twenty or thirty, but I don't know how many of them actually made it back to the Glendanon before she jumped out. Last I heard, two Jakers were trying to defend the Glendanon against some gunships, to buy time for the rest of the fighters to get aboard before she jumped away."

"We need to find the Glendanon," Jessica

commented.

"All in due time."

"Why?" Deliza wondered.

"If she's got twenty to thirty jump fighters on board, she's a formidable weapon," Jessica explained, "and a mobile one."

"We need to know his intentions," General Telles added.

"I know Captain Gullen well," Deliza told them. "He has family on Corinair. I am friends with his daughter, Sori."

"Do you have any idea where he may have been headed?"

"No, but I am sure his intentions were honorable. He is a good man," Deliza insisted.

"You're planning on fighting them, aren't you?" Loki realized.

"You sound surprised," General Telles said.

"Well, yeah," Loki replied. "They've got battleships, General. Battleships with jump drives, no less. And you've got what, a few hundred men, and *maybe* an old jump freighter with a couple dozen jump fighters stranded on her decks?"

"Not a few hundred *men*," General Telles corrected. "A few hundred Ghatazhak. There is a difference."

"Of course, but..."

"We will recon the Pentaurus cluster, then we will send word to Sol," General Telles explained. "The Alliance will send ships, and we will drive the Jung from this sector, just as we did from the Sol sector. Meanwhile, we should be prepared to harass the Jung as much as possible, prevent them from getting a firm foothold in the Pentaurus cluster. For if they do, they will undoubtedly spread throughout the entire sector, and beyond."

* * *

"You asked for more ships, we approved the construction of more ships," President Scott said irately. "You asked for better jump drives, so we developed better jump drives. You asked for better weapons, so we developed better weapons. Now you ask for more super JKKVs, even though you have how many? Fifty?"

"Fifty-seven," Admiral Galiardi replied.

"On how many platforms?"

"Twelve."

"It seems to me, Admiral, that you already have the ability to destroy the Jung Empire's entire industrial capacity with a single command," the president continued. "I fail to see how adding more super JKKVs strengthens our position."

"The Jung still have more than a hundred ships," Admiral Galiardi explained, "not including the six battle platforms currently protecting the Jung homeworld. And that number only represents the ships we have confirmed *within* the Jung sector. We have yet to determine the extent of their expansion efforts. There could very well be hundreds more out there. Perhaps even thousands."

"Don't you think you're overestimating the size of their forces just a bit, Admiral?" President Scott suggested.

"Better to overestimate an enemy's capabilities, than to underestimate them. The consequences are far less severe."

"And exactly how many more super JKKVs would you propose we build?"

"I think you misunderstand me, Mister President," the admiral corrected. "I am not proposing a finite number of these weapons. I am proposing that we continue to build them, as quickly as possible."

The president's eyebrow rose. "Until when? To what end?"

"Until the Jung realize they cannot beat us."

"They cannot beat us now, Admiral," the president argued. "Not without suffering irreparable damages."

"Short of complete annihilation, there is no such thing."

President Scott took a deep breath, letting it out slowly. "Of course, the Jung will do the same. For every super JKKV we build, they will build another ship. For every method we come up with to destroy their assets, they will eventually come up with a way to counter. It will not end. We will either be buried under all our weapons, or we shall be destroyed by them." President Scott shook his head. "I'm afraid either end is unacceptable. I cannot endorse such a plan, Admiral."

"If the leaders of the worlds we are sworn to protect will not give us the tools we need to do so..."

"Six years ago, you stood before me with a plan," the president interrupted. "A plan to protect the entire sector from Jung attack. A plan you swore would all but guarantee that the Jung would not attack any Alliance member worlds. We approved that plan, Admiral. *I* approved that plan, not so much because I believed in you, but because I did not want my son's sacrifice to be in vain."

"And because I had the support of the people of Earth," Admiral Galiardi corrected, "and you did not wish to empower me further by opposing me."

"I recommissioned you, Admiral," President Scott reminded him as he rose from his chair. "Let us not forget that." The president nodded at his aide, who signaled the guard at the door to open it, an open suggestion to the admiral that the meeting had ended.

"You are not the sole deciding vote in this Alliance, Mister President," the admiral said smugly as he too rose from his seat. "Let us not forget *that*."

"We have spent the last seven years protecting a fragile cease-fire. I shall not bet against that which my son gave his life to create." The president nodded to the general. "Good day, Admiral." President Scott turned his back to the admiral and walked back across his office toward his desk, paying no attention as the admiral exited the room.

"You know, building super JKKVs is not the same thing as deploying them," Miri reminded her father as she entered the room.

President Scott shot her a stern look, then turned to watch the admiral exit, the doors closing behind him.

"Relax, father. I activated the sound wall on my way in."

"It may not be the same thing, but it is the next step. As long as the weapons do not *exist*, they cannot *be* deployed."

"I'm not disagreeing with you," Miri insisted. "However, you could have been more diplomatic about it."

"The admiral needs to know that he cannot waltz into my office and bully me into granting him every weapon his black heart desires."

"I don't like the man any more than you do, father, but his interests are the same as yours."

"I'm not so sure about that," the president said as he took his seat behind his desk.

"You both want peace," Miranda reminded him.

"Except he wants it at the barrel of a gun, rather

than by mutual cooperation and understanding. Peace cannot be forced upon a people. They must *want* it."

"Most would argue that the Jung have no use for peace," Miri replied, "and that their so-called *negotiations* are nothing more than a stalling tactic to allow them to develop their own jump drive. After seven years of such negotiations, I'm finding it hard to reject that notion."

President Scott sighed. "I know how you feel," he admitted, "but we cannot give up hope."

"I know," she said, placing her hand on his shoulder. "I know. I miss him too."

* * *

Doran Montrose burst through the back door to his home, the others hot on his heels.

Terris suddenly appeared in the doorway from the living room. "What..." She spotted her husband and ran to him. "What is it, Doran? What's happening?"

"Everyone, into the living room, away from the doors and windows," Doran ordered.

"What is going on out there?" his wife demanded to know. "I heard reports of an invasion on the..."

"Not now, Terris," Doran insisted as he herded everyone into the living room. "We need clothing for everyone."

"What? Why?"

"Where are Nora and Dunner?"

"They are here..."

"Father!"

Doran embraced his daughter as she entered from the other room, followed by her younger brother. "Thank God you're both safe. Nora, see if you can find a change of clothing for Lael and Doctor Sato. Dunner, help Yanni and Doctor Megel find something to wear from my closet."

"What is going on?" Nora asked.

"Please, just do as I ask."

"Where did you get those weapons?" Doran's wife demanded.

"The weapons, of course." Doran looked at the others. "All your weapons are powered down, are they not?"

Yanni checked his energy rifle. "Yes."

"Give them all to me. I have a place to hide them, one that will shield them from detection."

The others placed their weapons on the couch as instructed.

"What are we going to do?" Yanni asked.

"You two are husband and wife," Doran said, pointing at Yanni and Lael. "Lael, you are a friend of my daughter's, visiting town with your husband and new child. Doctors, you two are my relatives from Federborough province. You are in town for the spring festival tomorrow. Understood?"

"Doran, please," his wife begged.

"It is important that everyone has the same story!" Doran insisted.

"Doran, you're scaring me."

Doran grabbed his wife by the shoulders. "It's the Jung, Terris. They have come."

Terris looked at her husband's eyes. She had not seen such fear in them for many years. "But, the Avendahl..."

"The Avendahl has been destroyed," Doran told her. "Darvano now belongs to the Jung."

Terris Montrose tried to fight back her tears as she clutched her husband. "What are we to do, Doran?"

"I don't know, yet," he told her as he held her

tight. "But I will think of something. I promise."

* * *

"Kind of tight in here, isn't it?" Captain Tuplo commented as he entered the Seiiki's cargo bay.

"That's what happens when you overbook your cargo," Marcus grumbled.

"A full ship is a happy ship," the captain replied as he ascended the port ladder.

Dalen came out onto the port landing, in front of the captain.

"I know," the captain said, holding up one hand as he stepped off the ladder onto the landing. "But we're full up. There's no room to shift cargo around."

"So what do we do if there's a problem and I need to get to the crawl spaces while under way?"

"I don't know, crack the back door and float some cargo outside temporarily?"

"Not funny."

"Relax, Dalen," Captain Tuplo told him. "This is a jump ship, and our next stop is Rama. Three hops at the most. I'm sure nothing will happen during the *grueling*, thirty-minute flight. After all, you take such wonderful care of all our systems, what could go wrong?"

Captain Tuplo didn't wait for Dalen to respond, moving quickly through the hatch on his way forward. By now, Neli had seated everyone, so the corridor past the boarding hatch leading to the cockpit would be free of passengers. Captain Tuplo didn't mind conversing with the various workers at the spaceports, but the passengers...they were always full of questions about what it was like to jump, or how the jump drive worked. For so many, the whole idea of traveling between star systems in a matter of minutes versus months was difficult to believe. Even those who had done so several times still had a hard time wrapping their minds around the concept.

Captain Tuplo entered the forward portion of the ship and moved quickly past the forward passenger cabin. "How are we doing?" he asked Neli as he passed the galley.

"Full house, Cap'n. All of them belted in and ready to go."

"Excellent. We should be lifting off straight away."

The captain turned the corner inward and ascended the steps to the cockpit, ducking as he entered the cramped space. He slipped past the engineering station and in between the seats, sliding down into the left seat as usual. "How are we looking, Josh?" the captain asked as he donned his comm-set.

"All systems are good. Preflight is complete, and we're ready to taxi."

"Ladila Ground, Seiiki, ready for rollback," the captain called over the comms.

"*Seiiki, Ladila Ground. Stand by.*"

"Did you see the girls in four A and B?" Josh asked.

"You know I never look in the passenger cabins, Josh."

"Yeah, well, you should this time. Trust me. I may have to go back there and stroll through in between jumps, if you know what I mean."

"It's a short flight, Josh."

"You could take a few minutes in between jumps, you know. Help a guy out, and all."

"The sooner we finish this circuit and get back to Palee, the sooner we get paid," Captain Tuplo reminded him.

"Seiiki, Ladila Ground. Cleared for rollback to pad four."

"Seiiki is cleared to roll back to pad four," the captain replied. "You want to do the honors?"

"Oh, boy, can I?" Josh replied sarcastically. He reached out and pushed the execute button, and the ship began to roll backward away from the terminal, controlled by the auto-taxi system required by the busier ports. "Why did you even install this thing?" he wondered as he sat idly, watching the exterior camera display.

"Hey, that *thing* opened up a lot of new routes for us, Josh, and you know it."

"Maybe, but between the auto-taxi, the auto-flight, and the auto-jump sequencer, all I ever do is push buttons."

"That's what commercial pilots do, Josh," the captain reminded him.

"It was more fun back *before* everyone had jump drives and automatic everything. Back when I got to actually *fly* the ship, instead of giving the computer permission to fly it."

"Don't worry, Josh. In a few more years, we'll have the money we need to complete our overhaul and head deeper out into space. Out where most people haven't even *heard* of a jump drive, let alone auto-flight systems."

"You've been saying that for the last two years, Cap'n."

Captain Tuplo switched comm frequencies. "Ladila Control, Seiiki. Ready for departure on pad four." Captain Tuplo looked outside, scanning both the ground and the skies above. "I promise, Josh, the next time we do a cargo-only run from a world without a controlled spaceport, I'll let you hand fly both the landing and departure."

"*Seiiki, Ladila Control. Cleared for liftoff on pad four. On departure, fly heading two five four and climb to the Boraliese sector for jump out.*"

"Ladila Control, Seiiki. Lifting off on pad four, on course two five four to Boraliese to jump out."

"*Safe flight, Seiiki,*" the controller replied.

"Take us to Rama, Josh."

Josh pressed the execute button on the auto-flight system. The engines fired, and the thrust slowly increased until the Seiiki rose off the pad and climbed slowly upward. A few seconds later, the auto-flight systems began to angle the ship's main thrust nozzles aft, causing the ship to move forward while climbing. Once they had cleared the terminal area and reached a high enough altitude, the ship accelerated rapidly, and her nose began to pitch up, her engines going to full power. The ship moved quickly through the broken layer of puffy, white clouds as it entered a slow, constant-rate turn to port onto its assigned departure heading. The climb out went like clockwork, just as it always did when the auto-flight computers controlled the ship. Once again, Josh was relegated to being a well-trained spectator.

"Approaching Boraliese sector," Captain Tuplo reported.

"Verifying jump sequence," Josh replied. "Sequencing for Rama is good. Jumping in five seconds......three..."

"*Attention all departing ships,*" the Ladila controller called over the comms.

"Two..."

"*We have an alert...*"

"One..."

"What?" Captain Tuplo said. "Wait..."

"Jumping."

The Seiiki's windows turned opaque as the ship executed its departure jump.

"Did he say an alert?" Captain Tuplo asked.

"Next jump in thirty seconds," Josh reported, ignoring his concern.

"Maybe we should wait for the message to catch up to us." Captain Tuplo suggested.

"It's probably just another stellar storm warning," Josh shrugged. "They get them all the time here."

"Yeah, you're probably right," Captain Tuplo agreed.

"Besides, we'll be long gone by the time it reaches Ladila," Josh added. "Next jump in ten seconds."

* * *

"Same as usual," Admiral Galiardi grumbled as he walked down the corridors of Port Terra on his way to his office.

"Then I take it you did not get the president's endorsement for your plan to build and deploy more super JKKVs?" the admiral's aide, Commander Macklay, surmised.

"Deploy? Hell, the idiot doesn't even want me to *build* them, let alone *deploy* them."

The admiral's aide looked around nervously, checking to see if anyone was within earshot of the admiral. "Sir, it might be better to refrain from calling the President of Earth an *idiot*, at least not within earshot of others."

Admiral Galiardi glanced at his aide as they entered the command center. "The president is well aware of my opinion of him, Commander."

"Of course, sir."

The admiral looked around the room, which

had recently been enlarged to include the adjoining caverns. As the Alliance fleet had grown, so too had the needs of its command center. The old rocky walls of the additional spaces were still in the process of being converted into smooth ones. It was a painstaking process that had happened all over the interior of the old Karuzara asteroid, ever since it had been turned over to the Unified Nations of Earth five years ago, and the admiral had been reinstated and put in command of all Alliance forces in the Sol sector. By now, ninety percent of the asteroid had been carved out, adding dozens of factory spaces, hangar bays, dry docks, and living areas. Even the exterior of the Karuzara was barely recognizable. So much had been built out from her rocky surface, one had to look closely to find surfaces that were still undeveloped. The massive rock orbiting the Earth was finally looking less like the Karuzara, and more like Port Terra.

Admiral Galiardi turned and headed into his office, his aide following close behind. "Any update from the Cape Town?"

"She is due to return to port later today," the commander replied. "Captain Stettner was quite pleased with the performance of his gun crews this time around. It seems they have worked the bugs out of their independent target tracking systems."

"Did he indicate a readiness date?"

"No sir, he did not," the commander replied. "However, he did not indicate that he expected to miss the original deadline, either."

Admiral Galiardi sat down at his desk. "You tell Buchard he needs to light a fire under his crew. I want that ship ready and on call *before* the Aurora goes in for overhaul, not after."

"Yes, sir," Commander Macklay assured the admiral. "Lieutenant Commander Ganis is waiting to speak with you."

"Send him in," the admiral replied as he turned on his view screen.

The commander left the office, replaced a minute later by the lieutenant commander.

"What do you have for me, Ganis?" the admiral asked.

"The second phase of the Sol protection grid passed its operational testing this morning. We now have a total of thirty-two jump missile launchers in operation around the world, which means we can put at least one hundred and twenty-eight missiles into space within two minutes of an alert. That gives us a protection radius of two light years in all directions."

"How long until we can start deploying the perimeter launch platforms?" the admiral asked. "I want that range doubled."

"The first twelve platforms will be ready for deployment in thirty-seven days, as scheduled."

"I hate those words, *as scheduled.* Just once, I'd like to hear someone say *ahead of schedule.*"

"Yes, sir."

"*Admiral,*" the intercom squawked. "*Alert traffic from Mu Cassiopeiae.*"

"What is it?" the admiral asked after pressing the intercom button.

"*Cobra One Four Seven reports spotting two Jung cruisers four light years outside the system.*"

"That's well within Alliance space," the lieutenant commander commented.

Admiral Galiardi was already out of his desk chair and heading for the command center just outside his office. "Commander Macklay!" the admiral bellowed as he stepped through the door.

The commander was already anticipating the admiral's next words. "The closest ship is the Aurora, sir," the commander informed him promptly.

"I thought she was prepping for overhaul?"

"She starts tomorrow," the commander replied. "She still has most of her crew and full armaments. However, her fighter wings have already rotated to the surface."

"What's the course of those ships?" the admiral asked.

"They're headed directly for Mu Cassiopeiae, at maximum FTL speed."

"Alert the Aurora. Have her prepare to get under way. And move the Tanna from Tau Ceti to Eridani. If this is the start of a coordinated attack, there will be more ships coming in from the direction of Patoray."

"What about the Cape Town?" Commander Macklay wondered.

"She's only got half her crew, and nowhere near her full armaments."

"She's got plenty of energy weapons, Admiral."

"No, get her back here and get more crew and weapons onto her decks as quickly as possible. We've only got one Protector-class ship on the line, and she needs to be here, protecting Earth."

"But we have the surface jump missile launchers now," Lieutenant Commander Ganis reminded the admiral. "Once detected, we can blow them to hell long before they get into attack range."

"Assuming we can detect them," Admiral Galiardi pointed out. "They just managed to get five light years inside our borders before we spotted them, and that's on an expected ingress route."

* * *

"All systems are good. We're go for the last jump into Rama."

"Set the jump sequencer for one minute," Captain Tuplo instructed.

"One minute, aye," Josh replied.

Captain Tuplo keyed the ship-wide intercom. "Ladies and Gentlemen, this is your captain. We are about to execute our last jump into the Rama system. As you may know, the government of Assengil does not allow jumps directly into the atmosphere, so we will be entering her atmosphere in the traditional way. Please, do not be alarmed by the red glow you will see outside. It is only the plasma wake caused by our shields hitting the atmosphere and heating up. Our shields will protect us. It may get a bit bumpy on the way in, but our inertial dampening systems should smooth them out nicely."

"Maybe you should record that for playback," Josh suggested. "I could add a trigger cue for it in the jump sequencer."

"I don't plan to make regular runs into Rama," Captain Tuplo said.

"Why not?" Josh wondered. "It's got plenty of traffic these days."

"Too close to Takara. I don't like my port fees lining the pockets of nobles," the captain explained bitterly. "Besides, it's a waste of propellant flying all the way down to the surface instead of just jumping in. All to keep from disturbing the damned *tranquility*."

"Thanks for giving me a few minutes before the last jump," Josh said.

"Did it help?"

Josh smiled impishly. "I got her contact number," he replied, his eyebrows bouncing up and down as a lecherous smile formed on his face. He glanced at the jump sequencer. "Five seconds."

Captain Tuplo smiled back.

"You know, you should trawl the ladies in the back once in a while yourself," Josh said. The windows turned opaque as the Seiiki jumped into the Rama system. "You might want to shave first, though."

"I like my beard," Captain Tuplo replied defensively. "It makes me look older, more experienced, more intelligent."

"And more scary," Josh added. "Assengil, dead ahead." He checked their course on his flight display. "Auto-flight is taking us right down the entry corridor."

"Scary, huh?" Captain Tuplo said.

"Yeah, scary," Josh replied. "And not like, *mean* scary. More like, *psycho* scary. No offense."

"I guess it could stand a little trimming," the captain admitted.

"A little?"

Captain Tuplo looked at Josh. "But I rather like the feeling of anonymity it provides."

"How the hell does it provide anonymity?" Josh wondered. "Everyone recognizes you with that thing. 'There goes Captain Tuplo, the guy with the psycho, out-of-control beard.' Try something new, like a goatee or something."

"I hate goatees," Captain Tuplo growled as he studied his flight displays. He glanced forward through the window, noting that the planet Assengil was growing larger. "Maybe we should start decelerating?"

"Relax, Cap," Josh replied, glancing at the auto-flight display. "Auto-flight has it. Decel burn is coming up in two minutes." He looked over at

Captain Tuplo, studying his face for a moment.

Connor felt Josh staring at him, and looked his way. "What?"

"Mutton chops, maybe?"

"You're joking, right?" the captain replied, his attention returning to his flight displays.

"Maybe with a handlebar mustache?" Josh suggested. "Anything besides the 'I've been hiding in a cave for the last twenty years' look you've got going on now."

"That bad, huh?"

"Isn't that why you've been avoiding running into passengers?"

"That obvious?"

"Just try trimming it shorter," Josh urged, trying to find a compromise. "At least make it look like you give a shit."

"All right, I get your point."

"And while you're at it, you might think about doing something with that hair of yours."

"I am your employer, remember?" Captain Tuplo reminded him.

"Just trying to help you get some action, Cap'n."

"I don't need any *action*," the captain argued.

"Everybody needs a little action once in a while," Josh argued. "Even psycho-looking ship captains."

"You just never worry about the possible consequences, do you, Josh?"

"Cap, it's all coming from a place of love, you know that."

An audible alert beeped several times.

Captain Tuplo looked at the sensor display. "Something is coming over the horizon of Assengil."

"A ship?" Josh assumed.

"Must be," the captain agreed. "Assengil doesn't

have any orbital structures to speak of." The captain's brow furrowed as he studied the image on the sensor screen. "It's awfully big to be a ship."

"The Avendahl, maybe?" Josh said. "I heard she comes out from Darvano now and again, just to remind the nobles that she's around."

"Nope. Bigger."

"*Bigger* than the Avendahl?"

"Wait," Captain Tuplo said. "It's not one ship, it's two. Two big ones."

"Takaran ships?"

"They're not squawking Takaran IDs," Captain Tuplo replied.

Josh noticed the look of concern on his employer's face. "Should I go to manual..."

"*Attention incoming jump ship,*" a voice called over the comms. The caller had an air of authority to his tone, one meant to strike fear in the hearts of those listening. "*Identify yourself, and state your intentions.*"

"What the..."

"This is the commercial transport ship, Seiiki," Captain Tuplo replied over the comms. "We are carrying cargo and passengers bound for the Assengil Spaceport from Ladila in the Paradar system. We are unarmed."

"Captain, more contacts," Josh warned. "Coming from those ships." He looked at the captain. "I think they're launching interceptors."

"*Seiiki, you are ordered to rendezvous with the Jar-Dortayo and land on her starboard flight deck.*"

"On whose authority?" Captain Tuplo inquired.

"*By order of Lord Dusahn, ruler of the Pentaurus cluster.*"

"Who the fuck is Lord Dusahn?" Josh wondered.

"I never heard of him," the captain replied.

"A Takaran noble?"

"I don't recognize the name."

Josh looked down at the sensor display again. "Those contacts are closing on us fast, Cap'n."

"We humbly request permission to land at the Assengil Spaceport and offload our passengers and cargo," Captain Tuplo responded, "after which we will depart your territory, never to return."

"You will follow our instructions, or you will be destroyed."

"What the..." Josh exclaimed. "Half the contacts just..."

Six jump flashes suddenly appeared directly in front of them, revealing menacing, black-hulled fighters trimmed in crimson and gold. The lead fighter fired his energy cannon, sending a stream of red energy bolts streaking directly over the top of the Seiiki's cockpit.

The fighters streaked past them, two on each side, and one above and below, all of them passing dangerously close to the Seiiki.

Josh's eyes widened as he watched the fighters speed past. He looked at his captain. "Those are Jung fighters, Cap'n."

"Are you sure?" Captain Tuplo asked in disbelief.

"Trust me on this," Josh insisted. "I've seen a lot of Jung fighters in my day."

"But I thought the Jung didn't have jump drive technology."

"Apparently, things have changed," Josh replied. "I'm going to manual," he added, pressing the auto-flight disengage button on the flight control yoke.

"Seiiki, this is your last warning," the voice said.

"Good idea," Captain Tuplo agreed. He looked out

the windows as the fighters swarmed up to escort them. Two on each side, and two in front.

"*Seiiki, Seiiki! Jotakh Leader!*" another voice called impatiently. This one had a heavy accent, one that Captain Tuplo could not quite place. "*Follow us to Jar-Dortayo. Make no attempt to deviate, or destroy you we must. Are you to understand?*"

"Yup, they're Jung, all right," Josh commented. "Same bad Angla."

Captain Tuplo watched as the fighters on either side fell back.

"They're surrounding us," Josh warned.

"*Are you to understand?*" the lead fighter pilot repeated.

"Can you get us out of here?" Captain Tuplo asked, looking at Josh.

"Watch me," Josh replied.

"*Seiiki! Respond!*"

"Fuck off," Captain Tuplo replied flatly over the comms.

Josh pushed the control stick forward and brought the main engines to full power. There was a thud, and the ship rocked slightly, as their shields turned an opaque yellow.

"What the hell was that?" Captain Tuplo asked.

"I had to push one of those fighters out of the way," Josh explained as he twisted the control stick to the right and pulled back slightly, putting the Seiiki into a climbing right, rolling turn.

"You what?"

"Don't worry, Cap, the shields protected us."

Captain Tuplo glanced at the sensor display, as the icon representing the Jung fighter they had just *nudged* out of their way disappeared. "Holy shit, Josh! You just destroyed one of their fighters!"

"Oops. I guess they don't have shields."

"Jesus," Captain Tuplo exclaimed as he looked to his left out the side windows.

"*Captain!*" Marcus called over the comm-set. "*What the hell is going on?*"

Red energy bolts streaked across their nose from the left, moving closer as the enemy continued firing. The ship rocked with the impacts of the bolts slamming into their port shields.

"*What the fuck! Is someone firing at us?*"

"Neli!" Captain Tuplo called over the comm-sets. "Get everyone in their seats! Now!"

"It's the fucking Jung, Marcus!" Josh called over the comm-sets.

"*Shit!*" Marcus swore. "*Get us the fuck out of here, kid!*"

"No shit," Josh commented to himself as he twisted the control stick and forced the Seiiki into another evasive maneuver.

"*Our shields aren't designed for this!*" Dalen warned over the comm-sets.

"We need an escape jump, Cap'n!" Josh yelled.

"I'm already on it!"

"Well get on it a little faster!" Josh insisted, as another energy bolt slammed into their right side.

"This ship isn't like those Falco fighters you used to fly, Josh..."

"Falcon, not Falco..."

"It doesn't have an escape jump button, you know!"

"Well, it would if you had ordered Dalen to install one, like I suggested!" Josh reminded him.

The ship lunged sideways, as more energy bolts slammed into her left side.

"We're losing our port shields! Aft section!" Josh

warned.

"Dalen!" Captain Tuplo called over the comms. "Port shields! Aft section! Can you boost them?"

"The fucking access hatches are blocked, remember!"

"Son of a..."

Another round of energy bolts slammed into the starboard side, sending the ship careening in the opposite direction.

"Captain!" Josh urged.

"I've got it! I've got it!" Captain Tuplo replied. "Jumping!"

The Seiiki's windows turned opaque, clearing a second later. The Jung fighters were gone, they were no longer being rocked by energy weapons fire, and the sensor screen was clear. There were, however, still plenty of warning alarms going off in the cockpit of the Seiiki.

"Now will you have Dalen install an escape jump button?" Josh demanded. He took a few breaths before continuing. "What do we do now?"

"We go to our next stop, Haven."

"Why? None of the passengers are going to Haven," Josh argued. "Maybe we should take them back to Ladila?"

"We told the Jung that we came from Ladila. If they wanted to track us down and destroy us, that would be the first place they would look," Captain Tuplo reasoned.

"Why would they want to do that?" Josh wondered. "We're just one little cargo ship."

"I don't know. Maybe because we destroyed one of their fighters?"

"Oh yeah, that." Josh started punching the destination into the jump navigation computer.

"Gonna be a hell of a culture shock for the passengers... Going from Ladila to Haven."

"Better than a Jung detention cell, I would imagine," the captain replied.

CHAPTER FOUR

Vladimir stood in the middle of the captain's ready room just aft of the Aurora's bridge, looking at the woman he had called his commanding officer and his friend, for the last seven years.

"So, this is it, I guess," Cameron said softly.

"*Da, da.*"

"Seven years of trying to get you to say 'yes', and you still say '*da*'."

Vladimir shrugged. "It is who I am."

"Yes, it is." Cameron rose from her seat and came around the desk to give her friend one last embrace. "I'm going to miss you," she whispered as she held him tightly.

"I will miss you, as well," Vladimir replied. "I will not miss the salads, mind you."

Cameron chuckled as she pulled away, wiping a tear from her eye. "Just try to eat one every so often, for me?"

"I will," Vladimir promised. "However, I will smother it with tons of creamy dressing and a modest portion of meat." A broad smile spread across his face.

"If that's what it takes."

Vladimir sighed. "You did it, you know."

"Did what?" Cameron asked.

"You became the first female starship captain in all of Earth's post-plague history."

Cameron smiled again. "The youngest too."

"Indeed," Vladimir agreed. "You should be as proud of yourself, as I am to have known you."

"And I, you," Cameron replied.

"Safe travels, Captain Taylor," Vladimir said, as

he came to attention and issued a perfect military salute.

Cameron understood the significance of her friend's gesture, which made it all the more difficult for her to hold back her tears. To her knowledge, Vladimir had only offered such a salute two other times in his life. To their friend Nathan Scott, when he surrendered himself to the Jung to save everyone, and later at Nathan's memorial service on Earth.

Cameron straightened up and returned the salute, in the same spirit that it had been given.

"*Captain, Comms. Flash traffic,*" the voice called over the desk intercom.

"Message?" Cameron asked, turning her head slightly toward the desk.

"*From Command, sir. We've been ordered to intercept a pair of Jung cruisers spotted inside Alliance space, en route to Mu Cassiopeiae at maximum FTL.*"

Cameron looked at Vladimir. "Your replacement isn't due for two weeks."

"You won't need him," Vladimir replied as he turned to exit. "I'll be in engineering," he added on his way out. "Cheng to Flight Ops. Have the line return my belongings to my cabin...and be careful with my cat."

Cameron followed Vladimir out of the ready room, continuing toward her command chair as her friend turned aft to exit. "Mister deBanco, contact the XO on Port Terra and have him rendezvous with us at the intercept point. Cancel all leaves, and recall all crew to the ship. They can meet up with us later, as well, if our mission is extended."

"Aye, sir," the communications officer replied.

"Tactical," Cameron continued as she took her seat in the command chair, "sound general quarters.

Helm, take us out of orbit and prepare to jump to the far side of Mu Cassiopeiae."

"Target plots coming in from command now," the tactical officer announced.

"Taking us out of orbit," the helmsman replied.

"Plotting jump to Mu Cassiopeiae," the navigator added.

"I have Commander Kaplan on the line, sir. She is asking if you'd like her to rendezvous immediately, or wait for some of the crew to report in and bring them along?" the communications officer asked.

"Who's in combat?" Cameron asked.

"Lieutenant Atchison," the tactical officer replied.

"That'll work for now," Cameron decided. "Tell the commander to bring a full load with her."

"Yes, sir," the comm officer nodded.

"The ship is at general quarters, Captain," Lieutenant Commander Vidmar announced from the tactical station directly behind the captain.

"Breaking orbit now," the helmsman reported.

"Mister Bickle?" Cameron said.

"It's pushing the limits, sir," the navigator replied. "The intercept point is just under four light years past Mu Cassiopeiae, which makes it just over twenty-eight light years away. We're going to have less than a full light year of jump range remaining upon intercept."

"Stretch the first jump to max range," Cameron ordered.

"Aye, sir."

Cameron pressed a comm-panel button on the arm of her command chair. "Cheng, Captain. I'm going to need you to rapid charge the number one jump drive once we get there."

"*It will not be a problem,*" Vladimir promised over

the intercom.

"On course for Mu Cassiopeiae," Lieutenant Dinev reported from the helm.

"First jump set for fourteen point nine light years," Mister Bickle announced. "Ready to jump."

"Execute departure jump," Cameron ordered.

"Departure jump, aye," the navigator replied.

"Load two spreaders with anti-FTL mines and prepare to launch," Cameron ordered as the blue-white light of the jump flash washed over the bridge.

"Two spreaders with anti-FTL mines, aye," the tactical officer responded.

"Preparing arrival jump," Mister Bickle reported.

"Jump flash," Lieutenant Commander Kono reported from the Aurora's sensor station. "Alliance comm-drone."

"Position update from Cobra One Four Seven," Ensign deBanco reported from the comm-center at the back of the Aurora's bridge. "Cobras One Four Two and Two Two Five are keeping positive tracks. No change in course and speed noted. Updated orders from command authorize maximum force."

"Very well," Cameron replied.

"Reactors one and two are now running at one hundred and twenty percent each," the systems officer reported.

"Very well," Cameron repeated. For a moment, she wondered if her next chief engineer would be willing to take such risks as easily as Vladimir.

"Arrival jump is plotted and ready," Ensign Bickle reported.

"Spreaders are loaded and ready to launch," the tactical officer added. "All weapons are charged and ready."

"Execute your jump, Mister Bickle," Cameron

ordered. "Tactical, stand by to launch spreaders."

"Executing arrival jump," the navigator announced.

"Spreader launch, standing by," the tactical officer confirmed.

Cameron watched the main view screen as the jump field energy poured out from the Aurora's emitters, spreading quickly over her hull, until its entire surface was bathed in the pale blue light. The blue light quickly intensified, becoming a brilliant blue-white flash a mere second later. Had the main view screen not been designed to greatly subdue the brightness of the jump flash, she would have surely been blinded, at least temporarily. The entire event took less than three seconds. It was a sight she had witnessed thousands of times before, yet it still amazed her as much as it had when she witnessed it during the very first test jump of the prototype nine years earlier. Despite the fact that she had been jumping all over the Sol sector for the last nine years, as well as to the Pentaurus cluster and back, the idea that a ship could jump fifteen light years in the blink of an eye still astounded her.

"Jump complete," the navigator reported.

"Knock them out of FTL, Lieutenant Commander," Cameron ordered.

"Firing spreaders," the tactical officer replied.

Cameron watched the main view screen as two jump missiles, one from each side, shot out of their forward launch tubes. The missiles adjusted their courses slightly, then disappeared behind their own jump flashes a few seconds later.

"Spreaders have jumped away."

Cameron waited patiently.

"Jump flashes," Lieutenant Commander Kono

reported from the sensor station a minute later. "And antimatter detonations, full spreads."

Cameron waited, breathing in a calm, regular fashion, until the next words came out of her sensor officer's mouth.

"New contacts," the lieutenant commander announced. "Two Jung cruisers...heavies...just out of FTL. Fifteen million kilometers and closing."

"Are their shields up?" Cameron asked.

"No, sir. Not yet."

"Comms. Transmit message in Jung. Message reads, 'This is the Alliance ship, Aurora. Reverse course and depart Alliance space immediately, or you will be fired upon. You have one minute from receipt of message to comply. There will be no further warnings.' End message."

Ensign deBanco swallowed hard. "Yes, sir."

"Targets are raising shields," the sensor officer reported.

"Load a full spread of jump missiles on all cats. Antimatter warheads on all six," Cameron ordered.

Lieutenant Commander Vidmar looked from his tactical console to his captain seated directly in front of him. "Confirming antimatter warheads on all six jump missiles, Captain?"

"That is correct," Cameron replied.

"Aye, sir," the tactical officer replied. "Loading all catapults with jump missiles, antimatter warheads." Lieutenant Commander Vidmar exchanged concerned looks with Lieutenant Commander Kono at the sensor station.

"Captain," Lieutenant Commander Kono began, "a single antimatter warhead is more than enough to take out a heavy cruiser."

"Relax, Lanea," Cameron replied, "I'm not going

to lead with them. I'll fire a few warning shots first, I promise."

"Yes, sir."

"Message should be reaching them now," Ensign deBanco reported from the comm station.

Cameron glanced at the ship's time display above the main view screen. "Very well." Cameron watched for exactly fifteen seconds. "Any change in target course and speed?"

"Negative, sir," Lieutenant Commander Kono replied.

"Lieutenant Commander Vidmar. Paint those ships, then lock all weapons on their targets and open the launch tube doors."

"Painting targets and locking weapons," the tactical officer replied. A few seconds later he added, "Opening launch tube doors."

Cameron glanced at the clock again. Thirty seconds had passed since the two Jung cruisers should have received their warning message. "Lock forward cannons on the targets. One turret on each ship."

"Locking forward plasma cannons on both ships," Lieutenant Commander Vidmar responded.

Cameron looked up at the time display. Forty-five seconds had passed. "Stand by to fire cannons... twenty-five percent power."

"Twenty-five percent power, standing by."

Cameron watched the last few seconds tick away. Exactly one minute after the moment the two Jung cruisers should have received their warnings, she gave the order. "Triplets, both cannons. Fire."

"Firing triplets, both cannons," the tactical officer replied.

Cameron watched the main view screen as

red-orange bolts of plasma energy fired from their forward plasma cannons, disappearing into the distant blackness of space ahead of them a split second later. Again, she waited.

"Direct hits, both ships," Lieutenant Commander Kono reported from the sensor station thirty seconds later. "Minor reduction in their forward shields. Still holding course and speed."

"Launch all missiles, but hold the jump until my command," Cameron instructed calmly.

"Launching all missiles, manual jump," the tactical officer replied.

She watched as six jump missiles, armed with antimatter warheads, left their port and starboard launch tunnels, moving ahead at a leisurely pace toward the still onrushing enemy cruisers.

"Six missiles away. All weapons are auto-updating their jump plots as they go."

"Very well," Cameron replied. She could feel the tension in the room. They had just launched enough antimatter to take out a small moon.

"Targets should detect the launches in ten seconds," Lieutenant Commander Kono announced.

"Stand by to jump all weapons to their targets to engage," Cameron instructed.

"Standing by," the tactical officer acknowledged.

"Three......two......one..." Lieutenant Commander Kono studied her sensor displays carefully, but said nothing.

Cameron looked at the sensor officer to her left. "Anything?" she asked, trying not to make it too obvious that she did not want to give the order to engage the weapons.

Five more seconds passed before the lieutenant commander had anything to report. "Targets are changing course. They're turning to starboard... Still turning..." The lieutenant commander breathed a sigh of relief, her stiff posture suddenly relaxing. "Targets are turning back toward Jung space, Captain."

"Safe all missiles, but maintain their tracks," Cameron instructed.

"Targets are going to FTL," the sensor officer added.

"All missiles are safed."

"Targets are gone, sir," the lieutenant commander finally reported.

This time, it was Cameron who breathed a sigh of relief. "Cancel the missile tracks and recall, Mister Vidmar. Comms, launch the missile recovery shuttles. And tell those Cobras to maintain a close track on those ships until they are clear of Alliance space."

"Yes, sir," the comm officer reported.

"Standing down all missiles and recalling," the tactical officer confirmed.

"That was close," Lieutenant Commander Kono commented from the sensor station.

"Too close," Cameron agreed.

* * *

"We're receiving recon data now," the communications tech reported to General Telles as he entered the Ghatazhak Command Center, along with Jessica, Loki, and Deliza.

General Telles stepped up to the main planning table, switching on the 3D display. An image of the Takar system appeared, floating in the air above the table. Red icons materialized over the system, most of them clustered around the many inhabited worlds of the Takar system, with the majority of them in the vicinity of the system's main world, Takara. The general touched one of the red icons with his finger, causing the icon to expand and change into an image of the ship it represented. He tapped the image again, expanding it further, allowing him to closely examine its markings and structure.

"Those are definitely Jung ships," Jessica commented.

"Indeed they are," General Telles agreed. "The question is, are the *Jung* the ones operating them?"

"Initial recon data shows a total of twelve ships currently occupying the cluster," Commander Jahal began. He glanced at his data pad. "Recon One reports that, on average, there are about eight ships in the Takar system, as ships are jumping in and out quite often. We're assuming those other four ships are patrolling the other systems of the Pentaurus cluster."

"What about Darvano?" Loki asked.

General Telles pressed several buttons on the side of the planning table. The image of the Takar system became smaller and slid to one side, making room for an image of the Darvano system next to it.

"There are currently four ships stationed within the area of the Darvano and Savoy systems," Commander Jahal said. "Recon Two reports no movement there."

"How many recon ships do you have?" Deliza wondered.

"Just the two," Jessica replied. "They're the Falcons that you converted into Super Falcons. Once the Alliance had enough jump fighters and gunships, they retired the line. We got the last two working ships, as well as two more inoperable ships to use for parts."

"And you've kept them going all these years," Loki commented in amazement.

"It was a challenge at times," General Telles admitted.

"What other ships do you have?" Loki asked.

"Four combat jumpers, two cargo jumpers, and a boxcar that spends more time in maintenance than on the line," Commander Jahal replied.

"Cycle the crews on the Falcons, and get them back out," General Telles ordered. "I want as much data as possible."

"What about old light?" Commander Jahal asked.

"We'll wait until that light gets well outside the systems," the general replied. "The Jung have not shown any sign that they have detected our recon Falcons, so let's keep them in close as long as possible."

"Or, they *have* detected them, and they just don't care," Commander Jahal commented.

"*Or*, they are *pretending* they aren't aware of our Falcons, and they plan on tracing them back to us."

General Telles pondered the idea for a moment. "By now, our presence on Burgess is known throughout the sector, and the Jung will undoubtedly be interrogating the populations quite vigorously. They will discover the threat we represent quite soon on their own, without tracing the Falcons back to this world."

"*Or*, they had spies on the surface and knew about us long before they invaded," Jessica suggested.

General Telles looked at Jessica. "You're not making this any easier, Lieutenant."

"Just tossing out ideas, Boss," Jessica quipped.

"Had they known about us ahead of time, we wouldn't be standing here talking about it,"

Commander Jahal insisted.

"Quite right, indeed," the general agreed. "Make sure the Falcon pilots are taking measures to prevent being tracked. And have everyone prepare to bug out, should it become necessary."

"General, there are over five hundred of us," Commander Jahal reminded him. "Twice that number if you count our wives and children. We do not have the capability to move that many people on short notice."

"I'm well aware of that, Commander."

"Of course, sir."

"Have the families disperse and blend into the general population of Burgess. They all have relatives on this world that they can stay with for now. We will pre-stage our equipment in another system, and we can fit all of our men in a single cargo pod, if necessary." The general raised his hand to stop the commander before he could object. "I agree, it is not the ideal solution, but it is the best one we have at the moment."

"When the Jung come, they will interrogate the people of Burgess as well. They will find our wives and children and use them as leverage against us." The commander objected.

General Telles looked at the commander. "Do you have an alternative?"

"I do," Deliza interrupted.

Everyone looked at her in surprise.

"The Glendanon," Deliza continued. "She's got more than enough room in her cargo bays to hold your entire operation. Soldiers, equipment, ships, and all your families as well."

General Telles looked at the commander.

"I'll get those recon ships examining the old light

to track her course right away," Commander Jahal said.

"Captain Gullen is an old friend of my father's," Deliza explained. "He served as a tactical officer aboard a battleship under Caius's regime. It will not be easy to track him."

"We will find him," General Telles promised.

* * *

"Admiral, we have another sighting," Commander Macklay reported.

"Where?" the admiral asked.

"You called it, sir. 82 Eridani. Three contacts, one large and two small, about three light years out."

"Damn it," the admiral swore, pounding the arm of his chair, getting the attention of everyone in the command center. "That's one of the most heavily patrolled corridors in the entire sector. How the hell did they get that far in without being detected?"

Commander Macklay had no response.

Admiral Galiardi sighed. "Order the Tanna to intercept. Same rules. Maximum force, single warning."

"Aye, sir," the commander replied.

"What's the latest from Mu Cassiopeiae?"

"The last report from the Aurora indicated that the Cobra gunships have not yet located the fleeing cruisers, and they have searched the length of their original departure course," the commander explained. "If they maintained that course, the gunships would have located them by now."

"Which means they purposefully changed course to try to elude us," the admiral added. "That means they never had any intention of leaving Alliance space." The admiral looked at the commander. "We need to know where those cruisers went to,

Commander."

"I've already sent additional gunships to the area," the commander assured him, "and the Aurora is examining the tracking data, trying to determine where the cruisers changed course by examining their old light."

Admiral Galiardi sat and thought for a moment.

"This could still be a coincidence, sir," Commander Macklay commented, noticing the admiral's concern.

"I don't believe in coincidences, Commander," the admiral replied resolutely. "Not where the Jung are concerned."

"No offense, Admiral, but I very much hope you are wrong," the commander replied.

"So do I, Commander," the admiral agreed, "for all our sakes."

* * *

"How are we going to get word to the Alliance?" Jessica asked. "We can't spare any ships, not if we might have to bug out at any moment."

"And the longer it takes to alert the Alliance, the longer it will take for them to send help," Commander Jahal added.

"Your company has its own jump comm-drone, does it not?" General Telles asked Deliza.

"Yes. It is kept in a midrange orbit, just inside Kassabol."

"Can we use it to contact the Alliance?" the general inquired.

"It doesn't have the range," Loki warned.

"What do you mean, it doesn't have the range?" Jessica challenged. "It has a mini-jump drive, doesn't it?"

"Yes, but it does not have the programming for such a long jump series," Loki explained. "Its jump navigation database only contains the systems within the Pentaurus sector."

"So it can't even find its way here?" Jessica asked, shocked by the idea.

"No, it cannot."

"No matter," the general said. "Better that we recover it elsewhere and bring it here." He looked at Deliza again. "Can you direct the drone to jump to an arbitrary point between systems?"

"I can send it anywhere within the Pentaurus sector," Deliza assured him.

"And you can reprogram the drone to make the trip to Sol?" the general inquired.

"Of course," Deliza replied. "However, I will need physical access to the drone."

"We will signal the drone to jump to the halfway point between the Darvano and Savahal systems," the general decided. "Then we will redirect it to the halfway point between Savahal and Ursoot, and we shall recover the drone there. That way, if the Jung attempt to track it, we should have enough time to recover the drone before they catch up to us."

"I will give you the access codes for the drone," Deliza replied. "Of course, you'll have to be *in* the Darvano system to activate it."

"Maybe we should try to contact Dumar while we're there," Jessica suggested. "Deliza *did* tell Montrose to try to find him before they jumped out. If they *did* contact him, at least we would know their status."

Deliza looked concerned. "You *are* planning on rescuing them, aren't you?"

"In due time, yes," the general replied.

"In due time?" Deliza frowned at the general's vague response. "What is that? In due time?"

"The Darvano system is occupied by at least four heavily armed, jump-enabled Jung warships," General Telles reminded her. "Each of which carries numerous jump-enabled fighters and shuttles. Furthermore, by now, there is a heavy Jung presence on the surface of Corinair. To make matters more difficult, we do not even know where your people are at the moment."

"If we jump in blindly and stir things up, we'll probably just make matters worse for them," Jessica added, placing her hands on Deliza's shoulders comfortingly. "Trust us, Deliza. After all, we *are* Ghatazhak."

"She's right," Loki told her. He suddenly turned his head and looked at Jessica after realizing what she had said. "Wait... What?"

* * *

"Our contract clearly states that we have the right to refuse making port at any designated stop if it puts the safety of the ship, the crew, the passengers, or the cargo at risk," Captain Tuplo argued.

"That contract also says we don't have to pay you for any uncompleted stops," the agent rebutted.

"All four of those were at risk," Captain Tuplo continued, ignoring the company agent's words. "If we hadn't aborted our approach and escaped, you'd be dealing with the fallout from not only the loss of your cargo, but probably the deaths of every passenger as well. How much do you think your premiums would go up if your insurance carrier had to pay out all *those* claims?"

"I am not disagreeing with your decision, Captain Tuplo," the agent said placatingly, "only with your assertion that you should still be paid for the run, which, as I pointed out, you did not complete."

"Why should I be out the propellant, *and* the cost of repairs?" Captain Tuplo argued. "It's not our fault the Jung suddenly decided to invade the Pentaurus cluster."

"Neither is it ours. Please, Captain, be reasonable. We are still willing to pay you for the remainder of your contracted stops, assuming of course that you complete them. We are even willing to cover the cost of your lost propellant. However, you will have to speak to your own insurance carrier about the cost of your repairs," the agent reasoned. "You *do* have damage insurance, do you not?"

"You know damn well we don't," Marcus sneered. "That's why you gave us the run, because we were cheaper than everyone else..."

"...Because we don't carry damage coverage," Captain Tuplo added.

"Not carrying such coverage is indeed a risk," the agent said. "However, it is a risk that you chose to take, not us." The agent stood for a moment, his eyes darting back and forth between Captain Tuplo and Marcus, worried that one of them might suddenly lash out at him. "Now, do you wish to complete the remainder of your contract, or should I find another ship?"

Captain Tuplo scowled, then looked toward Dalen, his engineer. "Is she safe to fly?"

"As long as we get to jump into the atmosphere," Dalen replied. "The shield emitters on the port side are completely fried, Cap'n."

"Paradar is a jump-down port, Cap," Josh reminded him.

"I know," Captain Tuplo snapped. He looked at the agent, scowling again. "We'll make the Paradar run on one condition," Captain Tuplo said. "You pay for our propellant back to Haven."

"I'll do you one better," the agent offered. "I'll give you a full cargo bay on your return trip to Haven."

Captain Tuplo stared at the agent in shock.

"Do we have a deal, Captain?" the agent asked, holding out his hand.

Captain Tuplo sighed. "Deal." He turned away from the agent and headed back up the Seiiki's cargo ramp, refusing to shake the man's hand.

"Captain, why do you want to come back to Haven?" Marcus asked, following the captain up the ramp.

"The port fees are cheaper," Captain Tuplo replied.

"So are parts," Dalen added.

Marcus winced as if he was in pain. "I fuckin' hate Haven."

"I'm not a fan of this dirt world either, Marcus," the captain said. "But if we're going to be laid up for a few days for repairs, better we don't waste our money paying higher prices on Paradar."

"How many days are we talking about?" Marcus asked.

Captain Tuplo looked at Dalen.

"I don't know yet," Dalen admitted. "I haven't had a chance to do a detailed inspection."

"Guess," Captain Tuplo insisted.

"Three, four days, maybe."

Marcus groaned. "Captain, please..."

"Stop whining and get this ship loaded, Marcus," Captain Tuplo ordered. "Dalen, help him. Josh, run full diagnostics on all flight systems."

"Where are you going, Cap'n?" Josh wondered.

"I'm going topside to check out the damage to my ship."

* * *

The cold blackness of space lit up with flashes of white light, as dozens of antimatter warheads suddenly detonated simultaneously. The blast created a wall of light that stretched over more than one hundred square kilometers of space. It was only visible for a few seconds, but was enough to disrupt the FTL fields of any ships attempting to pass through.

The wall of light vanished as abruptly as it had appeared, revealing three Jung warships: a cruiser flanked by two frigates. Seconds later, a blue-white flash of light appeared only a few kilometers behind the Jung ships. An Alliance destroyer, whose design closely resembled that of the Jung frigates, appeared from the jump flash.

Missile launchers atop both Jung frigates quickly rose from openings in their hulls, rotating to face astern. Within seconds, flashes of yellow-orange announced the launching of their weapons, as four missiles streaked away from each launcher, headed for the destroyer pursuing them.

"Multiple contacts!" Ensign Bottrell reported in earnest from the destroyer's sensor station. "Incoming missiles! Eight of them! Twenty seconds to impact!"

"Ready the escape jump," Captain Nash instructed. "XO, light 'em up."

"Firing all tubes," Commander Poschay replied from the tactical station.

"So much for the warning message," Captain Nash muttered.

"Ten seconds!"

"Torpedoes away!" the XO announced.

The Tanna's bridge flashed reddish-orange

several times as balls of plasma energy shot from the Alliance destroyer's mark four plasma torpedo tubes.

"Five seconds to…"

"Execute escape jump," the captain ordered calmly, not waiting for his sensor officer to finish his warning.

"Escape jump, aye," the young ensign at the Tanna's navigation console replied, as the subdued blue-white light of their jump filled their main view screens.

"Jump complete," the ensign continued.

"Position?" the captain inquired from his command chair in the middle of the Tanna's bridge.

"One light minute ahead of the targets, starboard of their course," the navigator replied.

"Lieutenant Gissel, turn forty-five to port and pitch up thirty degrees," the captain instructed. "Ensign Levitt, queue up a three-light-minute jump."

"Forty-five to port, and thirty up," the helmsman acknowledged.

"Three light minutes, aye," the navigator followed.

"Comms, dispatch a comm-drone and let Alliance Command know that we have been fired upon and are engaging all three enemy ships with intent to destroy," the captain ordered.

"Aye, sir," Ensign Nwosu replied from the communications station.

"Course change complete," Lieutenant Gissel reported from the helm.

"Mister Levitt, jump us out three light minutes. Then plot a return course. I want to make the next run on the cruiser, passing over her fore-aft, port-starboard."

"Aye, sir," the navigator replied. "Jumping ahead

117

three light minutes."

"Comm-drone is away," the communications officer reported.

The blue-white jump flash momentarily filled their main view screens once again.

"Coming about," the helmsman reported.

A tiny smile crept to the corner of Captain Nash's mouth. He knew that his helmsman enjoyed putting the pressure on her new partner, who had yet to finish plotting the new attack course. Lieutenant Gissel had been putting the young ensign on the spot whenever she had the chance, since he had joined the crew a few months ago. He had yet to fail at his task. However, this was his first time under real fire.

In fact, other than the Tanna's XO and her chief engineer, Captain Nash was the only one aboard who had seen actual combat...and plenty of it. Most of his crew had been reassigned to other destroyers as they had come online over the years. The steady flow of fresh recruits from the Alliance Training Academy on Earth had presented a challenge for the captain and his executive officer, requiring constant drills and reviews to ensure that their constantly changing crews were ready for action. Hopefully, today, those efforts would prove their worth.

"Don't let her rattle you, Ensign," the captain advised in his most reassuring tone.

"New course is ready," the navigator quickly replied.

Lieutenant Gissel peeked over her left shoulder at her captain, a mix of pride and satisfaction showing on her face.

Captain Nash smiled back at his chief pilot.

"Coming onto new attack course now," she announced as her attention returned to her console.

"Attack jump is plotted and ready," Ensign Levitt added in a relieved tone.

"Ready on the plasma cannons," the captain ordered. "Full power, triplets. Main guns on the frigates."

"Full power triplets on the cruiser, main guns on the frigates," Commander Poschay confirmed.

Amongst all the new faces on the ship, his second in command and chief tactical officer, Commander Poschay, was one of the only two who had been with him since he had taken command of the Tanna over seven years ago. Once a scrub ensign serving as the navigator on what had then been a frigate, Daryl Poschay had cross-trained in every department and rose quickly through the ranks, eventually replacing the Tanna's last XO when he had departed to take command of the newly commissioned destroyer, Nagoya.

Commander Poschay's efforts had paid off, as had Captain Nash's encouragement. The commander had been an excellent executive and tactical officer, having served in the position for more than a year now. Unfortunately, Captain Nash knew that the commander would be taken from him in less than a year, when the next round of destroyers was ready to leave the Tau Ceti shipyards.

"Execute attack jump," Captain Nash instructed.

"Executing attack jump," the navigator replied. A moment later, the screens filled with the subdued blue-white flash, as the destroyer instantly advanced nearly fifty-four million kilometers along its course. "Jump complete."

"Pitching down," Lieutenant Gissel announced from the Tanna's helm.

"Mains locked on the frigates and auto-tracking.

Opening fire," Commander Poschay reported. "Tubes coming to bear on the cruiser. Full power triplets, firing... Now."

The view screens flashed red-orange three times in rapid succession, as three pairs of plasma torpedoes left the destroyer's tubes.

"Frigate one is turning to port," the sensor officer reported. "She's accelerating."

"Direct impacts on their dorsal shields," the commander reported from the tactical station directly behind the captain.

"Cruiser's dorsal shields are down to fifty percent," the sensor officer added. "Frigate two is also breaking off and accelerating. Turning to starboard and pitching down."

"They're trying to spread out," Commander Poschay commented, "to get some maneuvering room."

"Which means they plan on standing and fighting, instead of slipping back into FTL as soon as their emitters come back online," the captain added.

"All targets are locking rail guns on us," Ensign Bottrell warned. "They're firing."

"Evasive pattern delta seven," Captain Nash ordered.

"Delta seven, aye..."

"Escape jump, three minutes, as soon as the maneuver is complete," the captain added.

"Three-minute jump after..."

"Tactical; jump missiles, frigate two. Launch when ready."

"Two jump missiles on frigate two. Launching!" the commander replied.

"Delta seven, complete," Lieutenant Gissel reported with her usual calm voice.

"Hold your jump one," the captain instructed, knowing his navigator was about to execute the escape jump.

"Missiles away," the commander reported.

"Jump," Captain Nash ordered.

"Jumping; forward three," Ensign Levitt replied as the jump flash filled the view screens again.

"Helm, turn us parallel to the cruiser's course track, opposite direction. Once on course, jump one minute out, come about one-eighty, and jump us directly beneath the target, stand off at two kilometers...and make sure our tubes are on her when we come out of the jump."

"Aye, sir," the lieutenant replied.

"Captain, I suggest we concentrate our fire on the target's dorsal shields," the commander urged. "They *are* down to fifty percent, after all."

"Which means her captain will shunt all power to those shields, expecting us to strike where we think she is weakest," the captain explained.

"Yes, sir," the commander replied.

"Did you manage to get any damage readings during the last pass?" Captain Nash asked his sensor officer.

"Yes, sir. No damage to either frigate. Minor weakening of their shields. The cruiser's status was unchanged."

"They've beefed up their shields," the captain observed. "We used to be able to take them down with just a few torpedoes."

"Turn complete," Lieutenant Gissel reported from the helm.

"You don't suppose that's why they're making a run at us?" Commander Poschay commented.

"Pitching up," the lieutenant added as she brought

the destroyer's nose up smartly.

"And risk a KKV strike against their homeworld?" Captain Nash scoffed. "Unlikely."

"Unless they're not worried about a strike," the commander said thoughtfully.

Captain Nash pondered the commander's comments a moment, then turned to his sensor officer. "Mister Bottrell, what are the chances the Jung could have a shield around their homeworld that we wouldn't know about?"

"Pretty much impossible, sir," the ensign assured him. "The emissions would be enormous. There would be no way to hide that from our recon drones."

"That's what I thought," the captain replied. "Stand by on all tubes, Commander. Same as before. Full power triplets on the cruiser, and don't stop firing until we jump away."

"And the frigates?" the commander asked.

"If they're still around, feel free to launch jump missiles at them."

"Aye, sir. All tubes are ready, and jump missiles are loading."

"Take us in again, Mister Levitt," the captain ordered.

"Aye, sir."

Captain Nash watched as the main view screen again filled with the momentary blue-white jump flash. When it cleared, the Jung cruiser hovered above, her ventral side facing them. Even from two kilometers away, the three-kilometer-long warship filled their view screen.

"Jump complete."

"All tubes are locked on target," the commander announced from the tactical station. "Firing all tubes."

More red-orange flashes of light on the main view screen announced the departure of round after round of plasma torpedoes. The enemy cruiser's shields glowed a pale yellow as the charges struck them. With each successive round, the intensity of the yellow glow increased.

"Any other contacts?" Captain Nash asked his sensor officer.

"Negative sir," Ensign Bottrell replied.

The Jung cruiser's shields finally gave up against the continuing bombardment, dropping with a wave of exploding emitters along the enemy ship's hull.

"Target's shields are down," Ensign Bottrell announced.

Two more rounds of plasma torpedoes struck the enemy ship's hull, breaking her open. The enemy ship broke in half across her midship line, after which internal secondary explosions blasted the rest of her apart.

"Cease fire," Captain Nash ordered, ending the assault. He stared at the view screen as the Jung cruiser continued to break up, rocked by one explosion after another. Ten seconds later, it was over. The massive warship was gone, leaving nothing but a spreading field of debris in every size and shape imaginable. The massive explosions, and the subsequent fires they had caused, quickly vanished as they were robbed of oxygen by the icy vacuum of deep space.

After all that Captain Nash had seen, after all the friends he had watched die years ago at the hands of the Jung Empire, the destruction of the cruiser had been surprisingly unsatisfying.

"I'm picking up one FTL signature, about two million kilometers to port," Ensign Bottrell reported.

"I'm betting you'll pick up another one on the other side in a few moments," the captain muttered darkly.

"Am I missing something?" Commander Poschay wondered. "Aren't the frigates supposed to protect the cruiser?"

Captain Nash thought for a moment. The commander was right. The fact that both frigates chose to cut and run the moment their FTL field emitters had come back online, and leave the cruiser to fend for itself, was troubling to say the least. "Ensign Nwosu, dispatch another comm-drone to command. Update the situation, and let them know we will be attempting to reacquire the remaining frigates."

Ensign Nwosu looked at his captain, noting the concern on his face. "Aye, sir."

* * *

Jessica and General Telles walked confidently out of the hangar toward the waiting combat jump shuttle that sat twenty meters away, engines idling.

"It is not necessary for you to go on this flight," the general said as they walked. "The flight crew is quite capable of transmitting the instructions to the comm-drone."

"I'm not going because of the drone, Lucius, and you know it," Jessica reminded him. "If we do make contact with Dumar, or Montrose, or anyone else from our days with the Alliance, they may need confirmation that it is us. At least, if they're smart, they will. Without any pre-established codes, it's going to require shared personal knowledge."

"I am not in disagreement with you on that point of fact, Jessica. I am merely pointing out that none of us has any duty or honor-bound commitment here."

Jessica stopped in mid-stride and stared at the general. "Well, *that's* an odd statement coming from a Ghatazhak."

"Our new life has required us to be more pragmatic. You of all people should know this."

"So you don't think we should help them?" Jessica challenged.

"I am not saying that we shouldn't. I am merely pointing out that we must consider our long-term survival. Getting wrapped up in this conflict may not be a good idea."

"I'm not planning on getting *wrapped up* in any conflicts, Lucius. I'm talking about rescuing our friends and their families."

"And that is the end of it?" This time it was the general on the offensive.

"That's the end of it," she assured him.

"I hope so," General Telles replied, sounding unconvinced. "As we are ill-equipped for anything more than a simple extraction at this point. So, do not make any promises beyond that."

"Understood," Jessica replied. She turned and continued walking, leaving the general standing alone, still ten meters from the jump shuttle. She tapped her comm-set as she approached the ship. "We good to go?" she asked over the jump shuttle's intercom frequency.

"*Ready when you are, Lieutenant,*" the pilot replied.

Jessica climbed up into the shuttle through its wide side door between the fore and aft engine pods. "Let's do it," she called over her comm-set, taking her seat along the back of the shuttle's utility bay.

The shuttle's engines began to spin up to full power, while the crew chief activated the door control.

The door slid smoothly forward as the combat shuttle rose from the tarmac. Once closed, the door pulled inward and sealed.

"Door secure," the sergeant called out.

"*Cabin pressure is good. Jump to orbit is ready,*" the copilot reported over the comm-sets from the cockpit.

"*Pitching up,*" the pilot announced.

The shuttle's four, side-mounted engine pods began to swing aft, as the shuttle accelerated and climbed. Jessica could feel the force of the shuttle's acceleration pushing her back in her seat.

"*Two minutes to jump altitude,*" the copilot, Lieutenant Latfee, reported.

"Are we going in and out, like the general said, or did you have something else in mind?" the sergeant asked Jessica.

"Nothing fancy, Sarge. We jump in, transmit the instructions to the comm-drone, and send a message to Dumar. Then we jump out and wait for an hour before we jump back in to get an answer. Simple as that."

"Right," the sergeant replied, looking unconvinced.

"What?"

"No offense, Jess, but things never go that smoothly when you're involved."

"You noticed, huh?"

"*Relax, Torwell,*" the pilot said. "*This one's a breeze.*"

"Jumping into the middle of a Jung-held system is a breeze? Since when?"

"Don't worry, Sarge," Jessica said confidently. "I'm sure the general told your boss not to let me do anything crazy. I'm just a comm operator on this one."

"Right," the sergeant replied.

Jessica smiled coyly at Sergeant Torwell, then turned to look out the window. She could see the city below, shrinking as they climbed. Down there, her parents, her brothers and their families, and her adopted daughter, Ania, were all going about their daily lives, unaware of what was transpiring in the nearby Pentaurus sector.

Her life had been good here. Training with the Ghatazhak was more intense than she ever could have imagined, and it involved far more discipline than she expected, but it had been just what she had needed after the war. The training gave her back what she had lost: her self-control. Although, at times the general had voiced doubt about how effective the training had been.

"Jump to orbit in three..."

More importantly, it had given little Ania a chance at a real life.

"...two..."

Therein lay the problem for Jessica.

"...one..."

No matter what the general said, she was not going to let the Jung take that chance away from her.

"...jumping."

One brush with death was enough, especially for a child. Jessica would not allow another.

The windows of the combat jump shuttle cleared again, and the view outside changed to that of the planet Burgess below.

"Jump series to Darvano, plotted and ready," Lieutenant Latfee reported.

"Everyone ready back there?" Commander Kainan asked from the pilot's seat.

Jessica glanced at the control panel for the portable comm-unit they had rigged into the shuttle's communications systems, in order to task Ranni Enterprise's jump comm-drone. The status screen showed that it was ready. She gave a nod to the sergeant sitting across from her.

"We're good back here," the sergeant replied.

"*Jump series in three......two......one......jumping.*"

The windows turned opaque again to protect the occupants from the bright, blue-white light of the jump flashes. It was over one hundred and twelve light years from Sherma to Darvano, and even with the shuttle's improved jump systems, it would take them more than an hour to reach their destination.

Jessica tapped her helmet control, dropping her visor and darkening it. "You know the drill, Sarge," she said as she moved her fingers to the comm-set controls. "Wake me when we get there," she added, after which she turned off her comm-set and leaned back in her seat to take a nap.

* * *

"I'm not bitching," Commander Ellison argued, "I'm venting."

"You're bitching," Captain Roselle insisted as he poured himself another cup of coffee. "You do so at least once a week, Marty."

"Well, I think I have a right to, don't I? Kes, Ollie... Hell, even Jobu got a command."

"Big deal. Those new destroyers are so damned automated a monkey could command them. I'm telling you, Marty, they're holding you for a Protector-class ship."

"Then why did they give the first one to Stettner? He doesn't have anywhere near my experience."

"Galiardi needed to get a Koharan in command of

that ship in order to get Tau Ceti on his side. It's all politics."

"I fucking hate politics," the commander sneered, pushing his plate aside. "They don't belong in the military."

"I couldn't agree more," Captain Roselle said. "But it's been that way ever since Dumar stepped down and President Scott caved in and reinstated Galiardi."

"And you didn't even *like* Dumar."

"I liked him a whole lot better than Galiardi, that's for sure." Captain Roselle set his mug down on the table and leaned back. "Just wait, you'll get a ship. I'd bet my life on it. Meanwhile, sit back and enjoy the easy duty."

"Easy duty my ass," the commander complained. "Easy for you, perhaps. You're not the one who has to deal with all these whiny-ass Koharan department heads every day."

"Again, politics. Tau Ceti *is* this ship's home port, you know. Technically, it *is* the property of the Cetians. You and I are just here to teach them how to operate the damned thing. That will also come to an end someday, at which point we'll both move on to bigger and better things," Captain Roselle insisted.

"Your mouth to God's ear..."

The intercom beeped. Captain Roselle turned to face the intercom panel on the wall. "Roselle."

"*Flash traffic from Alliance Command,*" the communications officer announced over the intercom. "*We've been put on alert, sir.*"

"On our way," the captain replied.

"Another damned readiness test," Commander Ellison groaned.

"Hey, at least we get to pretend like we're a real

combat ship, just like the good old days," the captain said as he rose from his chair and headed out of the captain's mess.

"You'd think command would ease up a bit by now," the commander said, rising to follow his friend. "I mean, it's not like the Jung are going to attack us or anything. Not with a few dozen super JKKVs trained on their primary worlds. Oh, and let's not forget the fact that our fleet has more than tripled in size since the cease-fire was signed."

"The Jung still have a lot of ships out there, Marty."

"Did I mention all the gunships? What is the count up to these days? Three hundred and something?" the commander commented as they entered the Jar-Benakh's command center.

"Captain on deck!" the guard at the entrance announced.

Captain Roselle and Commander Ellison walked over to the communications officer. "What have you got, Mister Bussard?" the captain asked.

The ensign handed the captain a message pad as he spoke. "We've been ordered to go to full alert and break orbit, but remain in the Tau Ceti system for now, sir."

"Did they say why?" Commander Ellison wondered.

"Holy shit," the captain muttered as he read the rest of the message. "A total of four separate contacts so far, all of them well within Alliance space," the captain said as he continued reading. "Both the Tanna and the Belem have confirmed kills."

"Jobu shot down a Jung ship?" Commander Ellison exclaimed in surprise.

Captain Roselle looked at his XO, one eyebrow

raised.

"Well, good for him."

"Increase patrols, and order our gunships to increase their current patrol range," Captain Roselle ordered. "I don't want those bastards sneaking up on us."

"What do you think they're up to, Gil?" the commander wondered. "Probing us, maybe? Testing our response?"

"Are we at war, sir?" the communications officer asked nervously.

"We just may be, Ensign." Captain Roselle looked at his XO again. "Set condition two throughout the ship."

* * *

"Holy, fuck!" Sergeant Torwell exclaimed from the gun turret atop the combat jump shuttle, after it came out of its last jump in the series. "You might want to warn a guy when you plan on coming out of the jump so damned close to a planet!"

"It's not a planet, it's a moon," Commander Kainan replied.

"It's still fucking close."

"Relax, Sarge, it's a small moon. You could fart and reach escape velocity from its surface," the commander said comfortingly.

"Torwell could, that's for sure," Lieutenant Latfee added.

"You guys did that on purpose," Sergeant Torwell accused. "I just may have crapped my suit, you know that don't you?"

"It was my idea, Sarge," Jessica admitted, as she activated the hailing call on her comm-panel. "We can hide here while we task the comm-drone."

Sergeant Torwell stared out at the moon to his

right. It was so close, he felt as if he could reach out and touch its icy surface. Then he turned to look further right. He noticed a strange amber glow on the frame of his turret's canopy, and turned to look behind him. His eyes popped open even wider with a start, and he nearly fell out of his seat at the sight of the massive gas giant behind them. "Jesus!" he exclaimed. After catching his breath, he continued. "Seriously, guys, you have to warn me before you do this kind of shit."

"What's the big deal, Sarge?" the commander asked. "We used to jump into atmo less than a hundred meters off the deck."

"Maybe, but I had nothing but sky above me when we did!" the sergeant argued. "And you guys are surrounded by the hull. I'm sitting up here in this little fucking bubble, remember? Besides, it's been years since we did those kinds of jumps, and I'm an old man now."

"What are you, like twenty-six, twenty-seven, maybe?" Jessica wondered.

"Earth years, maybe. But I'm thirty-two by Corinairan years...I think."

"You suck at math, Sarge," Commander Kainan commented. "You're only thirty Corinairan years old."

"Whatever."

"How's it going back there, Lieutenant?" the commander asked.

"Handshake is complete, and the control codes have been accepted. I'm sending tasking to the comm-drone now," Jessica reported. "Are you picking up any ships on passive?"

"Not yet," Lieutenant Latfee replied. "But our reception angle is pretty narrow right now."

"That's the plan," Jessica replied. "Tasking has been received. Just waiting for departure confirmation."

"You don't think it's going to raise some suspicion when the Jung see a comm-drone suddenly jump away?" Sergeant Torwell wondered.

"That's why we needed to act immediately," Jessica explained, "while there are still shuttles jumping in and out of the system. Once the Jung get this system locked down, nothing will be able to leave without getting tracked."

"What makes you think they won't track it now?" Lieutenant Latfee asked.

"They might," Jessica admitted. "That's why I routed the drone to about ten different systems before parking it in the Borada system."

"Borada?" Lieutenant Latfee said. "There's nothing in the Borada system."

"That's the idea," Jessica replied. "If the Jung do track the comm-drone, by the time they reach Borada, we will have already retasked the drone again and sent it on its way to Earth."

"Two minutes until we get line of sight on Corinair," Commander Kainan warned.

"That's it," Jessica replied. "I've got launch confirmation."

"And I've got the drone's jump flash," Lieutenant Latfee replied.

"Setting up the comm-array for directional beam," Jessica announced.

"How do you know where the recipient is located?" Sergeant Torwell wondered.

"We know Dumar lives on the side of Corinair that's facing us now, and from this distance, a directional beam will cover the entire planet. If he

133

has an active receiver, he'll get the message."

"And so will the Jung," the sergeant pointed out.

"The message is encrypted," Jessica replied.

"How does he know the encryption key?"

Jessica looked up at the sergeant in the turret above her, then looked forward between the engine bulkheads toward the cockpit. "Is he always like this?"

"I get talkative when I'm nervous," the sergeant said defensively.

"I'm trying to remember a time when you weren't running your mouth off, Torwell," Jessica commented as she prepared to send the message.

"That hurt, Jess."

"The encryption key is his son's birthday," Jessica said.

"How does he know that?"

"He's a smart man," Jessica replied. "He'll figure it out. And I'm seeding it with information that only he and I know."

"Like what?"

"Who his target was when he first came aboard the Aurora."

"His target?"

Jessica reached out and slapped the side of the sergeant's leg. "Jesus, Torwell. Enough already."

"Line of sight in thirty seconds," the lieutenant warned.

"I'll be ready," Jessica assured him.

"New contacts on passive," the lieutenant added. "A pair of fast movers, close together. Probably a patrol of two fighters."

"Where?" Jessica asked as she worked.

"Fifty thousand kilometers. They just came onto sensors. They probably just left the orbit of Corinair.

The planet is coming into our line of sight now. Ten seconds until you're clear to transmit."

"I'm ready," Jessica announced, her hands rising up from her console.

"Contacts are turning toward us," the lieutenant warned. "You'd better start transmit..."

Two jump flashes suddenly appeared less than a kilometer ahead of them, their light filling the interior from both the cockpit and the turret above Jessica, spilling into the utility area where she sat.

"Fuck!" Commander Kainan exclaimed as he pushed the shuttle into a spiraling dive to the right. "You got 'em, Sarge?"

"How the fuck am I supposed to get them while you're spiraling like a crazy bastard!" the sergeant yelled back.

The shuttle lurched to one side, flinging Jessica across the cabin.

"We're hit!" Lieutenant Latfee warned. "Port shield! It's down to fifty percent!"

"Level off so I can get a shot at them on their next pass!" the sergeant demanded.

"I need a clean shot with the comm-array to get this message out!" Jessica reminded the commander.

"They've split!" the lieutenant warned as the shuttle came out of its spiraling dive. "One to port, and one to starboard!"

"Which one is high and low?" the commander asked as he gunned all four engines.

The lieutenant checked the sensor display. "Port is high, starboard is low."

"Sarge, I'm going to turn into the fighter to port and show him our topside. That'll keep our port shield away from the starboard contact. Don't let that fucker pass on our left. If he hits our port shield again, we'll lose it."

"I've got it!" the sergeant replied.

"You'll have about ten seconds to get the message out," the commander told Jessica.

"I only need five," Jessica responded.

"Don't forget to give him the return message coordinates!"

"I did, I did!"

"Coming around now," the commander warned as he rolled the ship slightly to port and started his turn in the same direction.

"Shit! He jumped!" the lieutenant warned.

"Who jumped?" the commander demanded. "To where?"

"The guy on the right! Shit! He's on our left now! He's firing!"

"Jumping!" Commander Kainan announced.

The windows of the shuttle turned opaque momentarily as the ship jumped ahead a few thousand kilometers.

"Hang on!" the commander warned as he rolled the ship in the opposite direction and started another hard turn.

Jessica felt herself sliding to the left, all the while wondering why she hadn't put on her restraints.

"Jumping again," the commander warned.

Once again, the shuttle's windows turned opaque, clearing a few seconds later.

"That should buy us a few seconds," the commander decided.

"Corinair is at two one seven by one one four!" Lieutenant Latfee reported as the windows cleared again.

"How far did we jump?"

"About ten light seconds from our last position,"

the commander replied. "Start transmitting! Quick, before they figure out where we went!"

"I'm transmitting! I'm transmitting!" Jessica assured the commander.

"Two more contacts!" Lieutenant Latfee warned. "Fifty thousand clicks... FUCK!"

Two more jump flashes filled their forward windows as another two Jung fighters suddenly appeared in front of them and opened fire. Sergeant Torwell attacked with his double-barreled plasma cannon, sending bolts of red-orange plasma energy streaking toward the incoming fighters. The fighters split apart just like the previous pair, one to port, and one to starboard.

"Two more to stern!" the lieutenant warned. "I think it's the first two!"

"Message is sent!" Jessica exclaimed.

"We're out of here!" the commander added as he pushed the escape jump button on his flight control stick.

CHAPTER FIVE

Loki stared out the window of the Ghatazhak's flight operations office. On the apron sat the corporate jump shuttle he had flown for the last five years, its port side torn open by weapons fire.

It had been so long since he'd been fired upon in such a way. It seemed a lifetime ago. Yet, back then, it had been a fairly regular occurrence. Now, after so much time had passed, he failed to understand how he managed to get through it all. Even now, only a few hours after they had escaped, his hands still trembled at the thought of what might have happened. His wife. His child. They were all that mattered to him now. He would gladly live under Jung rule if it meant his family would be safe.

His perspective on the war he had been a part of so long ago had changed today. He viewed the war differently than he had as a single, young man with no one depending on him other than those who fought by his side. It had simply been him and Josh, together in the cockpit of that Falcon, challenging death at every turn and every jump... And winning. But now...little Ailsa. His little angel. The thought of her growing up without a father...

"How are you doing?" Deliza asked as she entered the office.

Loki wiped his eyes. "I'm okay... I guess."

"Yeah, me too," Deliza replied, handing him a cup of tea. "Try not to worry. They'll figure out a way to get them off of Corinair."

"I keep telling myself that," Loki began quietly. He stopped mid-sentence, unable to verbalize his next thought for fear he would break down. He looked at

Deliza. "You're not worried?"

"Of course I am," Deliza assured him.

"You don't look it."

"That's my father's influence," she said, sitting down in the chair next to Loki. She took a deep breath, letting it out slowly in a long sigh. "He always believed that worrying was a waste of time. He used to tell me, 'If there is something you can do about it, do it. If not, worrying about it isn't going to help. It's just needless suffering. Not only for yourself, but for those around you. And it certainly isn't helping those you might worry about.'"

Loki smiled. "Yeah, that sounds like Tug. Not Casimir, mind you, but Tug."

"Yeah, I think I liked him better as Tug, myself," Deliza said.

Loki looked out the window again, watching as several Ghatazhak technicians removed the body from the damaged cabin of their shuttle. "Did she have any family?" he asked, wanting to get his mind off his own problems.

"Biarra? A brother, I think. Her parents were killed when she was young, back when the Yamaro attacked Corinair."

"I remember that day," Loki said. "We were still flying the Aurora then." He turned and looked at her. "You were there. You and your sister, and your father."

"Yes, we were." Deliza smiled bashfully. "I had a bit of a crush on you back then, you know."

Loki looked surprised. "Really?"

"Who wouldn't? A dashing young pilot, one who saved our lives."

"Yeah, I was kind of smitten with you as well, I have to admit. I just never really had the nerve to say anything."

"Why not?" Deliza wondered.

"You were so smart, and your father was there, and I was trying to learn how to fly the Aurora... There just wasn't the time, really. Not with all that was going on. Besides, I was never very good with girls."

"You seemed to sweep Lael off her feet without any problem," Deliza grinned.

"Lael was easy."

"What?"

"I mean it was easy *with* her. She was so easy to talk to. I always felt so relaxed around her. We just hit it off without any effort. Simple, honest, and direct. It's like I couldn't say anything wrong with her. Even if I accidentally insulted her, it would just bounce off her like I had never said it."

"That's one of the reasons I hired her," Deliza said. "Because she's so honest and direct. It saves a lot of time when you don't have to dance around a person's sensitivities. That, and because she is so damned organized that it's frightening."

"Yes, she is," Loki agreed. "And yes, it is."

Deliza looked out the window as well. "Do you think it will fly again?"

"Probably," Loki replied. "The damage is mostly to the hull itself. All the systems are in the ventral box truss that runs under the deck. If we can get some scrap metal, we can probably just weld it in place to cover the hull, and the cabin will likely hold pressure just fine." Loki smiled. He knew that Deliza was trying to get him to focus on something else.

"Good. Once we fix her up, you, me, Yanni, Lael, and Ailsa will all load up and get as far away from the Pentaurus sector as possible."

"To where?"

"I don't know. Maybe back to Earth?"

"We don't have the range to get to Earth," Loki said. "We barely had enough energy to get here."

"We'll just have to get a better power plant, then. Maybe a mini-ZPED?"

"Where are we going to get a mini-ZPED, Deliza?"

"I've got money, remember?"

"Isn't it all on Corinair?" Loki argued. "The Jung, remember?"

"No one keeps all their wealth in one spot, Loki," Deliza said dismissively.

"I wouldn't know," Loki said with a wry smile. "I'm just a corporate shuttle pilot, remember?"

"Maybe, but I think I need to give you a raise after today."

"Or at least combat pay," Loki joked.

* * *

Captain Tuplo walked up the Seiiki's cargo ramp, a scowl on his face.

"Things went well, I take it?" Marcus greeted him from the top of the ramp.

"Could've gone worse, I suppose."

"How much are we left with?"

"Before or after the repairs?" the captain asked as he topped the ramp. He looked at Dalen, who was climbing out of the port crawlway hatch. "How bad?"

"We lost all the shield emitters on the port side, and the main port power bus is pretty much fried, as well."

"Can we fly on the secondaries?" the captain asked.

"We can, but why would we?" Dalen wondered.

"I got us another run."

"Cap'n," Marcus interrupted, "maybe we should

stay here a few days... Wait and see how things shake out in the cluster?"

"We can't afford the port fees here," Captain Tuplo explained. "Between the emitters, the power bus, and that hole in the hull, we'll be out of money in just one day here. Besides, we need the extra money if we're going to make repairs."

"Cap, I haven't even looked at the starboard side, yet," Dalen warned.

"Assuming the starboard side is no worse off than the port, can we make it to Haven as we are?"

"Fuck, not Haven *again*," Marcus groaned.

"What the hell is it with you and Haven?" Dalen asked Marcus.

"Can we make it or not?" the captain asked again in a more demanding tone.

"Assuming the starboard side is good, then yes. But would you mind if I looked around in there as well before we take off?"

"Make it quick," the captain ordered as he headed forward. "Cargo is on its way."

"You took a run without knowing if we could get off the ground safely?" Dalen exclaimed, shocked at the captain's recklessness.

"Everyone's in a panic," the captain said. "They're afraid to move any cargo for fear the Jung will take it and their insurance won't cover the loss. If I hadn't taken the run, this ship would be impounded in a few days and we'd all be on the streets." Captain Tuplo reached the top of the forward ladder, then turned back to face Dalen and Marcus. "Besides, I have faith in your mechanical skills, Dalen."

Marcus and Dalen watched as the captain disappeared through the forward hatch into the passenger compartment. A horn beeped from outside, and they both turned around to see a cargo hauler backing up to their cargo ramp.

"You best get your ass in the starboard crawlway, boy."

"Yeah," Dalen sighed. "Just don't load that shit in front of the hatch and block me in."

Marcus smiled. The thought had crossed his mind.

* * *

"*Mister President,*" Admiral Galiardi greeted over the secure vid-link to President Scott's office.

"Admiral."

"*I'm afraid matters have gotten worse, sir,*" the admiral began. "*Although the Aurora was able to turn away the ships bound for Mu Cassiopeiae, both the Tanna and the Belem were forced to return fire and destroy the targets.*"

"How many Jung ships were destroyed?"

"*Two in total,*" the admiral replied. "*One cruiser, and one frigate.*"

President Scott sighed. "How many men?"

"*Two to three hundred, combined. Furthermore, we've detected ships approaching the Alpha Centauri system.*"

"How many?"

"*A battleship, a cruiser, and four frigates,*" the admiral answered. "*We've dispatched the Cape Town to the Alpha Centauri system...*"

"I thought the Cape Town was still in trials?" the president interrupted. "Is she ready for action?"

"*No, sir, she is not. She is armed and can defend herself, and we needed to get some presence in the system. The Aurora is on her way there as well, but will not get there for fourteen hours. The Cape Town has been ordered to shadow the Jung ships and*" *remain out of range until the Aurora arrives. We're also moving the Cayene, the Bristol, and the Nagoya to the Alpha Centauri system, in case the Jung decide to stand and fight."*

"Do you really think they will do so?"

"At least two of their ships have chosen to do so thus far," the admiral reminded him. *"It's possible that those other encounters were meant to pull our forces away from Sol, in order to get another force through our defenses. Although, I would expect the force headed for us to be much larger."*

"How the hell did they get so deep into our territory without being detected?" the president asked.

"If you run the numbers based on known Jung FTL speeds for both ships and comm-drones, it is possible for all of these ships to have been launched after our initial attack on the Jung homeworld, and still have enough time to carefully sneak their way around our patrols. It would take an incredibly well-planned and well-coordinated effort on the part of the Jung, but it is possible."

President Scott closed his eyes a moment, rubbing his face. They had accomplished so much over the last seven years. They had brought the Earth back from the brink of another dark age, one that would have rivaled the great bio-digital plague of the twenty-fifth century that had swept over the entire core and sent millions fleeing to the stars. They had finally built up their defenses to the point where they had begun to feel safe again. And now, the Jung were at their doorstep once more. Again, the Jung were threatening to destroy not only Earth, but all of the Alliance worlds. "Recommendations?" the president asked, dreading the admiral's response.

"I recommend we move to defense condition two,"

the admiral replied without hesitation.

"Daily strike cycles." The president sighed again. "Are you sure that's wise? I mean, if even one of those ships fails to receive a launch cancellation order..."

"That is the way the system was designed, Mister President," the admiral reminded him. *"And we do use three jump comm-drones for every cancellation order."*

"I know," the president said. "Very well, Admiral."

"I need to hear the words, Mister President," the admiral prompted him.

President Scott straightened up, looking directly at the vid-link screen. "I authorize defense condition two."

"Authorization code?"

"One bravo, seven five four, foxtrot alpha, two zero one seven nine, lima tango."

Admiral Galiardi looked toward someone off screen for a moment, then turned back to the camera. *"Authorization code confirmed. All Alliance forces are now at defense condition two, Mister President."*

"Thank you, Admiral," the president replied. He switched off the vid-link. "Thank you for taking us one step closer to annihilation," the president added darkly after the link ended and the view screen turned off.

"Don't look at it that way," his daughter said, stepping forward from the side of the room where she had stood to remain out of the vid-link's view. "It's just another layer of assurance."

"It won't change anything," the president said, "especially since the Jung don't even know about the change." He turned to look at Miri. "At some point, we're going to have to meet with Ambassador Delhay."

"To what end?" Miri wondered. "You know he'll deny any knowledge of those ships."

"Perhaps we should try to open up direct lines of communication with the Jung homeworld."

"The cease-fire dictates that all communications between the Alliance and the Jung must be through the Jung ambassador..."

"Who will no doubt resist such direct contact as it reduces the power of his position," the president added.

"We must honor that agreement," Miri reminded her father.

"They have violated our space and fired upon our ships," the president replied. "If they are not going to honor that agreement, then why should we?"

"Because Nathan died to give us a *chance* for peace," Miri replied. "It is up to us to maintain it. If we do not, then my brother...your son, will have died in vain."

* * *

Travon Dumar sat in his living room with his wife. They both had their eyes glued to the view screen on the wall. The invaders had already shut down Corinairan news. Luckily, the planetary network itself was nearly impossible to turn off. It had too many redundancies, including satellite and radio segments. Short of setting off a series of strategically placed, electromagnetic pulses, it would be operational for at least a few days, if not longer.

Now, all they could see were random recordings from personal comm-units, uploaded by Corinairans from all over the planet. They were usually of poor quality, and were shaky and without any narrative to give any context as to what was going on. Occasionally, they would find one in which the operator would actually describe the events they were recording.

Two things were already obvious to Travon Dumar, a retired commander of the Sol-Pentaurus Alliance. The Jung had jump drives, and they had used them to invade the Darvano system. Travon was sure that the same thing was happening in every other inhabited system within the cluster, if not the entire sector. And if the Jung had only invaded the cluster thus far, the rest of the sector would soon follow.

The moment the reports had started coming in a few hours ago, Travon had gone into the secret room in his basement, and turned on the deep-space transceiver that had been given to him by Suvan Navarro, Captain of the Avendahl. He had no idea whether or not anyone would attempt to contact him, but if they did, he wanted to be ready.

His wife, of course, had objections to his even owning the transceiver, let alone turning it back on. She had forgiven his decades of deception, during which she had believed him to be working in importing and exporting, when the reality was that he had been commanding a covert, imperial anti-insurgent task force on Corinair. She also forgave him for being gone for three years while he commanded the Alliance forces in Sol, leading them in their rebellion and eventual stalemate against the Jung Empire. But now, with their world under attack by an even bigger threat than the old Takaran Empire, it was time for him to lie low. They were both getting older. It was time for the younger generations to step up and defend their worlds. She wanted him here, with her, running their little resort by the lake. He owed her that much.

"What is going to happen to us?" she asked

quietly, as she snuggled up to him on the couch.

"Nothing," Travon assured her. "The Jung don't want to kill us. They want our infrastructure and our economy to remain intact. They want us to produce what they need to continue their expansion. Destroying our cities, our factories, our worlds...it does not serve them." He paused a moment, looking in her eyes.

"What?" she asked, noticing his worried expression.

"If we disobey, they are most ruthless in their punishment. They will only put up with so much. It is a mathematical equation to them. Pure accounting. Profit and loss. If dealing with us proves too costly, they will simply wipe the planet clean and start over, populating it with their own people instead."

"Seriously?"

"I have seen them do this before," Travon told her. "They tried to do just that with Earth."

"It's difficult to imagine," she said, looking back at the view screen. "Even Caius Ta'Akar wasn't that bad."

"Yes, he was," Travon replied. "You just didn't see it. He was a master at media control and propaganda. And at outright purchasing the loyalty of those who might someday oppose him. The same animal, wrapped in different skins."

Travon's comm-unit beeped. He reached into his pocket and pulled it out.

"What is it?" his wife asked.

"I must go to the basement," Travon apologized as he rose. "I am receiving a message. A message from a ship in space."

She looked at him with pleading eyes.

"It is only a message, nothing more. It could be a

warning, one that could save our very lives."

She wasn't buying it. "Or one that will suck you back into the same world you promised me you had said goodbye to once and for all."

"It is only a message. An incoming one at that. It cannot harm us."

"Not directly, no," she admitted. "It's the events that follow the message that concern me."

"I promised you that I would never leave you behind again..."

"You promised me that you would stay *here*, Travon," she corrected.

"And it is a promise that I intend to keep, until my dying day," he assured her as he backed away from the couch, turned, and headed into the kitchen.

Travon passed through the kitchen and into the storm porch. He closed the inside door behind him, then removed his coat from its hook on the wall behind the door. With his free hand, he twisted the coat hook to the left, and the two vertical panels of wood parted, revealing stairs that led downward. Travon hung the coat back up and headed down the stairs, pressing a button on his way that closed the panels behind him, hiding the entrance once again. The lights snapped on, and the room below came into view.

The area itself was surprisingly large, with storage lockers on one side, a door that led to a bathroom, and several bunks. On the far side of the room was a gun rack, loaded with every conceivable weapon, most of which were not legal.

Travon moved to the workbench along one of the walls. The screen on the transceiver was glowing, displaying a short string of characters that made no sense. Just a collection of random numbers and letters. He knew the message had to be encrypted, for anyone sending him a message in such fashion would undoubtedly have a military background, most likely one in covert operations such as himself.

Travon immediately set to work attempting to decipher the message. He still had the old encryption algorithms used by the Alliance during his command, but he would have to figure out the starting value for the algorithm. He started with the obvious choices: his wedding anniversary and the birth dates of his two children. He fed the values into the system, and then had it try all two hundred algorithms using each of the dates.

The characters on the screen began to change, shifting as each algorithm tried to create a discernible message using each of the three dates he had entered. After several seconds, a readable message finally appeared.

Twenty-one alpha tango, version two five two. Date of Tug's death.

Travon checked the transceiver. There were two more messages in the buffer. That's when he realized that the message was not a message at all, but rather the first step in the decoding process. He quickly called up the next message, selected the indicated algorithm, and then entered the date of his friend's untimely demise. The second message immediately decoded.

Eighty-seven whiskey mike, version three five seven. Date of Na-Tan's death.

Travon Dumar smiled. He could only think of a handful of people that knew he still resided in this part of the galaxy. Fewer still who would know the date on which Nathan Scott, the mythical savior known as Na-Tan in the Legend of Origins, had been executed by the Jung as a war criminal.

He selected the next decryption algorithm and entered the date of Nathan Scott's execution.

But the message did not decrypt.

Travon entered the date again, but with the same negative result. He looked down for a moment. *Did I get the date wrong?* It didn't seem possible, since it was a date he would never forget. For he, then Admiral Travon Dumar, had been the one who had put the young captain into the very situation that led to his surrender and eventual execution. He had not known that it would happen, but he knew the mission would be a dangerous one. Perhaps the most dangerous mission Captain Scott had ever faced.

He checked again. The date was correct, but still the message refused to decode. Then he remembered something. Something that Commander Telles had said to him at Nathan's memorial service back on Earth. 'Legends never die.'

Travon entered zero as the algorithm's starting value, and the message appeared. His eyes grew wide as he read the message. When he finished, he glanced at the clock on the wall. He had very little time before he had to answer the message, and much to do before then. It would require many steps to ensure that the Jung could not trace the call and discern his location. Although he doubted any such measures would be taken so soon after their initial invasion, it was a chance he could not take. Many lives were at stake, and not just those of himself and his dear wife.

* * *

"Just make sure you get this damn ship fixed as quickly as possible," Marcus said as the last of the cargo containers were rolled down the Seiiki's cargo ramp. "I don't want to stay on this dusty-ass rock any longer than need be."

"It's going to take us a couple days, at least, Marcus," Dalen warned. "You could help, you know, seeing as you're in such a hurry and all."

"I don't fit in those crawl spaces very well," Marcus shrugged. "I'll leave that to you and Josh." Marcus looked around. "Where the hell did he get to?"

"I don't know," Dalen replied, picking up the cargo straps from the deck to stow them. "Maybe he went with Neli for supplies?"

"Josh, voluntarily going with Neli?" Marcus sneered. "Not likely."

"With the captain, then?"

"Captain left the moment we touched down, before Josh shut everything down."

"*Hey!*" a voice called from outside.

Marcus turned to look down the ramp, but saw no one who looked like they were shouting for his attention.

"*Hey!*" the voice called again. It was Josh's voice.

Marcus headed down the cargo ramp, looking for Josh, followed by Dalen. As he neared the bottom of the ramp, he spotted Josh running across the busy space port, dodging cargo carts and other workers.

"Hey! Marcus!" Josh yelled as he approached, panting.

"What the hell's going on?"

"The Jung," Josh said in between breaths. "They've captured... the entire... cluster... Everything... all at once... I heard."

"Where'd you hear that?" Dalen asked.

"I was at the port controller's office, updating our time fixes and charts. I heard them talking."

"Talk is just talk, boy. You know that," Marcus

said, waving him off.

"No, it's true."

"How do you know that?"

Josh paused a moment to catch his breath. "While I was there, word came through on the comm-jumper. Takara, Corinair, Savoy, Taroa, Korak..."

"What about Dobson?" Dalen wondered.

"Dobson, Haydon, Devi, Borne," Josh continued. "All of them. The Jung took 'em all, Marcus. I'm telling you. And every damned one of their ships, big and small... They've all got fucking jump drives."

"So? What does that mean?" Dalen said, still confused. "I mean, I know the Jung are bad guys, but..."

"Imagine Caius, but a hundred times worse, and with a hundred times more ships and troops," Marcus explained.

"I was ten when Caius fell, Marcus," Dalen reminded him.

"Trust me, kid, this is bad news... Very bad news."

Josh looked at Marcus. "What do we do?"

"What do you mean, what do we do?" Marcus asked.

Josh looked around, his brow furrowing. "Do we tell him?"

"I'm pretty sure the captain already knows about the Jung invasion, there, Josh," Dalen remarked, his voice dripping with sarcasm. "They did shoot at us a few hours ago, remember?"

Marcus and Josh exchanged knowing glances.

"He's right," Marcus said. "Besides, he's in the load master's office, so he's probably already heard."

"Right," Josh replied, realizing his error.

"Best thing we can do is to keep the captain and the rest under wraps as best we can," Marcus explained. "I never thought I'd say this, but Haven is probably the best place for us right now, all things considered."

"Why is that?" Josh asked.

"Because there ain't shit here on Haven that the Jung would give a damn about, so it's the last place they'll waste time invading."

* * *

Doran Montrose's comm-unit beeped, alerting him to an incoming call. He reached into his pocket to retrieve his comm-unit and looked at its display screen.

"Who is it?" Yanni wondered.

"There is no ID," Doran replied, concern in his tone.

"Are you going to answer it?"

Doran activated his comm-unit and held it up to his ear. "Hello?"

"*Doran?*" the caller's voice greeted. "*It's Ardum.*"

"Hello, Ardum," Doran replied hesitantly, still unsure of who was speaking to him.

"*I've been trying to get through for nearly an hour,*" the caller exclaimed. "*Are you guys alright? Are your children home and safe?*"

"Yes, yes, they are," Doran replied. "And yours?" he asked, fishing for information that might help him identify the caller. The voice was garbled, but seemed familiar.

"*They are fine. We are all fine. Did your sister's family arrive safely, as well? And their friends?*"

"Yes, they are all here with us."

"*And the baby? She is uninjured?*"

"Yes, the baby is fine." Doran looked at Yanni, furrowing his brow and shaking his head, still not knowing the identity of the caller.

"That is wonderful. Terribly frightening what is happening, is it not?"

"Yes, it is. Will you be alright, Ardum? Do you need anything?"

"No, thank you. We are planning on going to our cabin in the mountains, until things settle down. We have supplies there... Several months' worth, in fact. You and yours are more than welcome to join us."

"I appreciate the offer, Ardum. When will you be leaving?"

"The sooner the better, I would imagine. No later than tomorrow, I think."

"I will discuss it with my wife and the others, and let you know."

"Yes, please do. And if you cannot reach me directly, try my niece, Jessica. I spoke with her earlier, and she plans to call me back soon. You may have better luck contacting her, as she is using an exchange that is not as busy."

"I'll remember that," Doran promised.

"Be safe," the caller said before disconnecting.

Doran deactivated his comm-unit and looked at Yanni.

"Who was it?"

"Somebody named Ardum." Doran looked at Yanni again. "I don't know anyone named Ardum."

"There's an Ardum in legal. Could it be him?"

"I don't even know the guy," Doran replied. "This guy was talking like we were old friends."

"What did he say?"

"He wanted to know if my wife's family and friends arrived safely, and about the baby."

"Ailsa?" Lael wondered. "Did he ask about her by name?"

"No, but he did know she was a girl." Doran's

comm-unit played an alert tone. "I've got a message," he said, looking at the comm-unit again. "It's from the same guy, Ardum."

"What does it say?"

Doran looked at the message. "'Ardum 12345.34512.'" Doran thought for a minute. "Of course!" he exclaimed a moment later. "It's Dumar! And his niece Jessica, on a different, less crowded exchange... He's talking about Jessica Nash. She must have made contact with him. But how did she know..."

"Deliza must have gone to her for help!" Yanni realized.

"Then Loki is alright?" Lael asked.

"He must be," Doran replied. "The Sherma system is more than one hundred light years away. It is doubtful they would already know about the invasion. Even less likely that Jessica would come all this way so quickly, unless Deliza asked her to." His comm-unit made another alert tone. "There's more. An encryption algorithm ID. Old Alliance encryption, and a starting value."

"What's the value?" Yanni asked.

"The date of my brother Kyle's death."

"How can we be sure it is really Dumar?" Yanni questioned. "It could be the Jung, trying to lure us out into the open."

"Doubtful," Doran argued, as he programmed his phone to decrypt the next message. "It is too soon, and we are very low value targets to them, if anything. Besides, very few people would even know I had a brother, let alone when he died. It's Dumar. I am sure of it." His comm-unit played the alert tone yet again.

"What does he say?"

"One moment while the message decrypts." After several long seconds, he finally spoke. "It is an address to rendezvous. He intends to smuggle us all out of the city and hide us until we can be extricated by the Ghatazhak."

"Hide us? Where?"

"He has a small resort on Lake Macumby."

"I never heard of Lake Macumby," Yanni admitted.

"It is about two hundred kilometers southwest of the city. Very secluded, and a long and difficult drive. It is not well known. His business is all word of mouth. Mostly for hunters and fishermen. It is closed this time of year due to the cold at that altitude."

"When are we to rendezvous?" Lael asked.

"Not until tomorrow."

"I'm ready to go now," Doctor Megel insisted.

"He needs time to drive down into the city."

"Where are we to meet?" Yanni asked.

"At a small market a few minutes' walk from here." Doran began typing a return message into his comm-unit.

"What are you doing?" Yanni asked.

"Answering him."

"There's no way the Jung can trace these things, can they?" Doctor Sato asked worriedly.

"Of course they can," Doran replied.

It was not the answer they were hoping for.

"But I am sure the admiral took precautions by routing the signal through multiple exchanges," Doran continued. "Besides, it is unlikely the Jung will be taking such measures at this point."

"What about the message you are sending?" Doctor Megel wondered.

"The message will take the same path back. It is the way it is designed," Doran explained.

"To decrease the workload on the routing servers," Yanni realized.

Doran looked at Yanni with surprise.

"I used to work in IT back on Earth, remember?"

* * *

"Admiral, Cobra One Nine Five has detected a Jung battleship just this side of Arae."

"Another battleship?" the admiral replied. "So that's two now. Two Jung battleships within Alliance space."

"Yes, sir," Commander Macklay confirmed. "One near Alpha Centauri B, and one near 41 Arae."

"No escorts?"

"In the Arae system? No, sir."

Admiral Galiardi grimaced. This was the fourth instance of Jung ships inside Alliance space on this day alone. Granted, most of the sightings had been near systems located at the outskirts of Alliance space. However, the ships detected near the Alpha Centauri system would have to be in transit for at least eighteen months to reach the Centauri system. *A year and a half in Alliance space, all without being detected.* That thought alone was unsettling.

But why now? And why all at once?

"There has to be a reason for this, Admiral," the commander insisted.

"Yes, but what? Are they testing our response? There are much less risky ways to do that than showing themselves *thirty light years* inside our borders. Such a thing makes no tactical sense whatsoever. If you can get that deep inside enemy territory without being detected, then you can get deeper. Hell, you can get anywhere you want. Why not just sneak all your ships in at once, and then attack?"

"Because they know we'd wipe their homeworld out with our super JKKVs," the commander replied.

"Exactly," the admiral agreed. "But that is also a good enough reason *not* to reveal their ships so deep inside our borders. Like I said, it makes no sense."

"Maybe they just want to show us that they can strike whenever and wherever they wish?"

"To what end?"

"To gain leverage at the negotiating table, maybe?" the commander suggested. "To force a better arrangement?"

"I don't think so." Admiral Galiardi shook his head. "No, there is more to it than any of that. There's something missing. Something that we're not seeing, here."

"Do you wish to dispatch ships to intercept the battleship near 41 Arae?" the commander asked.

Admiral Galiardi sighed. "Not yet. If they are testing our response, then it does us no good to jump every time they appear. And if this *is* an attempt to draw our forces away from Earth, then we'd best not take the bait. Besides, that ship is no threat to any Alliance worlds at this point. Have Cobra One Nine Five continue tracking. If the target turns back toward Arae, then we'll jump a few destroyers out there to deal with it."

CHAPTER SIX

"Well, it looks like we may be here for more than a single night," Captain Tuplo reported as he entered the Seiiki's galley.

Marcus leaned forward over the table, his head dropping in disappointment.

"No runs?" Josh assumed.

Captain Tuplo poured himself a cup of coffee. "Nothing is moving. No passengers, no cargo, nothing. Everyone is afraid the Jung are going to confiscate their cargo *and* their ships, never mind what might happen to passengers and crew."

"I don't get it. Why would the Jung give a damn about little ships like us?" Dalen wondered.

"Control," Josh replied. "Confiscate all the jump ships, and they'll have complete control over all movement of goods and people. That's what they did in the Sol sector, except it was FTL ships. A hundred credits says they don't bat an eye at sub-light ships, or even FTL-only ships."

"You could be right," Captain Tuplo agreed, taking a sip of his coffee, "but I wouldn't want to chance it."

"But surely that's not everywhere," Neli commented as she moved the pot of stew she had prepared for their evening meal from the stove to the table.

"From what I hear, nothing is moving in or out of the cluster," the captain replied. "Although, I did hear a rumor that some of the lesser Pentaurus worlds don't always have a Jung ship present."

"You think they're jumping around the outer worlds with just one or two ships?"

"Makes sense," Captain Tuplo agreed. "It had to

take quite a few ships to take down both the Takaran fleet *and* the Avendahl, at the same time. I imagine they're keeping the bulk of their fleet in the main Pentaurus worlds until they are completely secured. After that, they'll probably spread them out more evenly."

"How many ships do they have?" Josh wondered.

"No one really knows for sure," the captain said. "I've heard reports ranging from six to twenty. Best I can tell, no one has seen more than six Jung ships together at once, though. And according to reports, they are jumping around like crazy. Problem is you only see them jump in or out, not both. And nobody hangs around long enough to ID each ship, that's for damn sure."

"Anyone have a guess at how long it's going to take for things to shake out?" Dalen wondered.

"I told you not to bring us here," Marcus groaned, his head still buried in his arms on the table.

"Once we get the ship fixed, we'll probably move further out. Start taking runs around the outer edges of the sector, possibly even outside the sector," the captain said.

"There ain't shit outside the sector," Marcus reminded him, his face finally coming up from the table. "Leastways not nearby."

"True enough," the captain agreed. "We'll have to jump a few hundred light years, most likely. Maybe more."

"We'd better get more weapons, then," Josh warned.

"Well, we're on the right world for *that* at least," the captain admitted. "You can buy them on the streets, here on Haven."

"There's a reason for that," Marcus grumbled.

"Now might be a good time to start thinking about adding some sort of defensive ship-to-ship weapons, Cap'n," Dalen suggested.

"How do you figure?"

"We've already got a hole in the top of the hull, just inboard of the port nacelle. And it's right above the main power line. All I'd have to do is clean up the hole a bit, and we could mount a small plasma turret up there."

"We'd need a targeting system to control it," Josh reminded Dalen.

"Plasma turrets ain't cheap," Marcus said.

"Neither are targeting systems, I imagine," the captain added. "Let's just concentrate on fixing what we've got for now. Speaking of which, how long is it going to take?"

"Starboard side was good," Dalen replied, "so it shouldn't take more than a day, assuming we get the parts quick enough."

"Shouldn't be any problem getting parts," Josh said. "Haven's a fucking junkyard."

"Give me a list, and Josh and I will find what you need after dinner."

"You got it, Cap'n," Dalen replied as he scooped another serving of stew into his bowl. "I'll get started pulling the damaged parts tonight."

"I'd appreciate that," the captain said. "Haven's port fees may be the cheapest around, but they're still fees, and they'll add up quickly. Besides, if we *are* going to move further out, we're going to need the extra credits to buy supplies and such to make it through until we find work. We've got no idea if the worlds further out will accept Pentaurus credits. I want to be flush with food, water, propellant, and spare parts, *before* we leave the sector."

"Assuming that we *do* have to leave the sector," Neli pointed out.

"Oh, we do," Josh insisted.

"Maybe the Jung are only interested in the cluster worlds," Neli suggested hopefully.

"She could be right," Captain Tuplo said. "Outside of the PC, no one else has much industrial capacity. Maybe the Jung will be satisfied with just the cluster."

"No, they won't," Josh said confidently.

"He's right," Marcus sighed. "As soon as they secure the core PC systems, they'll secure the fringe worlds. Then the ones outside the PC. Hell, for all we know, they've been conquering worlds all the way from the Sol sector to here, and spreading out in all directions to boot."

"It's what they do," Josh added.

"I hope you're wrong," Captain Tuplo said, "because if you're right, it won't matter how far out we go. Sooner or later, the Jung will catch up to us."

* * *

"Jump complete," the lieutenant announced as the shuttle windows cleared.

"Scanning all channels," Jessica replied.

"Four contacts," the lieutenant added, "twenty thousand kilometers; tracking left to right."

"Are they turning toward us?"

"Negative," the lieutenant responded, "targets are maintaining course and speed."

"This sucks!" Sergeant Torwell complained, sitting in the gunner's chair hanging from the ceiling of the jump shuttle's utility compartment.

"Shut up, Torwell," Jessica instructed as she monitored her long-range communications console.

"Four more contacts!" the lieutenant warned, his

voice apprehensive. "Bearing one five seven, twenty-five degrees up relative. A third group is bearing two one five, sixty degrees down, relative."

"If they're not coming toward us, I don't give a shit," Jessica informed him.

"Just hurry up and get the message, so we can get the hell out of here," the sergeant whined.

"Shut up, Torwell!" Commander Kainan ordered.

"Jump flash!" the lieutenant interrupted. "Dead ahead! Thousand kilometers and closing fast. Sensor profile indicates a Jung gunship."

"It's message plus thirty, already!" the sergeant moaned. "Has he replied, or not?"

"I swear to God, Torwell! If you don't shut your yap..."

"Incoming message!" Jessica announced, interrupting them.

"Thank God," the sergeant exclaimed.

Jessica studied the incoming signal for a moment, waiting for an ID code.

"Who else would it be from," the lieutenant said.

"What does he say?" the sergeant wondered.

"Hold your horses," Jessica replied, "I still have to decrypt it."

"One-fifty and closing," the lieutenant warned.

"Just a few more seconds," Jessica begged, "I've almost got it."

"The gunship will have range on us in fifteen seconds," Lieutenant Latfee reminded her.

"Ready the escape jump," the commander ordered.

"Already done," the lieutenant assured him. "Five seconds..."

"I've got it! I've got it!" Jessica shouted.

"Jumping!"

The jump shuttle's windows instantly turned

opaque as the ship disappeared in a blinding flash of blue-white light. "Please, tell me that was Dumar," the sergeant said nervously as the turret bubble surrounding him cleared again.

"Jesus, Torwell," Jessica sneered, "you should stay away from recon work. You don't have the nerves for it."

"Were you under the impression that I volunteered for this mission?" the sergeant replied dryly.

"Well, was it?" the lieutenant wondered as well.

"Yup," Jessica replied, "it's from Dumar."

After several seconds of silence, the lieutenant and the commander turned and looked aft of the cockpit. At the same time, Sergeant Torwell rotated his gun turret around and peered downward between his feet at Jessica.

"Well?" the sergeant asked again.

"He made contact with Montrose," Jessica told them. "Yanni, Lael, the baby, Sato and Megel... They're all safe, for now."

"Is that it?" the sergeant wondered. "We risked our asses for that?"

"There's more," Jessica replied, as she swung the comm console to the side and leaned back in her seat. "Just get us the hell back to Burgess for now."

"Well, I hope Dumar's got some idea how to rescue them," the commander said as he turned back around in his seat, "because this place is crawling with Jung."

* * *

"The sudden, unexpected arrival of Ambassador Delhay at the presidential compound here in Winnipeg has many speculating that his visit is somehow connected with the sudden deployment of the Aurora, the Cape Town, and several other Alliance ships.

While President Scott's press secretary insists there is no connection, and that such impromptu meetings are common, it is rare for the ambassador to leave the Jung Embassy compound, especially after last year's attempt on his life, and the lives of his family."

"Well, it didn't take long for them to put that together," Miri said, as she picked up the remote from the president's desk and turned off the view screen.

"I will never understand how the press manages to keep tabs on the position of all our ships," the president said, shaking his head.

"All it takes are a few well-placed telescopes and the jump-comm-net."

"Ah, yes," the president sighed, "the double-edged sword of near real-time interstellar communication."

"Mister President," the guard standing just inside his office door called. "The ambassador is on his way up."

"Thank you." The president turned to look at his daughter. "How do I look? Hopefully not as tired as I feel."

Miri straightened his tie and smoothed out the wrinkles in his suit jacket. "You look fine," she assured him. "With just the appropriate amount of concern on your face."

"I'm getting way too old for this."

"You're only as old as you feel," Miri reminded him.

"Today, I feel about a hundred and forty."

"The ambassador is in the outer office," the guard updated him.

President Scott took a deep breath, letting it out slowly in an attempt to put himself in a new frame of mind. He moved out from behind his desk and into the middle of the room, readying himself to greet the ambassador.

A moment later, the main doors to his office swung open. Two more guards moved just inside the doors as Ambassador Delhay entered the president's office.

"Mister Ambassador," President Scott greeted with a smile, his hand extended.

"Mister President," the ambassador replied, smiling back. He reached out and took the president's hand in the customary gesture of friendship. "It is a pleasure to see you once again. I am pleased to see that you're in good health, despite the rumors often perpetuated by your news media."

"I may be old, but I'm not dead yet," the president replied with a light chuckle. "I hope you are also doing well?"

"Indeed, I am. Life on Earth seems to agree with me."

"And your family? I assume they are also doing well?" the president asked, attempting to keep the small talk going while the others cleared the room. "Please," he added, gesturing toward the sitting area.

"Yes, yes, they are all quite well, thank you," the ambassador replied, taking his seat opposite the president, on the other side of the small sitting table. He was well aware of the required choreography of such meetings. While the effectiveness of their conversations required complete privacy, the president's guards would be watching the ambassador's every move. Once the customary handshake had been completed and the ambassador had taken his seat, he would no longer be able to approach the president without being immediately overrun by guards bursting through the doors. "I was quite surprised by your request to meet. I do hope the purpose of this meeting is nothing dire."

President Scott paused a moment, waiting for the last guard to exit and close the soundproof doors behind him. Once he was satisfied the room was secure, he spoke. "I'm going to get straight to the point Mister Ambassador. There have been four separate sightings of Jung ships on this day alone. Near the Mu Cassiopeiae system, the 82 Eridani system, the 41 Arae system, and even more troubling, near the Alpha Centauri B system. As you know, these encroachments upon Alliance space constitute serious violations of the cease-fire agreement, and represent a great threat to the ongoing peace that both our peoples have shared for the last seven years, and hope to continue sharing long into the future." The president paused a moment, studying the reaction of the ambassador.

"Are you sure that your detections were accurate?" the ambassador asked without missing a beat. "It is not uncommon for…"

"Two Jung cruisers near the Mu Cassiopeiae system," the president said, interrupting him, "a cruiser and two frigates near 82 Eridani, and a battleship each in the 41 Arae and Alpha Centauri B systems."

Concern began to creep into the ambassador's expression. "You are saying that these detections were indeed confirmed."

"Not only were they confirmed," the president replied, "but in three cases these *detections* were engaged, and at least two of them were destroyed by our warships. So, Mister Ambassador, you can understand the nature of my concern."

Ambassador Delhay fought to preserve his neutral

facial expression. After a moment, the look of mild concern that had spread across his face moments ago disappeared altogether. "Mister President, I can assure you that I have no knowledge of the positions of our warships. Furthermore, I am unaware of any such purposeful incursions on the part of my government into Alliance space. I can further assure you that the Jung Empire respects the cease-fire it currently enjoys with the Alliance and has no desire to see it come to an end."

President Scott contemplated the ambassador's response. It was exactly the answer he had expected. "Mister Ambassador, I shall take you at your word. However, I find it difficult to believe that your government is unaware of these incursions."

"I believe we have stated, on more than one occasion, that we cannot guarantee all of our ship commanders will honor the terms of the cease-fire..."

"And we accepted that, in the beginning," the president replied, cutting him off mid-sentence, "as it took time for new instructions to reach every ship in the Jung fleet. But, it has been seven years now. That excuse is no longer valid."

"There is still much animosity among our warrior caste," the ambassador reminded him.

"As there is among my people toward yours."

"It would not surprise me if one or two commanders chose to demonstrate their ability to penetrate deeply into Alliance space in the hopes that our leaders might reconsider their 'peaceful coexistence' policy in regards to the Sol-Pentaurus Alliance."

"We are not talking about one or two ships, Mister Ambassador," the president argued.

"I'm not defending their actions, assuming these alleged ships are indeed ours. However, I'm also not going to lie to you, Mister President. The majority of the Jung general population still despises your Alliance, in particular the people of Earth. In the warrior caste this animosity is nearly unanimous."

"We're talking about seven warships," the president said. "Seven of them, Mister Ambassador, not one or two. Seven warships, in four different locations. All of them well inside Alliance territory. Territory agreed upon in the formal cease-fire agreement that both our peoples signed. I suppose an argument could be made that three of those incursions were merely navigational errors—although that would be a bit of a stretch—the incursion near the Alpha Centauri system can only be interpreted as a purposeful violation of the cease-fire agreement."

Ambassador Delhay did not respond at first, and instead took a moment to carefully consider his words. "Mister President, what is it that you wish me to say? I was honest with you when I said I had no knowledge of these incursions prior to this meeting."

"And I believe you," the president replied.

"Speaking only from my own personal opinion, and not representing the opinions of my government, I would be quite surprised to learn that these incursions were ordered by our leaders." The ambassador looked at President Scott, looking directly into his eyes. "Especially since they are aware of the numerous kinetic kill vehicles your Alliance has trained upon not only the Jung homeworld of Nor-Patri, but also numerous other worlds and tactical assets. Such actions would be tantamount to suicide."

"Please do not take what I say personally, Mister Ambassador, but the Jung Empire has demonstrated, on more than one occasion, a general disregard for human life, especially when those lives stand between the empire and its goals."

"You are suggesting that the Jung Empire would willingly sacrifice millions of its own citizens in order to justify a war that would most likely cost millions more lives? The very idea is absurd!"

"I'm not suggesting anything, Mister Ambassador," the president replied calmly. "I am merely stating facts. Surely you cannot dispute that the Jung Empire has, in the past, taken such actions."

"Again, I ask you, what is it that you ask of me, Mister President?" Ambassador Delhay said with forced patience.

President Scott stared at the ambassador, trying to identify a sign indicating he was lying. He knew it was unlikely that Ambassador Delhay was aware of either the actions or intentions of the Jung leadership cast, or those of the Jung warrior caste. The ambassador was at great disadvantage due to the limitations of linear FTL-based methods of interstellar communication. Because of this, President Scott, against the objections of Admiral Galiardi, had authorized the use of a dedicated jump comm-drone long ago to provide near real-time communications between Ambassador Delhay and the Jung homeworld. However, it was unlikely the Jung would allow any sensitive communications to be conveyed by an Alliance-controlled jump comm-drone. "I realize you will first need to communicate with your leaders," the president began. "However, I need your assurance, and the assurance of your leaders, that these incursions were not authorized, that they shall not happen again, and that the commanders of the ships who committed the incursions will be properly dealt with by the Jung Empire."

"I am confident that once I have communicated with my superiors, such assurances will be forthcoming," Ambassador Delhay promised.

"I must also inform you that our KKV platforms, along with our entire fleet, have been put on alert, and that we are now at defense condition two." A stern look came over the president's face. "It is not only the terms of the cease-fire that require me to issue such warnings, but also my own sincere desire to maintain the peace that has existed between us all these years."

The ambassador stared at the president for several moments, squinting, unable to read his political adversary. "I assume that such a provocative move was at the behest of Admiral Galiardi?"

A controlled look of disapproval came over the president's face. "Do not assume for a moment that the people of the Alliance are not in control of *their* military forces. It would be a grave mistake on your part."

President Scott leaned back in his chair, folding his hands in his lap. Ambassador Delhay studied the president's calm, confident demeanor. For a man approaching ninety Earth years of age, he was a picture of strength and resolve and, like his son Nathan, was not a man to be taken lightly.

"I will communicate all that we have discussed with my leaders," the ambassador promised. "I shall contact you as soon as I get the reply."

"That is all I can ask of you," the president said, as he rose from his seat.

The Jung ambassador stood up. "Mister President." He paused a moment, waiting for the guards to enter the room once again before he offered his hand to the president.

"Thank you for coming, Mister Ambassador," the president said, taking the ambassador's hand once more.

Ambassador Delhay released the president's hand, nodded politely, and exited the room. President Scott waited until the doors had closed before returning to his desk.

"Do you think he is telling the truth?" Miri asked as she entered the office from a side door.

"I believe that *he* believes he's telling the truth," the president replied as he sat at his desk. "We'll see if his position changes after he speaks with his superiors."

* * *

Strange voices echoed throughout the ship. Distant voices, speaking in hushed tones, as if from the far side of a large room. The voices sounded familiar, yet he was unable to identify them. The voices were pleading, crying out, begging him to protect them, but from what he did not know.

He found himself on the Seiiki's bridge, alone, but the voices were still there. He gazed out the forward windows at the Jung ships in the distance. The vessels grew larger with each passing moment. Flashes of blue-white light obscured his view of the approaching warships. Rail gun rounds collided with his shields, causing them to glow with brilliant yellow opacity. Then the shields failed, and the projectiles found the Seiiki's hull, ripping it open.

Captain Tuplo found himself sucked through the hole and into space. The first thing he noticed was the overwhelming cold. Everywhere, everything, cold. He could see his ship being torn apart by Jung rail gun fire. Chunks of the Seiiki's hull were flying in all directions. Her hull opened in several more places. Passengers were swept out as well, joining the sea of his ship's debris as it came apart under the constant rail gun bombardment by the Jung ships. Their bodies were motionless, faces frozen in horror, lives immediately extinguished.

Yet Captain Tuplo was still alive, floating unprotected in the void of space, watching his ship, his crew, and his passengers.

How am I still alive? He had only the question, but no answer. *Why am I still breathing while they are not?*

The Seiiki continued to break up, until finally the enemy gunfire found her antimatter reactors. There was a blinding flash of bright white light, as the release of antimatter instantly annihilated all matter in the vicinity. The white light washed over the captain as he floated in space, yet he felt nothing.

His head began to spin, his thoughts becoming confused. Nothing made sense. *Why did the Jung attack his ship? Why was he still alive? What did he do wrong? Why was he unable to protect the only people he cared about?*

And what the hell is that beeping noise?

Captain Tuplo sat bolt upright in his bunk, his body drenched in a cold sweat. He blinked several times, then turned toward the beeping sound. *The hatch alarm.* The captain jumped out of his bed, slipped on his shoes, and grabbed his weapon from its holster hanging from the wall as he exited his cabin.

Once in the corridor, the captain headed aft for a few steps, just far enough to reach the door to Josh's cabin. He pounded several times on the cabin door. "Josh! Wake up!" The Captain headed forward again, moving quickly down the corridor and through the hatch of the forward end. He made his way alongside the forward passenger section, raising his weapon and pressing his charge button as he approached the boarding hatch.

The captain could hear muffled voices from outside. A moment later, Josh came stumbling down the corridor, rubbing the sleep from his eyes. He spotted the captain, noticed his raised weapon, and turned around to run back to his cabin.

Captain Tuplo looked at the boarding hatch control panel. The outer door was open, but the inner door was still locked. The captain stood at an angle, trying to get a clear look at the intruders, but they were both huddled to one side, working to override the door lock. He glanced at the boarding hatch control panel again, noticing that three of the six numbers required to unlock the inner hatch had been successfully entered.

Josh came running back up the corridor, his own gun in hand. Captain Tuplo gestured for him to slow down and be quiet. The captain pointed at the inner door and held up two fingers, indicating there were two men trying to break in. He moved back around the corner, held up his weapon and took aim at the inner hatch. Josh did the same, moving into the galley hatch and training his own weapon in similar fashion.

A fourth digit appeared on the boarding hatch control panel. Josh charged his weapon and held it steady, aiming at the inner hatch. Had either of the intruders taken the time to occasionally peek through the window, they would've spotted at least one of the two armed men inside, and would have quickly abandoned their efforts. But thieves were rarely so intelligent.

A fifth digit appeared.

Captain Tuplo readied himself, moving his finger to the trigger of his weapon, as the sixth digit appeared and the inner hatch slid open. "Take one step beyond that hatch and we will burn holes through you both!" the captain warned.

They heard nothing.

"Now, I know you can hear me," the captain continued. "What I *don't* know is if you speak Angla. Either way, in five seconds we start shooting. Five..."

There was immediate movement inside the boarding airlock as the two men quickly exited the ship, skipping the ladder they had originally used, and jumping the two meters to the tarmac below.

"I guess they spoke Angla after all," Josh said.

Captain Tuplo came back out around the corner to inspect the boarding airlock.

"What the hell's going on out here?" Marcus demanded as he came down the corridor, Dalen and Neli hot on his heels.

"Just a couple of Haven's finest," Josh joked as he powered down his weapon.

"Locks don't appear damaged," the captain said as he examined the controls. "Nevertheless, we should probably change the codes." The captain looked at Dalen.

"Now?"

"Now," the captain replied.

"But I was sleepin'."

"And the sooner you change those codes, the sooner you can get back to sleep," the captain said as he came out of the airlock and headed forward to the cockpit.

"Where you going?" Josh wondered.

"Someone's got to take first watch," the captain

replied, "in case those two are dumb enough to come back and try again."

"They can't be that dumb, Captain," Josh argued. "They know we're here, and they know we're armed."

"Never underestimate how stupid someone can be," the captain said, as he ascended the short ladder to the cockpit.

"He's right," Marcus agreed. "Besides, there's more than enough dumbasses to go around on this world. That's why the overnight fees are so low on Haven, and why no ship captain in his right mind would want to spend the night on this dusty rock." Marcus turned to head back to his cabin. "Neli and I will relieve you in four hours."

"I'll put on some coffee," Josh said.

Dalen watched as everyone else left him standing there by the boarding airlock inner hatch.

"*Get on it, Dalen!*" the captain bellowed from the cockpit.

"Son of a bitch," Dalen cursed.

"*You want some coffee?*" Josh asked from the galley.

"No thanks," Dalen replied. "Besides, this will only take ten minutes."

"*Then why the hell are you bitching?*" Josh called back.

"Because it's the middle of the night," Dalen reminded him, surprised that he had to ask.

* * *

A blue-white flash appeared in the evening sky over Lawrence. A moment later, it was followed by the distant thunderous clap that accompanied all jumps into the atmosphere.

Although Lawrence was Burgess's capital city, and by far the largest city on the only inhabited world in the Sherma system, it rarely received more than a few jump ships per day, especially after sundown.

Loki and Deliza ran out of the Ghatazhak hangar office, peering up at the night sky as they came outside. Several kilometers away they could see the flashing lights of the approaching ship, though it was still too distant for them to identify.

"*Lawrence Control, Jumper One Golf,*" the pilot's voice crackled over the speakers in the open hangar, "*inbound for landing on pad one four.*"

"Is it them?" Deliza asked Loki.

"I'm not sure," Loki admitted.

"It is," General Telles assured them as he approached from behind.

"*Jumper One Golf, Lawrence Control,*" the speakers blared. "*Clear direct for pad one four.*"

"*Jumper One Golf, clear direct, pad one four.*"

The three of them watched as the combat jump shuttle descended quickly toward them, leveling off on the far side of the spaceport ten meters above the surface. The shuttle transited the spaceport quickly, rotating to port and sliding sideways to starboard as it descended the last few meters and touched down on the tarmac before them.

Loki and Deliza both turned their backs toward the landing shuttle to protect themselves against its considerable thrust wash. The general only squinted.

The shuttle settled onto its landing gear, and its thrust wash suddenly disappeared, while the engines stopped screaming and began to spin down. Loki and Deliza turned back around as the shuttle began to roll toward the open hangar. Its large side door slid opened, revealing Jessica and Sergeant Torwell inside. Her data pad in hand, Jessica hopped down from the rolling shuttle and jogged toward them.

"Please, tell me they're alive," Loki begged, noticing the look of concern on Jessica's face.

Deliza had also noticed Jessica's expression, but was unable to speak, her hands covering her mouth.

"They're alive," Jessica assured them as she came to a stop. "All of them. Yanni, Lael, Ailsa, Michi, and Tori. They are alive and well, and hiding out at Doran's."

"Oh, thank God," Loki exclaimed.

Deliza also breathed a sigh of relief. "Do *they* know *we're* alive?"

"Yes," Jessica replied, "I included that in the original message to Dumar." She continued walking, leading them all back to the hangar office.

"Did they say anything else?" Loki wondered. "Did they say how... Did they say where... I mean... How do we rescue them?"

"Slow down, Loki," Jessica insisted. "One thing at a time. Let's get inside first."

Jessica exchanged glances with General Telles. He knew she had bad news.

Moments later, they entered the office. Jessica removed her helmet and life support pack, setting them down next to the door. She turned back around before speaking, in order to face the others as they entered. "Okay, like I said, they're all alive, they're all fine, but that's pretty much the end of the good news. Dumar's reply was far more detailed than we expected. I don't know how he did it so quickly, but he provided us with quite a bit of information about the invading forces, and how they're spread out across Corinair. Every major city on Corinair has been occupied by the Jung. Dumar estimates at least a battalion, perhaps even a brigade or a division in the larger cities. Aitkenna definitely has at least a division on the ground. We're talking close to half a million men planet-wide."

"If the Jung have put that many men on the ground, then it means their goal is to take that world with its infrastructure still intact," the general said.

"Dumar also thinks the Jung have captured Donegan and Kurzweil as well; however, he has no confirmation."

"If their intention was to take the Darvano system without damaging her infrastructure, then surely they would do the same to the Takar system," Commander Jahal added as he entered the room.

"Indeed," General Telles agreed. "Darvano and Takara were the only armed systems in the Pentaurus cluster. They would have to be taken simultaneously in order to utilize the element of surprise to their advantage." General Telles looked at Jessica. "Then it is confirmed?"

"I'm afraid so," Jessica replied. "The Avendahl was completely destroyed. She left a debris field at least a hundred kilometers wide, and that's after half of it fell back to Corinair and burned up in its atmosphere."

"How are we going to rescue them?" Loki demanded. "We have to get them out of there."

"It's not that easy, Loki," Jessica insisted.

"Yes, it is!" Loki replied stubbornly. "Just give me a jump shuttle and I'll go get them myself!"

"You'd be intercepted before you touched down, Loki," Jessica explained. "We were intercepted less than a minute after we jumped in. Both times. And we were in deep space."

"We can jump into a canyon or something. They'll never see us."

"That won't work!" Jessica protested.

"Sure it will!" Loki argued. "You guys used to do it all the time," he continued, looking at the general. "Isn't that right?"

"Corinair has an extensive satellite surveillance network," General Telles reminded him. "It was put in place to allow more accurate tracking and control of jump ships due to the increase in traffic over recent years. If the Jung have control of that network, and we must assume they do, then they will see your jump flash, and respond quickly."

"This isn't like before, Loki," Jessica said. "They didn't have jump drives. They've got jump fighters all over the place. The moment you jump in, the nearest Jung fighters will jump to your location and you'll be dead, as will everyone you meant to pick up."

"But we can't just leave them there," Loki argued. "It's only a matter of time until the Jung find them."

"Why would the Jung wish to find them?" the general wondered.

"Because *we* were trying to rescue them," Loki replied. "Us, and three of the Avendahl's fighters. Don't you think the Jung are going to be curious about someone to whom such resources would be committed?"

Jessica looked at the general. "He's got a point."

"Indeed," the general agreed. "However, that changes nothing. As you said, their fighters would be on us before we even touched down. We may be forced to wait until things settle down on Corinair before we can attempt a rescue."

"But..." Loki began to argue.

"That's probably what Dumar is thinking as well," Jessica said, cutting Loki off. "He has arranged to get them out of Aitkenna and to the safety of his resort in the mountains."

"What good would that do?" Deliza asked. "Those satellites can see Dumar's resort as well, can't they?"

"Of course," the general admitted, "but it will be some time before the Jung get around to inspecting such facilities. I suspect they will be safer there than any place else on Corinair, at least for the time being."

"But..."

Jessica held up her hand, interrupting Loki yet again. "The admiral used to command a counterinsurgency unit on Corinair... A covert one at that. He knows what he's doing, Loki. We have to trust him." Jessica put her hand on his shoulder in comfort.

Loki sighed. The idea of his wife and child stranded without him on a Jung-occupied world was more than he could stand. "I don't know if I can," he admitted, his voice trembling.

Deliza placed her hand on Loki's other shoulder. "Travon Dumar is a good man, a smart man. My father trusted him without reservation, and I trust him as well."

"Come, you both need rest," Commander Jahal said, as he led both Loki and Deliza out of the office.

Jessica and General Telles watched them leave, then the general turned to Jessica. "How did it really go?"

"That system really is crawling with Jung," Jessica replied.

"Any idea what the admiral is up to?"

"Gather the troops, lie low, and wait for an opportunity, I guess. I'll tell you one thing, though. Whatever plan he does come up with, is not going to be an easy one."

* * *

Josh placed the two mugs of coffee on the deck of the Seiiki's cockpit, then climbed up the short ladder to the cockpit's deck. He picked up the mugs and moved forward. "Coffee, Captain?"

"Thanks," the captain replied, taking the mug offered by his copilot. "You don't have to stay up, Josh. I can handle the watch by myself."

"I can take the first one, if you'd like," Josh offered as he slid into the copilot's seat. "I'm already wide awake."

"That's okay."

Josh took a sip of coffee. "Trouble sleeping?"

"Something like that."

"Wanna talk about it?" Josh asked.

Captain Tuplo frowned at him.

"Just thought I'd offer."

The captain took another drink of his coffee as he stared out the windows at the dimly lit spaceport. "Why does Marcus hate Haven so much?"

"You mean besides all the dust, the stink, the crappy food, and let's not forget all the wonderful people just waiting to rob you blind when your back's turned?"

"It's not the only shithole in the sector."

"Just the shittiest," Josh replied.

"You guys lived here for what, ten years?"

"Ten or twelve, I don't rightly know. I always get confused trying to calculate Haven years to Earth years to Corinairan years... Doesn't really matter. Let's just say I was just outta diapers when my mom got shipped here to serve her debt, and full grown by the time we left."

"How old were you when she passed?" the captain asked.

"Not very... Not old enough to remember, that's

for sure."

"That's when Marcus took you in?"

"Yup. He was always sweet on my mom, always bringing her stuff... Little things like extra blankets, extra food, toys for me. I don't know that she ever returned his kindness, if you get my meaning, but it don't matter. He took care of me, nonetheless. He's the only father I really had. Never knew my real father. My mom never talked about him, at least not that I can remember. As best I can tell he ran out on us when I was still a baby."

"So Marcus took good care of you, then."

"I suppose so," Josh said, leaning back in his seat. "It's not like he was the perfect father. I suppose he was as good as any. Gave me a place to live, food to eat, made sure I learned what I needed to know, smacked me around when I needed it." Josh smiled. "And trust me, I needed it." Josh took another drink of his coffee. "To be honest, I probably wouldn't be here if it wasn't for Marcus."

"How so?"

Josh looked at the captain. "You're full of questions, aren't you?"

"Sorry if I'm prying," the captain apologized.

"No matter," Josh assured him. "It wasn't easy for Marcus, either. The company treated everyone like shit, Marcus included. On Haven, you can cheat, steal, hell, you can even kill someone, and no one gives a damn. But being a debtor? Well that's just about the worst thing you can be on Haven. And me being from outside the sector didn't help much. That's the second worst thing you can be on Haven."

"I didn't realize you were from outside the Pentaurus sector," the captain said. "Not that I give a damn." The captain took another sip of his coffee.

"Any idea where you were born?"

"Not a clue."

"Your mother didn't leave anything behind when she passed? Something that might suggest your place of birth?"

"Does it really matter?"

"I suppose not."

Josh stared out the window for a moment, watching the dust swirl around in the night breeze. "I used to think about it a lot, actually. I used to wonder if maybe I had relatives somewhere. Somewhere like Palee, Volon, or maybe even Takara for that matter. Truth be told, it used to bother me quite a bit. But then I got all swept up in the rebellion, and then the Alliance. After that, it didn't seem to matter as much. Hell, I figure I've been more places, and seen more things, than most people could ever dream of. So why should I care where the hell I was born, as long as I know where I've been?"

Captain Tuplo said nothing, only nodding his agreement. They sat there for several minutes, both of them staring out the windows, saying nothing as they drank their coffee.

"What about you?" Josh asked. "You remember much about your past?"

"Bits and pieces, really," the captain replied. "The crash wiped out most of my memory. I'm surprised I can remember how to pilot a ship." The captain took in a deep breath and sighed. "I remember her face though."

"Whose face?"

"My mother's... I think. Short brown hair, big green eyes. And I remember that she never really got mad, or at least she didn't look it. Of course, like I said, there's not much left of my memories. And what few things I do remember don't make sense."

"Whattaya mean?" Josh wondered. "Like there's pieces missing or something?"

"No, it's like I'm watching someone else's life. Little snippets here and there, but I can't put them together. It's like watching a few minutes from a bunch of different vids, and then trying to string them together into a cohesive story."

"That sounds really fucked up," Josh chuckled. "Sorry, Cap'n. I didn't mean to make light of your condition."

"I know. And you're right, it is fucked up."

"Do you remember anything about the crash?"

"Not a thing. Not a damn thing. Nothing before and nothing during. Other than the bits and pieces I talked about, my memory only goes back five years to when I woke up in the hospital after the crash. That's another thing that drives me crazy. I'd really like to know what happened, so I could avoid it ever happening again."

"Do those doctors think you'll ever get your memories back?" Josh asked.

"They have no idea," Captain Tuplo said with a sigh. "They just keep telling me that I'm lucky to be alive, as if that should be enough." The captain turned to look out the window again. "I suppose it should be, but it isn't."

"But you do know who you are. Where you were born, where you grew up, who your parents were, that kind of stuff."

"Only because I read it in a file they gave me," Captain Tuplo said. "It doesn't make it any more real to me, no more so than *you* dreaming about where *you* were born." The captain looked at Josh again. "I guess I'll just have to follow your lead, Josh, and just look forward instead of back."

Josh raised his mug of coffee. "Here's to always looking forward, Cap'n."

* * *

"Coming up on jump point," Lieutenant Commander Vidmar announced from the Aurora's tactical station. "All anti-FTL jump missiles are running straight and true."

"Cape Town confirms she is ready to jump on schedule," Ensign deBanco reported from the comm station.

Captain Taylor looked around the Aurora's bridge, its features tinged with the red lighting accents that signified her ship was at general quarters. It was the second time she would take the Aurora into combat in as many days. Up until the previous day, the Aurora had gone seven years without firing a single shot in anger. To many, it was a captain's dream... going so many years without being put in harm's way. To Cameron, it had been a relief. After two years of battling the Jung, she had welcomed the cease-fire. There was nothing glorious about war. It was nothing but death and suffering...and waste, so much waste.

At least now, both her ship and crew were properly equipped and trained. The Aurora was the oldest ship in the fleet, a distinction that had been passed to her upon the retirement of the last of the Earth's early scout ships turned gunships. She had seen more than her share of combat, and her share of upgrades. She was so much more than she had been when Cameron had first set foot on her decks more than seven years earlier. More importantly, the Aurora was a legend...both in the Sol and the Pentaurus sectors, as was her previous captain.

"Jump point in ten seconds," the tactical officer warned.

"Jump all missiles on schedule," Cameron ordered.

"Aye, sir. Jumping all missiles in three......two...... one......"

Cameron watched the Aurora's main semi-spherical view screen as several dozen tiny flashes of blue-white light, laid out in a perfectly symmetrical pattern, appeared before them.

"Anti-FTL missiles are away."

"Five degrees to starboard and ten up relative, Lieutenant," Cameron instructed her helmsman.

"Turning five degrees to starboard and coming up ten relative," the lieutenant replied in her usual, confident demeanor.

"Stand by to jump us ahead, five light minutes," Cameron instructed.

"Five light minutes, aye," the navigator confirmed.

"Anti-FTL missiles should have detonated," the tactical officer reported.

"On new heading."

"Jump us ahead five, Mister Bickle."

"Jumping ahead five," the navigator replied as the blue light from the Aurora's jump emitters quickly poured out across the hull, then flashed in a brilliant blue-white as the ship jumped ahead five light minutes along her course. "Jump complete."

"Launch the first wave of jump missiles, delayed jump," Cameron ordered calmly. "Lieutenant Dinev, bring us about, onto an overhead intercept course."

"Launching jump missiles," Lieutenant Commander Vidmar replied.

"Coming about to intercept course," the helmsman answered.

"Cape Town should be jumping in to engage the targets," the lieutenant commander added. "Jump missiles away, delayed jump."

Cameron glanced at the main view screen as six jump missiles, three from each side of the Aurora, streaked ahead of them. Once far past them, the missiles turned to port in a graceful arc, heading toward the Jung battle group five light minutes away. By now, the antimatter charges on their anti-FTL jump missiles had spread out, detonated, and disrupted the mass-cancelling fields of the Jung ships, forcing them back to subluminal velocities. As they turned back toward the enemy battle group, the Alliance's first Protector-class ship, the Cape Town, was jumping to a position directly in the Jung battle group's path, engaging all seven ships with her massive plasma cannons.

"The Cape Town should be engaging the Jung battle group by now," Lieutenant Commander Vidmar reported.

"On intercept course," Lieutenant Dinev reported from the helm.

"Hold course and speed," Cameron instructed. "We'll jump in ten seconds after our weapons jump away."

"Holding course and speed, aye."

Cameron continued watching the main view screen. By now, their jump missiles were too far ahead for her to see, but in a few seconds, their jump flashes would be visible.

They were about to kill hundreds of Jung, a fact that was always lingering in the back of any captain's mind, and Cameron was no exception. But Admiral Galiardi's orders were clear; there would be no warning hail this time. These Jung ships were too deep in Alliance space for their presence to be an 'accident', or a 'navigational error'. It was a clear violation of the cease-fire agreement, one that required a decisive response. It was also an overt act of aggression, and was one the Alliance would meet with equal, if not superior force.

Six flashes of light appeared on the main view screen, so far ahead of them that, had she not been expecting them, they might have gone unnoticed.

"Weapons have jumped away," Lieutenant Commander Vidmar reported.

Cameron took a deep breath, letting it out in a slow and steady manner, giving their weapons a chance to do their jobs before taking her ship in to attack. "Jump us in, Mister Bickle."

"Attack jump in three......two......one...... jumping," the navigator said as the blue-white light of the Aurora's jump flash briefly illuminated the main view screen.

"Contacts," Lieutenant Commander Kono announced. "Eight of them. Seven Jung warships, and the Cape Town, sir..."

"...The Cape Town is currently engaging all seven targets..." Lieutenant Commander Vidmar said, appearing impressed.

"...Jump flashes!" Lieutenant Commander Kono added. "Twelve Cobra gunships! They're attacking the frigates!"

"Helm, bring us onto the nearest cruiser and hold steady," Cameron ordered. "Tactical, prepare a full spread of plasma torpedoes. Full power triplets."

"Steering toward the near cruiser..." Lieutenant Dinev replied as she altered the Aurora's course slightly.

"...Both cruisers' shields are down to fifty

percent," Lieutenant Commander Kono reported from the sensor station. "Battleship's shields are still at ninety-eight percent. Two of the four frigates have shield strengths of less than thirty percent!"

"All tubes show ready to fire, Captain..."

"...Battleship is bringing some of her main guns onto us," Lieutenant Commander Kono added.

"Full power to forward and port shields," the captain ordered. "Put the shield energy where it counts."

"I have a firing solution on the near cruiser, Captain," the lieutenant commander announced.

"Fire on all tubes."

"Firing all tubes..."

"...The battleship is firing her guns," the lieutenant commander reported as the bridge lit up with the red-orange flashes of the plasma torpedoes leaving their tubes and racing toward the enemy cruiser.

"...Torpedoes away..."

"Rail gun impact!" the systems officer reported. "Forward and port shields!"

"Put our nose on the battleship, Miss Dinev," Cameron ordered calmly.

"Torpedo impacts in ten seconds..."

"...Turning onto the battleship, aye..."

"Another full power spread of triplets, Mister Vidmar," Cameron instructed. "This time on the battleship. Stand by on the escape jump."

"Preparing another spread..."

"Missile launches!" Lieutenant Commander Kono warned. "All four frigates! Thirty missiles total in action! Plotting their courses now!"

"Be ready on that escape jump, Mister Bickle."

"The Cobra pack just took out one of the frigates," the lieutenant commander reported.

"All tubes are ready to fire," Lieutenant Commander Vidmar announced from the tactical station.

"I need to know where those missiles are going..."

"Yes, sir," her sensor officer replied. "All missiles are headed... They're headed for the Cape Town, sir! All of them! They're engaging point defenses!"

"I have a firing solution on the battleship..."

"Fire all tubes," Cameron ordered.

"Cape Town is knocking them down, one by one..."

"...Firing on all tubes..."

"...Cruiser two is locking her main guns on us," the sensor officer warned.

"Torpedoes away!" the tactical officer reported.

"...Port and forward shields are down to eighty percent," the systems officer announced.

"...Cruiser one's shields are failing," Lieutenant Commander Kono reported from the sensor station. "She's maneuvering, diving fast and turning to starboard. Cape Town's guns are tracking her."

"...Torpedo impacts in five seconds..."

"...Shields are down to seventy percent and falling..."

"Roll us over," Cameron instructed. "Show them our dorsal and starboard sides. Sideslip us, Lieutenant. Don't give them any more of our forward shields to shoot at than necessary."

"Torpedo impacts!"

"Yes, sir," the lieutenant replied, as she rolled the Aurora to starboard and swung their nose away from the approaching Jung battleship, so their forward shields would be at an oblique angle.

"Battleship's topside shields are down to fifty-two percent!" Lieutenant Commander Kono reported with surprise.

"Are you sure about that?"

"Yes, sir. Now at fifty and dropping."

"All plasma cannons on that battleship, Mister Vidmar."

"Another frigate is down!"

"Another round of torpedoes will knock their..."

"Can't do it," the captain replied, cutting her tactical officer off. "We can't afford to show them our weak shields. Let go another round of jump missiles: high arc, double jump, to apex and back to target. Let them go as we pass so the battleship won't see them launch. Helm, pitch up forty-five degrees to help out with the launch angle. Systems, keep shifting power to the shields between us and that battleship."

"Cruiser one is destroyed!" Lieutenant Commander Kono reported. "The Cape Town took her out!"

"What about those missiles?"

"The Cape Town's point defenses took them out, as well!"

"Missiles programmed and ready," Lieutenant Commander Vidmar reported from the tactical console.

"Nose at forty-five up, Captain," the helmsman reported.

"FTL fields are building! All ships!" the sensor officer reported.

"Firing plasma cannons!" the tactical officer announced.

Cameron called up the starboard ventral cameras on the main view screen. The Jung battleship appeared in the center of the screen, as if passing under them, while the Aurora's four main quad-barreled plasma cannons pounded away at her surprisingly weakened topside shields.

"All targets are going to FTL!"

The captain continued watching as the image of the battleship began to elongate, her mass-cancelling fields reaching full power. The ship suddenly stretched forward like it was made of rubber, its aft end following, disappearing in the distance an instant later.

"All Jung ships have gone to FTL," Lieutenant Commander Kono reported.

"Cobra Leader is asking if you want them to pursue, Captain," Ensign deBanco announced from the comm station.

"Was their departure course in the direction of Sol?" Cameron asked her sensor officer.

"Negative, sir," Lieutenant Commander Kono replied. "Best guess would be Rho 1 Cancri, nearly forty-three light years away."

"They could still turn toward Sol," the captain thought out loud, "at least for a few weeks, assuming their top FTL speed hasn't changed." She turned her chair aft, toward her comm officer. "Instruct the Cobras to pursue and track. Notify if the targets turn towards Sol, or any other Alliance world, for that matter. Update command every hour."

"Aye, sir," the comm officer acknowledged.

Captain Taylor looked at her tactical officer, Lieutenant Commander Vidmar. "Damned odd, wouldn't you say?"

"Yes, sir, I would."

"Cobras are jumping away," the sensor officer reported.

"Threat board?"

"No threats in the area," Lieutenant Commander Vidmar replied.

"Stand down from general quarters," Cameron instructed as she rose from her seat. "Have the XO and the cheng report to me in my ready room in twenty minutes," she added as she headed aft.

"Aye, sir," the comm officer replied.

"You have the conn, Mister Vidmar."

CHAPTER SEVEN

"I do not understand why you are taking such a risk," Rorik said to his father as they finished loading the last of the partially filled wine barrels into the back of the delivery truck.

"The Jung must be stopped," Travon told his son. "You know that as well as anyone."

"This isn't stopping them," his son protested. "Smuggling your friends out of Aitkenna and back here is not only going to put your life at risk, but it will put all of our lives at risk. Have you thought of that?"

"You know that I have, Rorik, but as I have already told you, doing nothing puts us *all* at risk."

"But you don't know that," Rorik insisted, frustrated that his father would not see the reasoning behind his argument.

"Yes, I do." Dumar turned to his son. "You do not know the Jung like I do. Few do. I have seen what they can do. And now that they have jump drives..." He stopped and took a deep breath. "Do you think I *like* risking my life this way? Do you think I enjoy knowing how much you, your mother, and your sisters...how much you all worry? Believe me when I tell you that we must take action. All of us must do everything we possibly can to impede the Jung's progress at every turn."

"But will they not simply wipe us all out of existence if we become too much trouble? Isn't that what you said they did to Tanna? Isn't it better to be subjugated but alive, than free but dead?"

Travon looked down at the ground, sighing. He stared back up at his son's troubled face. "That is a question each man, each woman, must answer for themselves. Do you not remember what it was like to live under the Ta'Akar Empire?"

"The empire that you served?" Rorik replied. "And without our knowledge, I might add."

Dumar sighed again. He was not proud of that chapter in his life. "Caius was nothing compared to the Jung. Caius was an egomaniac, a buffoon dressed in royal robes. The Jung are cold, calculating, and without remorse. They will let us live only so long as they need us. Eventually, they will replace us with their own people. I have seen it on other worlds."

"But you said that takes decades, sometimes even centuries," Rorik argued. "Please, father, at least wait and see... Wait for things to calm down. Perhaps then..."

"No," Dumar interrupted, "we cannot wait. The longer we wait, the more entrenched the Jung will become, and the more dangerous it will be."

"Then let me come with you," Rorik pleaded.

"Out of the question," his father replied with a wave of his arm.

"I can fight as well as..."

"We do not go to fight, Rorik. And you do not have the training for such operations. If this were to be a stand-up fight, I would surely want you by my side. But for now, I need you here, with your mother and sisters. You must prepare the rooms for our guests. You must act as if everything is as it should be."

"And if you do not return?" Rorik asked, his voice trembling slightly.

Dumar looked his son in the eyes, putting his hands on the young man's shoulders. "Then you must protect your mother and sisters, and take care of your wife and child. You must pretend that I went into town for supplies, because we feared shortages due to the invasion. That is all that you know. Do you understand?"

"Yes."

Dumar gave his son a slight shake. "Do you understand, Rorik?"

Rorik looked back into his father's eyes. He had always known that his father was a strong man, but until this moment, he had not realized just how strong he truly was. "Yes, father, I understand."

Dumar hugged his son, then turned and climbed up into the passenger side of the delivery truck to join his comrade.

* * *

"It's really just a matter of wiping the system's base navigational command priorities and replacing them with new ones," Deliza explained as she tapped on her portable console in the back of the combat jump shuttle. "The biggest problem is that this unit wasn't really designed for such long trips. Its navigational database is rather limited."

"But it *can* make it back to Sol, right?" Jessica asked.

"Assuming nothing abnormal happens, yes. But with its limited data storage capacity, it will only be able to follow the course I specify, and will not be able to improvise, should any anomaly occur during transit. That's why I'm giving it the same course that's in your boxcar's database from when it was doing runs between Corinair and Earth," Deliza continued. "Except that its starting point will be from here instead of Corinair. From here, it will jump to the Gaiperura system, which would normally be the first point along the route from Corinair to Sol. From that point, it will continue on to Sol. Since that was a well-established route, it shouldn't have any problems navigating."

"Then why did you even bring it up?"

"Because the limited data capacity means I can only include star data along a very narrow corridor... A tunnel with a radius of no more than ten light years in fact. That means, at some points along its journey, it is only going to have the bare minimum of three star fixes from which to calculate its position and course for the next jump."

"I always assumed they just jumped a straight line from departure to destination," Jessica said reluctantly, admitting her ignorance about jump navigation.

"The majority of the jumps are indeed along a straight line," Deliza confirmed. "However, there are at least twenty-eight points along the route back to Sol that require a course change of at least five to eight degrees." She looked at Jessica. "Space is not exactly empty, you know." Deliza glanced back down at her console, as she continued explaining. "Granted, the odds of colliding with anything bigger than a grain of sand *are* astronomical. However, the likelihood of a collision increases with proximity to star systems, hence the need to steer *around* several systems along the way."

"How much longer?" Sergeant Torwell asked.

"What are you worried about?" Lieutenant Latfee wondered. "There isn't a Jung ship within twenty light years of this system."

"I'm not worried," the sergeant replied, "I'm hungry. It's way past dinner time."

"I've finished uploading the navigational database. I'm uploading the message for Sol Alliance Command now," Deliza told them. "Just a quick systems check..."

"We're coming up on the launch window in thirty seconds," Lieutenant Latfee warned. "If we miss it, we'll have to wait for the drone to make another lap around the planet."

"I knew I should have brought some snacks," the sergeant muttered.

"All systems are good," Deliza announced. "The drone is ready to launch."

Jessica reached into her pocket and pulled out an energy bar, handing it to the sergeant.

"Bless you, sir."

"Ten seconds to launch window."

"I'm transmitting the launch order now."

"I get whiny when my blood sugar gets low," the sergeant said as he took a bite of the energy bar.

"*Get?*" Jessica commented skeptically.

"Jump comm-drone is powering up its jump field emitters," Deliza announced. The back of the jump shuttle momentarily filled with a blue-white light. "Drone is away."

"How long will it take to get to Sol?" Jessica asked.

"Not more than twenty hours," Deliza replied.

"I thought jump comm-drones routinely made the trip between the PC and Sol in six hours?"

"The ones that are *designed* for such trips, yes. I've instructed our drone to pause for several minutes at each jump point and get multiple navigational fixes, just to be safe." She looked at Jessica. "I assumed that *getting* the message to Sol was more important than how long it took to get there. After all, even if they send help immediately, it will take them some time to reach us, depending on their jump capabilities."

"No, you're right," Jessica agreed. "Good thinking."

"Can we go home now?" Sergeant Torwell wondered. "We've been jumping around all damn day."

"One bar wasn't enough to shut you up, huh?" Jessica laughed.

* * *

"Captain on deck!" the guard at the door barked as Captain Taylor entered the Aurora's command briefing room. The officers, gathered around the conference table, immediately moved to stand.

"As you were," Cameron insisted as she walked to the head of the table. While she usually enjoyed the respect that came with her position, there were times when it was not needed. "Let's get straight to it," she said as she took her seat. She glanced around the room briefly, taking a quick head count. Other than her CAG, all of her command staff were present. "As of thirteen twenty-seven, Earth Mean Time, our gunships lost contact with the surviving ships from the Jung battle group that we engaged a few hours ago." Cameron paused a moment, taking note of the looks of frustration and disappointment on the faces of her officers. "The report is the same as before. One moment, they had good tracks, and the next moment they were gone."

"How is that even possible?" Commander Caro, the ship's chief medical officer asked.

"I have to wonder the same thing," Lieutenant Commander Vidmar agreed. "The frigates I could understand. They don't give off a lot of emissions, especially when they're running cold. But Jung battleships are like Christmas trees on our sensors, Captain."

"Even battleships can rig for cold running," Commander Kaplan, the ship's executive officer, commented.

"Maybe, but a Jung battleship is five kilometers long," the lieutenant commander reminded her. "Even if they're running cold at sub-light speeds, they'll light up if you are sweeping with actives."

"The targets were slipping in and out of FTL, constantly changing course at random intervals and in random directions," Lieutenant Commander Kono, the Aurora's lead sensor officer, explained. She turned to her captain. "I briefly went over Cobra Two One Four's sensor logs, Captain. The Jung were aggressively trying to shake our gunships."

"What about old light?" Commander Caro asked. "Can't they back off and try to catch it from further out?"

"I'm afraid not," Cameron replied. "It's not always that easy."

"Especially when you're trying to track FTL signatures," Lieutenant Commander Kono added.

"But everything gives off *some* emissions," the commander insisted.

"If they went cold as soon as they came out of FTL, then launched a decoy *back* into FTL, it would be easy for the gunships to miss," Lieutenant Commander Kono explained. "And by the time you figure out you've been tricked, the original target has changed course and gone back into FTL in a different direction." The sensor officer turned to address Captain Taylor. "That's probably what happened, sir. And shortly after going to FTL, the decoys probably went back to sub-light and shut down. And they're small enough that they'd be hard to find."

"Which would explain why the targets just *disappeared*," the Aurora's XO, Commander Kaplan, commented.

"Precisely what I was thinking," Cameron replied.

"Still, shouldn't we keep looking for their old light?" Lieutenant Commander Vidmar, the Aurora's senior tactical officer, suggested.

"The Cobras will continue searching," Cameron replied. "But truth be told, by the time they pick up their trail, they will have already changed course and speed at least a dozen times."

"Captain," Vladimir began, "am I the only one who thinks the Jung are only making themselves detectable when they *wish* us to detect them?"

Cameron looked at her chief engineer. "Why would they *want* us to detect them?"

"To draw our ships out of position," Lieutenant Commander Vidmar suggested.

"To test our response," Commander Kaplan added.

"Or to test their capabilities," Vladimir chimed in.

"Are you suggesting the Jung have some sort of stealth capabilities that we aren't aware of?" Cameron asked her chief engineer.

"Like some sort of cloaking technology?" the executive officer added.

Vladimir shrugged. "I have no idea. I'm only pointing out how odd it is that they were able to get so *deep* into Alliance space *without* being detected, and then, at a time of their choosing, they are able to vanish. What is that game? Cat and mouse?"

"We just destroyed four of their ships," Lieutenant Dinev, the ship's lead helmsman said, finally joining the debate. "That's a really expensive way to play cat and mouse, don't you think?"

"Four ships, and probably close to a thousand lives," the XO added. "And that's just from the battle at ACB. How many other ships were destroyed in the

203

other engagements?"

"The number of ships and crew lost is irrelevant at this point," Captain Taylor insisted, trying to maintain control of the meeting. "Regardless of what the Jung are up to, we are technically at a state of war once again."

The room suddenly became quiet.

"Granted, none of our ships have suffered any damage, and no Alliance lives have been lost, either military or civilian," Cameron continued. "However, by the letter of the cease-fire agreement, both unauthorized trespassing in Alliance space, and firing on Alliance ships, constitute acts of war."

"You don't think Galiardi will launch the SJKKVs, do you?" Lieutenant Commander Vidmar wondered.

"It's not the admiral's call," Cameron reminded him. "It's the president's."

"Thank God for that," Commander Kaplan muttered.

Cameron shot a disapproving glance at her executive officer. It wasn't the first time Lara had voiced her disapproval of the admiral. And although Cameron didn't much care for him, she had warned her second-in-command to keep such opinions to herself while in the presence of junior officers. "SJKKV strikes would be warranted, at least legally," Cameron continued. "However, I doubt that the president will approve any use of SJKKVs unless Alliance assets are directly attacked."

"Uh, we *were* fired upon, Captain," Lieutenant Commander Vidmar reminded Cameron. "More than once I might add."

"But in each instance, Alliance ships fired first," Lieutenant Commander Kono pointed out.

"Because they were invading our territory,"

Lieutenant Commander Vidmar argued. "Hell, we even warned them!"

"That's enough," Cameron chided. She paused a moment, waiting for things to settle down. "I know that, for many of you, this has been your first time under fire, so I'll cut you some slack. But the fact is, we have to be ready to fight a war. Why is irrelevant, at least for us. We go where we're told to go, and fight when we're told to fight. It's as simple as that. Now, I didn't call you here to debate the issues. I called this meeting because I want to know exactly how prepared for combat this ship really is." She looked at her executive officer. "Commander?"

"We are currently at seventy percent staffing levels throughout the ship," Commander Kaplan said. "Unfortunately, that's as good as it's going to get for now. Some of our crew was transferred to the Cape Town, since we were a day from going down for refit. We were due to get replacements straight out of the academy once we were back in service."

"Will that be enough?"

"If I shift some people around a bit, yes. But we'll only be able to field three shifts instead of four, which means six-hour rotations instead of four."

"Schedule some floaters from each shift to come in and relieve people at key positions for short breaks," Cameron suggested. "And make sure we have plenty of coffee on board."

"That's going to be a bit of a problem," the commander responded. "We're low on just about everything. In fact, we don't even have a supply officer."

"Let me guess. He was transferred to the Cape Town," Cameron said.

"Yes, sir. I sent a message to command logistics,

and told them to send us everything... To just pretend like they were stocking a new ship. They said they'd get on it."

"Any word when we'll get those supplies?"

"Nothing solid. A few days, at the most."

"I'm assuming we're good on ammunition," Cameron said.

"We weren't scheduled to offload the rail gun rounds until our reactor cores were removed," the commander explained. "I guess they wanted us to remain armed until we absolutely could not be asked to get under way at a moment's notice. However, we're only at fifty percent jump missile capacity."

"I'll keep that in mind," Cameron replied. She turned to her tactical officer. "Lieutenant Commander Vidmar, feel free to keep me apprised of our jump missile count at all times."

"Yes, sir."

"Commander Caro?"

"I'm short two physicians, four nurses, and a few med-techs," the chief medical officer counted. "And I only have two rescue teams. However, we were also waiting for the reactor cores to be removed before we shut down completely, so supply-wise, we're in good shape. However, if we do suffer heavy casualties, we're going to need to jump them back to Earth as quickly as possible, at least until I get fully staffed again."

"Your people were transferred as well?"

"No, sir. Doctor Borrison's rotation was up, and he went to his next specialty rotation back on Earth. He can be recalled if necessary. Doctor Lorenz is having treatment on his knee. If you remember, he injured it while on leave. As for the others, they will be returning in a few days. But the two replacement physicians could take several weeks. Fleet medical is trying to get a few trauma surgeons to volunteer for temporary duty in the meantime."

Cameron looked at Vladimir wearily. "Please tell me you don't have any bad news."

"I'm afraid I do," Vladimir replied. "In light of the Jung transgressions into Alliance space, Fleet has canceled my transfer." Vladimir smiled. "I guess you're stuck with me a while longer, Captain."

A small smile crept into the corner of Cameron's mouth as she turned away from Vladimir and back toward her executive officer. "Get me a new duty roster, and an updated supply count, Commander. And designate someone to take over as supply officer."

"Yes, sir."

* * *

Jerrot faced straight ahead, but his eyes flicked back and forth nervously as he watched the Jung guards inspect the vehicle. "This is the fifth checkpoint in not even as many kilometers."

"I know." Travon Dumar's demeanor was the exact opposite of Jerrot's.

"What is it they are looking for?"

"Weapons, people trying to get out of the city," Dumar explained calmly. "Anything that doesn't sit right with them. Mostly, they are just trying to get a feel for what the normal flow of traffic might be. This is why they issued a bulletin on the net just after the invasion, stating that everyone should go about their business as usual, but to expect delays in transit."

"How do they expect us to function normally when they stop us at every other intersection?"

"Relax, Jerrot. It will not be this way forever," Dumar assured his nervous friend. "They only seized control yesterday. In time, things will settle back down to normal."

Jerrot rolled his eyes. "Normal, you say. How are things going to ever be normal under Jung occupation?"

"We lived under occupation before, and we can live under it again."

"I cannot believe I let you talk me into this," Jerrot muttered, his eyes still on the guards in front of them.

"Try not to appear nervous. You'll draw attention to yourself."

"I'll likely draw *more* attention if I do *not* appear nervous." Jerrot looked at Dumar. "Remember, you promised to get me and my family off of Corinair in exchange for helping you."

"You have my word, Jerrot."

"I still don't understand how an importer ended up being a retired Alliance admiral. Someday, you must explain that one to me, Travon."

"Someday. For now, keep your mind focused on your job," Dumar insisted. "You are delivering wines to market, just as you always do, twice weekly. And I am here to help you move the barrels because your usual assistant did not show up for work today."

Jerrot studied Dumar's calm demeanor for a moment. "How do you do it, Travon?" he asked, a puzzled expression on his face. "How do you remain so calm? They have guns, after all. Lots of them."

"I have faced men with guns before, Jerrot."

Jerrot shook his head in amazement. "Yes, there is much you still have to tell me about yourself, Travon."

The soldiers detaining the vehicle in front of them stepped back and waved it forward through the checkpoint. Then they turned to look at Jerrot's truck, gesturing for him to advance to the inspection area.

Jerrot took a deep breath and rolled the truck forward a few meters.

"Present identity cards to be inspected," the Jung soldier demanded. His accent was thick, and his pronunciation of the Corinairan language was difficult to understand.

Jerrot handed his card to the soldier outside his window, as Dumar passed his to the soldier on his side of the vehicle.

"What purpose are you to entering this city?" the Jung soldier said curtly.

Jerrot recoiled at the sudden questioning. It was the fifth time a Jung guard had asked him the same question today, but this one had the poorest Corinairan yet. "Uh, my *purpose* is to deliver garant spice wine to the market."

"What is this...*wine*?" the soldier asked, one eyebrow rising in suspicion.

Jerrot looked at Dumar, confused. Then he looked back at the soldier standing in his window. "Uh, it's a warm beverage, made from garant fruit. You drink it," he added, miming the act of drinking. "It is very popular on this world. It makes you feel good." Jerrot offered an exaggerated smile for the soldier.

"And why are you to come with him?" the soldier on Dumar's side of the truck inquired.

"To help him move the barrels of wine off the truck."

The soldier looked at Dumar, taking note of his age.

"My usual helper did not show up for work today," Jerrot explained.

"This is work for younger man," the soldier chuckled. "Much younger, I think."

"I am not too old to move a few barrels of wine, my friend."

The soldiers laughed at Dumar's response.

"From where does this *wine* come?" the first soldier wondered.

"Dakon Province, eighty kilometers to the west," Dumar replied quickly, before Jerrot could mistakenly give the guards the true origination point of their product, which was just south of Dumar's resort.

"And how many times to usual do you make such deliveries?"

"Two times per week, on average," Jerrot replied.

Dumar glanced at the rear camera view on the truck's console, watching as one of the other soldiers walked slowly along the side of their vehicle, scanning it with a handheld sensor unit. The man paused at the tail of the vehicle for a moment, staring at his scanner, then looked forward and signaled to the soldier standing next to Dumar that everything was in order.

"Your identity card," the Jung soldier outside Dumar's window said. "Have a good day, Mister Oslo," he added in an expression of politeness that seemed completely unnatural.

"Thank you," Dumar replied as he accepted the card back. "To you, as well."

"You may proceed," the other soldier instructed, as he handed Jerrot's ID card back to him and signaled the soldiers at the gate to allow them to pass.

"Thank you, sir," Jerrot replied, trying to hide the overwhelming feeling of relief washing over him. He put the ID card back in his shirt pocket and moved the vehicle slowly forward. After pulling through the gate and driving a full block, he was finally able to relax a bit. "They asked more questions than the previous checkpoints."

"That is to be expected, as we move deeper into the city," Dumar told him. He reached over and patted Jerrot on the shoulder. "You are doing well, Jerrot. How much further to the market?"

"Less than a kilometer, I think."

"Good. Then it is unlikely we will encounter any more checkpoints. At least, not until we attempt to leave the city."

Jerrot looked at Dumar again. "I just hope your plan works. If it does not, I fear what they might do to us."

"You have nothing to fear, Jerrot," Dumar replied, "as they will undoubtedly kill us on the spot."

Jerrot looked at him in horror. "You're not helping matters, Travon."

* * *

"Cap'n," Marcus greeted as he and Neli reached the top of the Seiiki's cargo ramp and found the others gathered in the cargo bay.

"Marcus," Captain Tuplo replied. "What's the good news?"

"Nothin' good, that's for sure." Marcus and Neli set their cloth satchels of food they had purchased from Haven's local street markets down on the deck beside them. "There's not much in the way of payin' runs, I'm afraid. The Jung have got the PC locked down so tight, everyone's afraid to fly anywhere within the cluster, let alone in or out of it."

"That's what I was afraid of," the captain sighed.

"Runs gotta start popping up eventually, right?"

Josh said. "I mean, people gotta eat. Even the Jung gotta eat. And people gotta move around from system to system. Goods gotta move..." Josh looked at the captain, then at Marcus. "I mean, if the Jung want to take advantage of the PC's infrastructure, then they ain't gonna shut it down completely. Sooner or later, the wheels gotta start turnin' again, don't you think?"

"Of course they will, Josh," Captain Tuplo agreed. "The question is, can we wait it out?"

"Sure we can," Josh insisted, undaunted by recent developments. "In the meantime, we can do that maintenance shit Dalen's always complaining about not havin' enough time to do."

"This ship costs me credits just sitting in port, Josh. Credits I can't afford to spend. And that maintenance you're talking about? That costs credits as well. Credits for parts. Credits to feed us. Credits to pay all of you."

"Won't be the first time we've had to go without pay, Cap'n," Marcus reminded him. "Likely won't be the last. Frankly, I'm okay with that."

"Me too, Cap'n," Dalen added.

"That's right," Josh agreed.

Marcus nudged Neli.

"Me, too," Neli chimed in, although not as readily as the rest.

"I know you are, and I appreciate it, I do." He paused a moment to think, taking in a deep breath and letting it out in a long sigh. Then he looked at Neli. "How many days do you think we're stocked for?"

"Including what we bought today? A week? That is, if Josh can refrain from eating twice his weight each day."

"I have a very high metabolism," Josh defended.

"What you have are hollow legs," Marcus quipped. "Ever since you was knee-high."

"How are repairs going?" the captain asked, looking to Dalen.

"Shields are back up, but the port shield generator is on its last legs, Cap'n. I can't promise it's gonna last much longer."

"Best guess?"

Dalen shrugged. "Four, maybe five reentry cycles. After that, we're really gonna be pushin' our luck."

"I don't suppose you could overhaul it again?"

"I can try, I suppose," Dalen replied. "But truth be told, there's not much left to overhaul. One good spike and it'll fry for sure."

The captain looked at Marcus. "How much does one of those things cost?"

"More than we've got," Marcus replied. "Even for a refurb."

"Maybe it's time we pulled up stakes and left this sector behind for good," Neli suggested.

Everyone became quiet. It had been discussed many times before, and Neli always seemed to be the one to bring it up.

"I can't believe I'm agreeing with Neli," Josh said, "but maybe she's right, Cap'n. Maybe it *is* time."

Captain Tuplo studied each of their faces briefly. "Well, suppose we do jump out of the sector for good. If we're lucky, we pick up a job before our food and fuel runs out, and before we lose that shield generator once and for all. We'll have a whole new set of rules to learn. A whole new set of contacts to make, and relationships to build. And because we'll be short on everything, we won't be able to be very picky about what jobs we accept or who they're for. That could very well lead us into a lot of trouble. And remember, there are not a lot of jump ships operating outside the Pentaurus sector."

"But that's an advantage," Neli insisted.

"Perhaps," the captain replied. "But it also makes us a target, not only for nefarious types like the two we scared off last night, but for any businessman or would-be potentate looking for an edge over his competitors."

"Kinda goes with the territory, though, don't it?" Marcus said.

"Yes, it does. But what if we *don't* find work right away? What if the first port we set down in *sees* the potential in our ship and squeezes us out of work so we won't be able to pay our port fees and our ship gets impounded and auctioned off? Or worse yet, make us fly for them for peanuts, just so we can keep our heads above the red line?"

"Cap'n, we can always lift off *before* we run out of funds for the port fees," Josh said. "It's not like we haven't done it before."

"And what? Float around in space until someone takes pity on us, or worse yet, we hand our ship over so we don't starve to death adrift in space? Hell, we don't even know if they'll *accept* PC credits outside of this sector." Captain Tuplo shook his head, frustrated by the situation. "No, if we're gonna leave the Pentaurus sector behind once and for all, we've got to have the resources to do so in a safe manner."

"You keep sayin' that, Cap'n," Josh said. "But every time we get together enough to head out, something happens, and we get stuck again."

"It's not like I'm not trying, Josh."

"I know…"

"The problem is you're not willing to take risks,

Captain," Neli said, interrupting Josh.

"Nel..." Marcus scolded.

"Well, it's true!" Neli looked at their faces. "You all know it is!" She turned to address Captain Tuplo. "No offense, Captain, but you *always* play it safe. It's not that I'm complaining, mind you. I appreciate that you're always thinking about our safety, I truly do. But sometimes, ensuring our safety *means* taking risks."

Everyone was silent, stunned by Neli's bluntness. Captain Tuplo examined their faces one at a time to read his crew's reactions. He could tell they agreed with her. He even half-agreed with her himself.

Finally, the captain sighed and looked at Marcus. "You said there's not *much* in the way of paying runs, right? So, what *was* there?"

"Just three runs," Marcus replied. "Two of them from people with enough to pay some dumbass a ton of credits to jump to either Corinair or Savoy to evac family or friends, or some shit."

"Gotta be nobles, if they're paying so much," Josh stated.

"And the third?" Captain Tuplo asked.

"Evac a bunch of passengers, crew, and cargo off a ship that lost main power half a light year outside of Rama."

Captain Tuplo thought for a moment, rubbing his chin. "Well, there's no way I'm going anywhere near Corinair or Savoy. I may be desperate, but I'm not stupid."

"Doesn't matter," Marcus explained. "Both those runs were snatched up quicker'n shit."

"Seriously?" Captain Tuplo replied, surprised. "Who the hell was that stupid?"

"The pay was pretty damn high, Cap'n. The pickup

at Corinair alone was payin' a hundred thousand credits. Seventy for the Savoy job."

"Shit," Dalen muttered. "One hundred thousand would've been enough to fix *everything* on this ship, good as new, *and* get us out of this sector. *Way* out."

"Assuming we'd survive to collect," the captain pointed out. "What about the Rama run? Anybody take it?"

"Not yet. It only pays twenty, and it would take most ships currently in port half a dozen round trips to complete the job. There's more than three hundred people aboard."

"Why is it paying only twenty thousand?" the captain wondered.

"I guess you're worth a far sight more if you've got noble relations," Neli commented with disdain.

"Daschew says it's a cake run, that they aren't even in the shipping lanes," Marcus answered.

"*Sigmund* Daschew?" the captain asked. "He's the one paying for the Rama run?"

"Yup."

"That's why the payout is so small," the captain surmised. "Siggy's a cheap little bastard. Did you try and haggle with him?"

"I didn't bother. I was sure you wouldn't be interested," Marcus replied.

Captain Tuplo sighed again. All his instincts were telling him *not* to take the run, but Neli's words were still gnawing at his conscience. That, and they needed to replace the port shield generator. "Will twenty be enough to replace that generator, *and* leave us with a few weeks of operating expenses?" the captain asked Marcus.

"Thirty would be better."

The captain looked at Dalen next. "Are we good

to go?"

"Good as we're gonna get, without spending any more credits."

Captain Tuplo shot a disapproving look at Dalen. "You know what I mean."

"Yeah, Cap'n. We can handle the Rama run. Atmo here is on the thin side, so we can probably handle six or seven reentry cycles."

The captain stood still for a minute, arms crossed, a million scenarios playing in his head... Most of them not good. "Very well," he finally said with a sigh. "Go sign us up for the Rama run, Marcus."

"Yes, sir."

"But try to get thirty outta that weasel," the captain added.

* * *

The delivery truck full of wine barrels moved off the main boulevard and down a side street, turning left into the small alleyway behind the market. It came to a stop, then backed up carefully to the market's delivery entrance.

"Good afternoon, Jerrot," the owner of the market greeted. "You are late."

"My apologies, Anji. So many checkpoints."

"Yes, yes. They tell us it is for our own safety. We shall see. You have my usual order?"

"Yes, sir. Eight barrels, as usual," Jerrot promised, as he climbed up onto the truck to unlash the barrels.

Anji looked at Dumar, cocking his head to one side. "And the cost?"

"At a *deep* discount today," Dumar assured him, "because you are such a good and cooperative customer."

"Your show of appreciation will not be easily

forgotten. I only hope that I can continue to be such a *good* customer."

"Our hopes as well." Dumar gestured toward the door. "May I use your restroom?"

"Of course."

"What about the barrels?" Jerrot asked.

"I will have one of my boys help you," Anji promised. "It is the least I can do."

Dumar entered the market and made his way through the back storeroom. After stepping through the doors into the market itself, he looked around, noting the locations of every person in the store, both shoppers and employees. As expected, there were not many customers today. Most people had chosen to stay home and wait to see how things played out for the next few days. While it did help decrease the amount of time they were to actually spend in the city, it also increased their visibility to some extent. It was an unavoidable eventuality, as Doran Montrose was certain that the Jung would soon be conducting door-to-door searches for those who had been involved in a running gunfight from Ranni Enterprises the previous day.

Dumar queried a passing employee as to the location of the restroom, then headed across the back side of the store. He glanced down each aisle as he passed. When he spotted Doran Montrose and his wife, he made eye contact. Without breaking his stride, Travon signaled with his eyes for Doran to follow him.

Doran nodded, excused himself from his wife for a moment, then headed down the aisle to follow Dumar.

A moment later, Dumar entered the restroom, and immediately turned on the water to wash up. As he did so, Doran entered the restroom, and stepped up to the next sink and turned on his faucet, as well. Dumar signaled for silence as he turned off his water. He dried his hands, then pulled his comm-unit out of his pocket. He activated the device and used it to scan the room while Doran continued to wash his hands.

"It is safe to speak," Dumar finally said, putting his comm-unit back in his pocket. "Have your people slip into the back. One or two at a time, so as not to draw the attention of the other shoppers."

"We are practically the only shoppers in the store. What about the employees?"

"They are all members of the owner's family, who is an old friend. Their cooperation has been secured."

"There are cameras," Doran reminded him.

"Which are not working today."

"How are you going to get us out of the city without raising suspicion? There are checkpoints everywhere. They are inspecting everyone. We almost didn't make it here ourselves."

"We have a plan," Dumar assured him. "You must trust me."

"You know that I do, Admiral."

"Do not refer to me in that way, even when we know it is safe."

"Of course. My apologies."

Dumar patted Doran on the shoulder. "I hope you like the smell of garant wine," he said as he headed for the door.

"What?" It was too late. Dumar had already left the restroom. Doran turned off the water and dried his hands, then left, as well. He walked across the back of the store, turning up the aisle when he spotted Yanni pushing a shopping cart and Lael strolling alongside him, carrying baby Ailsa. Doran walked toward them, pretending to search the shelves for something. He nodded politely at them as he passed, ducking in just behind them as if to grab an item off the shelf.

"Go to the restroom in the back," Doran instructed in a whisper as he picked an item off the shelf from behind Yanni. "Then duck into the storeroom to meet Dumar," he continued as he inspected the item. "But first, pass the same message on to Michi and Tori, and tell them to pass it on to my children."

"Understood," Yanni whispered as Doran walked away, item in hand.

* * *

"Jump series complete," Josh reported as the Seiiki's cockpit windows cleared. "The Asa-Cafon should be nearby."

Marcus stood behind Josh's seat wearing a pressure suit, staring down at the sensor display in the center of the console. "So where are they?"

"Are you sure you calculated for drift and..." Dalen started to ask.

"I know how to plot a jump, Dalen," Josh snapped, cutting him off, "and I know how to calculate for drift. It should be here."

"Maybe the Jung already got to them?" Dalen said.

"Unlikely," Marcus insisted. "Not this far outta the shipping lanes."

"Just be patient," Captain Tuplo said. "We didn't jump in that close. It will take a few..." The captain was interrupted by an alert tone from the sensor display. "You see."

"I told you," Josh said.

"Is it them?" Marcus asked.

"I'm picking up their distress beacon. I'll paint 'em with active briefly." Captain Tuplo reached down and switched the sensors to active mode, sending out a brief pulse of energy to better identify the ship. Everyone watched anxiously, waiting for the return. After thirty seconds, it came. "Size matches. Database confirms it. The Asa-Cafon. The only emissions she's putting out is her beacon, though. Nothing from her reactor core, and barely any thermal readings. In fact, her pressurized spaces look mighty frigid. If they're still alive, they're freezing their asses off." The captain turned to look over his shoulder at Marcus. "Are you sure that docking system you rigged is going to work?"

"If she's got standard hatches like her registry specs say, it will," Marcus assured him. "If not, we'll have to break out the rescue bubbles."

"You couldn't pay me to get into one of those bubbles," Dalen said stubbornly.

"You wouldn't say that if they were the only thing between you and space," Captain Tuplo insisted. He looked at Josh. "ETA to docking?"

"Seven minutes."

"You got a fix?"

"You bet."

"Then I'm shutting down the active scanners," the captain said. "If there *are* any Jung ships in the area, I sure as hell don't want to broadcast our position to them." The captain turned back toward Marcus and Dalen. "Better head aft and get ready."

"On our way," Marcus replied, as he and Dalen turned to exit the Seiiki's cockpit.

"Make damn sure you get a good seal before you pop their hatch, Marcus. And remember, send them up the catwalks and into the side corridors so we

221

can use those as inner airlocks. That way, if we lose a seal, we won't lose the whole ship."

"I remember," Marcus replied, as he waited for his turn to descend the ladder to the deck below.

"And don't forget to hook up!" the captain added as Marcus started down the ladder.

Marcus paused, his head still in the cockpit. "This ain't my first dance, Cap'n."

"Asa-Cafon, Asa-Cafon," the captain called over the comms. "This is the Seiiki. Do you copy?"

"You're using directional, low-power, right?" Josh asked.

"This ain't my first dance, either, Josh."

"Just checkin'."

"Asa-Cafon, Asa-Cafon. This is the Seiiki, in the blind. We are approaching from your starboard side. ETA is six minutes. We intend to link up to your port, midship boarding hatch. If you can copy me, have your passengers ready to disembark. We can only carry about one hundred and fifty people at a time, so we'll have to make two trips just to get the passengers off."

"I think I can see her running lights," Josh said, pointing out the forward windows. "She must still have battery power."

Captain Tuplo looked out the window as well. "Yup, that's her." He keyed his mic again. "Asa-Cafon, Seiiki. If you can hear me, shut off your running lights. We have your position, so conserve your power for life support."

Captain Tuplo and Josh stared out the window at the approaching ship's lights. Finally, they went out.

"Yes!" Josh exclaimed.

"Asa-Cafon, Seiiki. Your running lights are off, so we know you can hear us. If we're clear to dock to your port, midship boarding hatch, flash your running lights twice." Captain Tuplo gazed out the window as the Asa-Cafon's running lights flashed on and off two times. "Excellent," the captain said, keying his mic again. "Asa-Cafon, Seiiki. Hang tight. We'll be there in a few minutes." The captain looked at Josh. "You up for this?"

"Walk in the park, Cap'n."

Captain Tuplo looked at Josh, puzzled. He had heard a lot of unusual expressions from the young man over the years, but this was a new one. "That's good, right?"

CHAPTER EIGHT

Doran Montrose and his wife walked up to the restroom doors at the back of the market. Doran looked back over his shoulder, checking to see if anyone was looking their way, then guided his wife toward the storeroom door.

"What are…"

"Ssh," Doran cautioned her quietly, pushing her gently away from the restrooms and toward the door to the back. "Quickly."

They slipped through the door and were met on the other side by a young man. "This way," he whispered. They followed him across the storeroom, around several stacks of boxes, and into a back corner on the far side, shielded from view.

As they rounded the corner of the stack of boxes, they spotted Dumar, standing next to two large wine barrels, with a small, wet dog beside him.

"Quickly. Into these barrels," Dumar said, gesturing for Doran and his wife to step up on the wooden boxes and into the barrels.

Doran and his wife exchanged a confused look. Doran stepped up onto the box and looked inside the barrel. "But, they still have…"

"The contents have been calculated to allow for your body mass," Dumar explained in hushed tones, "and the wine is warm enough to mask your body heat from the Jung scanners. They are using simple devices. They will see only full barrels of wine."

"How can you be sure?" Doran asked.

"They did not detect Max," Dumar replied, pointing at the dog next to him.

Doran's wife looked afraid, pausing hesitantly

after stepping into the warm, burgundy liquid. "How will we breathe?"

"The wine should only come up to your chin, and there are holes in the lids to allow air inside. It will work."

Doran lowered himself down into the barrel, the wine coming up around his body as he squatted down, until it was lapping at his chin. "And if your calculations are incorrect?"

"Then drink some of the wine," Dumar replied with a grim smile. "If nothing else, it will make the journey more tolerable."

Doran's wife settled down into her barrel as well, slowly allowing the wine to rise up around her body.

"How long must we be in these barrels with the lids closed?" Doran asked.

"At least until we are well clear of the city. Then, you may at least crack the lids open to make it easier to tolerate the smell," Dumar explained.

"How did you manage to get baby Ailsa into one of these?" Doran's wife wondered.

"In her mother's arms," Dumar answered. "And, I injected the child with a mild sedative, so that she would sleep."

Doran squatted down as Dumar prepared to put the lid in place. The wine crept up over his chin and then lips, forcing him to lean his head back to keep his nose and mouth out of the liquid. "This smells horrible."

"I said it would work," Dumar replied flatly as he placed the lid on top of the barrel, sealing Doran inside. "I did not say it would smell good."

* * *

The Seiiki drifted slowly over the much larger Asa-Cafon, passing over her midship. As she cleared the larger ship's hull, the Seiiki fired her braking thrusters, stopping her forward motion completely. Several more tiny squirts of thrust sent the smaller vessel downward, her descent stopping a few moments later by opposite thrust.

The Seiiki's aft cargo ramp began to swing downward, as the ship thrust, yet again, to begin a gentle translation backward toward the port side of the Asa-Cafon's midsection. Her cargo ramp passed its normal position, continuing to swing until it was hanging down at a forty-five-degree angle.

As the Seiiki continued to back toward the Asa-Cafon, a large docking collar began to extend from the back of her cargo bay, reaching its full extension only a few seconds before it made contact with the Asa-Cafon's hull.

Marcus stood at the forward end of the Seiiki's cargo bay, sealed up inside his pressure suit, his hands against the hatch of the docking apparatus. The ship rocked, as a metallic *clank* translated through the Seiiki's hull. The sudden motion nearly knocked Marcus off his feet.

"*Contact,*" Josh announced over Marcus's helmet comms.

"*No shit,*" Dalen commented back.

Marcus worked the controls beside the docking apparatus hatch. "Docking collar has a good lock. I'm pressurizing the seal now." After a few seconds, a red light on the panel turned green. "I've got a good seal, and the tunnel is pressurized. Permission to pop the inner hatch, Cap'n."

"*Pop it and get the first group aboard,*" the captain instructed over the comms.

"Poppin' inner hatch."

"Dalen, Neli," the captain continued. *"Remember, do not open those hatches until the ones at the other end of those corridors are closed and locked. It's your own asses you're protecting. Just remember that."*

Marcus pulled open the hatch on the docking apparatus and moved inside. "I'm in the boarding tunnel. Making my way to their outer hatch."

"Marcus, are you carrying?" Captain Tuplo asked.

"You bet your ass I am."

"If those passengers panic, don't be afraid to use that thing to keep them under control."

"Don't you worry none about that, Cap'n. I'm quick on the trigger."

"Just don't shoot any holes in my ship. I can't afford to fix them unless we finish this job."

Marcus reached the hull of the Asa-Cafon, and pressed the control panel for the outer hatch. The hatch sank into the hull, then slowly slid to one side, revealing a small airlock. Marcus could see the face of a young man looking through the porthole in the middle of the Asa-Cafon's inner hatch. "Come on, kid," he said, gesturing to the young man to open the hatch. "Don't be shy."

The young man in the window shook his head, refusing to open the hatch.

"What the hell is wrong with this guy?"

"What's going on down there?" Captain Tuplo asked over the comms.

"This idiot won't open the hatch," Marcus replied.

"He probably isn't sure if the airlock is pressurized," the captain surmised.

"Well what the fuck does he think I'm doin' in here?"

"Is your visor still down?"

"Oops." Marcus raised his visor to show the

nervous young man that it was safe to open up. A moment later, the hatch began to slide open, more slowly than he expected.

"I don't think they have any power left," Marcus said. "They're cranking their hatch open manually."

"*Copy that.*"

"Thank God you're here!" the young man exclaimed from the other side.

"Yeah, yeah, yeah. Save the pleasantries, kid. The sooner you get your first group aboard, the sooner we can get back for the rest of you."

"You don't know how happy we are that you came!"

"That's real nice. You can buy me a beer later. Now let's get movin'."

Marcus turned and headed back down the boarding tunnel toward the Seiiki. He stepped through the hatch at the end, into what little space remained in the cargo bay, which was mostly filled with the docking apparatus they had installed for the mission. "Come on, people! We ain't got all day!" he chided as he turned around to face the passengers coming down the boarding tunnel toward him. "First twenty-five to port, second twenty-five to starboard! Head aft along the sides and up the ladders! Then forward through the hatch and into the corridor! Last man closes the hatch behind him! If you don't, you won't be let into the main compartment!"

Marcus stood there, repeating his instructions as the passengers moved out of the docking apparatus, filed along its sides to the aft end of the cargo bay, and ascended the ladders to the catwalk above. Once they reached the catwalk, they did as instructed and stepped through the aft hatches into the corridors.

When Marcus noticed the passengers bunching

up, he waved his hands for them to stop. "Hold up! Hold up! Everyone hold on while we cycle the first group in!" Marcus turned away from the passengers momentarily. "That's twenty-five per side. I'm waiting on you guys."

"*I've got a good lock on the aft hatch,*" Neli reported over comms. "*I'm letting my first group in.*"

"Talk to me, Dalen," Marcus called.

"*I still show the hatch on my side as open!*"

"Starboard side!" Marcus yelled. "Close your aft hatch!"

Passengers from the Asa-Cafon continued to push forward in the boarding tunnel, despite the fact that the line had stopped moving.

"I said to hold up, goddamn it!"

"*I've got it!*" Dalen reported. "*I've got a good lock. I'm letting my side in.*"

"*Port corridor is ready for more passengers,*" Neli reported.

"Port side!" Marcus yelled. "Open your hatch and get inside the corridor. Twenty-fifth one in closes the hatch! And don't forget!"

Josh stared at the Seiiki's sensor display, as Captain Tuplo switched between the various cameras inside the Seiiki's cargo bay and corridors, keeping an eye on the activity elsewhere in his ship.

"Neli," the captain called over his comm-set. "Get to the main compartment and tell those people to move up into the upper compartment to make room for the next group. We've got to keep this thing running smoothly."

"*Right away, Captain.*"

"How are we looking, Josh?" the captain asked, as he watched Neli on the monitor.

"So far, so good. No ships in the area, and our docking seals are holding up."

"Marcus, as soon as those hatches close, you drop your visor, close the Asa-Cafon's hatch, and disconnect," the captain instructed.

"*I can squeeze maybe ten more along either side of the docking apparatus, Cap'n,*" Marcus offered.

"Bad idea," Captain Tuplo objected. "That thing is sealed up with our inner cargo hatch ring using nothing more than temp-bond and prayers. You said so yourself, remember?"

"*It'll hold 'till we get the ramp up and locked, Cap'n. Just don't go jerkin' us 'round too much before I get the boarding tunnel retracted and the ramp closed.*"

"It's your call, Marcus. You installed the damned thing."

"*I got it, Cap'n,*" Marcus replied. "*Just don't let that little shit use any more than one percent on the translation thrusters until my say so.*"

Captain Tuplo looked at Josh. "I'm sure it was a term of endearment."

Josh rolled his eyes.

———

Neli made her way past the passengers crowded around the entrance to the main passenger compartment, pushing her way in between them as she yelled instructions at the top of her lungs. "Everyone! Move to the upper level and strap in! If there are no seats, sit on the floor! When you run out of room up there, sit on the platform or the steps! No one takes a seat down here until every centimeter of space up *there* is filled with bodies!"

———

Marcus counted off the twenty-fifth passenger for each side as they came out of the boarding tunnel.

"You and you," he commanded, grabbing them by the arms. "As soon as you get inside those hatches up there, you close and lock them."

"Then they'll let us in?" one of the two passengers surmised.

"Negative. You all will ride back in the corridor."

"Is it safe?"

"Safer than stayin' here," Marcus said. "Don't worry, it's a short trip. Just don't forget to close those hatches."

Marcus released the two passengers, allowing them to continue aft along either side of the docking apparatus.

"*We're standing room only, Cap'n,*" Neli reported over comms.

"Ten more, down here!" Marcus ordered.

"*What about the forward corridors?*" the captain asked.

"Five per side, and that's it until the next trip!" Marcus added.

"*Forward corridor as well. Port side is full up, I'm telling ya!*" Neli replied.

Marcus yelled over the heads of the passengers in the boarding tunnel, trying to get the attention of the crewman in the Asa-Cafon's hatch at the other end. "That's all! That's all we can fit! We'll get the rest on the next trip!"

"*We're full up to starboard, too, Cap'n!*" Dalen reported.

"*That's it, Marcus,*" the captain said. "*Get your last ones aboard and close it up!*"

"Come on, people, squeeze in there! All the way back!" Marcus yelled. He reached in and helped a young boy and his mother through the hatch, then looked down the boarding tunnel. At the opposite end, the Asa-Cafon's crew was having trouble holding back the rest of the passengers to close their hatch.

"No!" one of the passengers trying to get past the crewman cried out. "You've got to take me with you!"

"Get your ass back inside!" Marcus demanded.

"I can pay you!"

"Sorry, pal! You'll have to wait for..."

"There's no way..." The man overpowered the crewman and charged down the boarding tunnel, three more panicked passengers following behind him.

Marcus drew his weapon, pressing the charge button as it slid clear of his holster. The man continued to charge forward, determined to get past him. Marcus stepped inside the boarding tunnel and punched the charging man directly in the nose, knocking him off his feet.

The man fell to the ground, but quickly scrambled back to his feet, only to find the fully charged energy pistol pointed at his forehead. At the other end of the arm holding it was Marcus, with a big smile on his scruffy face.

"Get your ass back in there," Marcus ordered in a menacing tone, "or so help me I'll burn a hole in your head and giggle about it later."

Two of the Asa-Cafon's crew charged into the tunnel, grabbing the other men and dragging them back into the ship. The young man who had originally been overpowered came into the tunnel next, accompanied by another, more burly, crewman.

"Go, we've got this!" the burly one yelled as he grabbed the man kneeling at the end of Marcus's weapon and dragged him back to the Asa-Cafon.

Marcus watched as the two crewmen dragged the passenger back through the hatch. "Get that hatch closed!" he instructed as he stepped back through the hatch behind him and into the Seiiki's cargo bay. "We'll be back in half an hour, max!"

"We'll be here!" the crewman replied as they began cranking the hatch closed.

Marcus closed his hatch as well, then watched through the hatch portal until the Asa-Cafon's outer hatch was closed and mated back up with the seams of her hull. "Breaking docking seal," he announced over his helmet comms as he deactivated the docking ring locks on the far end of the boarding tunnel.

The sound of rushing air filled the room, as the pressure inside the boarding tunnel escaped into space. Several of the passengers crowded around the docking apparatus screamed out in fear, thinking the cargo bay was losing pressure.

"Clean disconnect," Marcus added. "Retracting the boarding tunnel." As he holstered his weapon again, he looked down at the young boy standing in front of his mother to his left. "That's what happens when you don't do as you're told."

"Thrusting away, one percent only," Josh announced as he fired the Seiiki's docking thrusters to push away from the Asa-Cafon. "You wanna call up the return jump series?"

Captain Tuplo stared at the monitor, transfixed by the expressions of absolute terror on the faces of his passengers. He could not imagine what they had been through. The loss of power. The frigid temperatures. All the while, not knowing if anyone was going to come to their rescue, or even worse, if they would freeze to death, trillions of kilometers away from their homes.

Connor Tuplo knew that he had been in a horrific

233

crash. But he had no memory of it. Not before, not during, and not after. His only memories were from the moment he had awakened in the hospital, six months later. All he knew of the crash was what he had read in the reports, and the pictures he had seen of the wreckage. He didn't even remember his life before the crash. That too was now just a collection of facts from his personnel file. Facts he had committed to memory in order to feel somewhat normal...as he imagined everyone else felt. Everyone who *remembered* their past.

The faces. He wondered if the faces of his passengers had been the same, fear and panic, the kind that only comes with the knowledge that certain death is inevitable.

Connor had been told the accident was not his fault. Some part, some tiny part deep within the ship he had been flying, had failed at exactly the wrong moment. He had even been given compensation for his pain and suffering... Enough to buy the Seiiki, *and* learn how to fly all over again. But that hadn't brought back the lives that had been lost. The lives that *he* had been responsible for as the pilot that day. It hadn't even brought back his life...only a superficial facsimile of it.

"Cap'n?" Josh called again.

"Uh, yeah," the captain replied, snapping out of his daze. "The return series, coming up."

"*Boarding tunnel is retracted,*" Marcus reported over the comms. "*Ramp is coming up.*"

"Coming about and climbing relative to the Asa-Cafon," Josh reported as he eased the throttles of the main engines forward.

"*Take it easy,*" Marcus warned. "*The ramp ain't up, yet.*"

"Relax, old man," Josh replied. "Cap'n, you got those jumps loaded?"

"Loaded and ready," the captain answered. "Let's get these people back to Haven as quickly as possible, so we can come back for the rest of them while there's still time."

"What's the hurry, Cap'n?" Josh asked. "You know somethin' I don't?"

"I don't know. Something just doesn't feel right."

* * *

Jerrot and Dumar wheeled the last two wine barrels out of the market and toward the truck.

"I have learned that the checkpoints on both Eighty-Second and Dinsmuir have been moved," Anji said in a low voice as he stepped up alongside Dumar. "To where, I do not know. But if you take Normund Boulevard south, you will likely have only the one checkpoint on the edge of the city to deal with. That should help you get to your next delivery on time."

"Thank you," Dumar replied, shaking his hand in sincere gratitude. "I will not forget this, my friend."

"We do what we must, and we fight however we are able," Anji replied. "It is the Corinairan way."

"Indeed it is," Dumar replied with a wry smile. He turned and watched as Jerrot and two of Anji's men loaded the last two barrels of wine onto the truck and lashed them down. It would be a long and bumpy ride, especially for those submerged up to their chins in the spiced wine. Dumar thought for a moment, wondering just how Lael was going to manage keeping both her and the infant's faces out of the water. He had taken some of the wine out of that barrel, and placed it at the front of the truck's cargo bed, in the hopes that the Jung's simple handheld scanners would not notice the heat signatures above the level of the fluid. It was a risk, but was one they had to take for the sake of the child.

Jerrot checked the cargo straps to ensure they were taut, then jumped down off the cargo bed. "Let us depart."

Dumar nodded politely at Anji, then turned and climbed up into the passenger side of the truck's cabin. A moment later, they were rolling away from the market.

* * *

"Come on, folks, let's keep it moving," Dalen instructed, as he helped passengers clear the bottom of the boarding stairs at the spaceport on Haven. "There's still a lot of people left on the Asa-Cafon."

"I didn't find anything out of place," Marcus said as he came out from under the Seiiki's port engine nacelle. "Nothin' on the starboard side, neither. You sure you aren't just imaginin' things, kid?"

"I'm telling ya, something didn't feel right during touchdown. The vibrations were wrong. They were... out of sync, or something."

Marcus tapped his comm-set. "Cap'n, everything looks good down here. You find anything on your end?"

"*Nothing*," the captain replied over comms. "*Diagnostics all look good. How long before we can lift off?*"

"*Last of the passengers are exiting now*," Neli reported.

"I'm telling you, something wasn't right," Dalen insisted.

"Go look for yourself, then," Marcus grumbled. "I'll get the last of them down and clear."

"I don't know, Cap'n," Josh said, as he studied the diagnostics readout on the engineering display at the back of the Seiiki's cockpit. "There *was* a drop in power in the port, outboard engine as we flared, but it was less than two percent of what we were asking of it." Josh turned to look at Captain Tuplo. "It ain't the first time it happened, you know."

"I know, I know," the captain admitted with slight frustration. "But the last time it happened and we ignored it, we were down for a week to repair it, and it was *not* cheap."

"That time was way more than a two percent drop, Cap'n," Josh argued. "Two percent we can handle, especially if we're runnin' light. When it starts droppin' ten or twenty percent, then I'll start sweatin'. Besides, if we don't finish this job, we don't get paid, remember?"

"*Last passenger is headed down the gangway now, Cap'n,*" Neli called over comms.

"Finally," Captain Tuplo replied, glancing at the ship's time display. "Marcus, Dalen; as soon as that last passenger is clear of the pad, you two get your asses back on board. I want to be wheels up and jumping in two minutes."

* * *

Travon and Jerrot had been waiting in line at the checkpoint on the southern border of Aitkenna for more than half an hour. Their cargo bed was loaded with twelve barrels of wine, four of which were empty, while the other six contained not only wine, but also the six adults and one infant they were attempting to smuggle out of the city.

"How are you holding up, Jerrot?" Dumar asked, as he watched the Jung soldiers finish inspecting the vehicle in front of them.

"I am fine. I just want this to be over with. It is like my entire future hangs on the next few moments."

"That's because it does," Dumar replied, as he glanced back through the window at the wine barrels, checking that their lids were still in place. "As does that of your family."

"You need not remind me, Travon. Believe me."

"Well, at least this is the last checkpoint."

"And there are no others in the countryside?"

"None that I am aware of," Dumar said.

"But there might be."

"It is possible. However, considering this is only the second day of Jung occupation, I would expect their focus would be on securing the major cities first. The countryside will come later."

"Hopefully we will all be long gone by then," Jerrot commented.

"Indeed."

The vehicle in front of them began to roll forward through the checkpoint gate, and the Jung soldiers signaled for them to pull forward. Jerrot eased the truck ahead, coming to a stop a few meters further, as the gate came down in front of them. All Jerrot could see was the road on the other side of the gate. The road represented freedom, and life. Both without the Jung. All they had to do was get past this checkpoint and drive back to Dumar's resort in the mountains. The drive would be long, but it would likely be without incident. All they had to do was get past the gate in front of them without raising suspicion.

"ID card," the Jung soldier instructed.

Jerrot handed the soldier his ID card, as the other soldiers began scanning his truck, carefully passing their scanners up and down, side to side, checking for any signals that would indicate they were carrying prohibited cargo.

Dumar handed his ID card to the Jung soldier at his window as well, while the other soldier scanned his side of the vehicle.

"You entered city from opposite," the guard said, an air of suspicion in his tone. "Why for you to exit here, not there? Are you not to be going home?"

"No, we are not," Jerrot replied, remaining as calm as could be expected while a tired, apparently irritated and armed soldier was interrogating him. "Our next delivery is in Jerston, the next city to the south. It made sense to exit here, rather than backtracking. I apologize if we were supposed to exit the same way we came in. I was unaware of this requirement."

The soldier looked at Jerrot, one eyebrow raised. He checked the ID card, then compared its photograph with Jerrot's face. "You are carrying garant spice wine, yes?"

"That is correct."

"It is good to drink, I hear. Maybe I should take some? For my men and I. What you think of this?"

"Help yourself," Dumar offered.

Jerrot glanced at Dumar.

At the back of the truck, one of the soldiers holding a hand scanner noticed a leaking spigot. Wine was dribbling onto the bed of the truck, down the end, and onto the street. The soldier barked something in Jung to the soldiers at the front of the vehicle, then reached down and filled his cupped hand with the burgundy liquid. He brought his hand up to his mouth and sipped at the liquid, spitting it out a moment later and cursing in Jung.

The soldier at Jerrot's window laughed, then

looked back at Jerrot. "My men do not want your rancid liquid," he said, handing the ID card back to Jerrot. "You may pass."

"Thank you, sir," Jerrot replied, as he prepared to drive.

"On your way!" the soldier ordered, signaling the gatekeeper to let them through.

The other soldier handed Dumar his ID card and stepped back. Dumar nodded politely, as the vehicle pulled slowly forward.

Moments later, they were through the gate and rolling down the boulevard, away from the city.

"Finally," Jerrot sighed with relief.

"It is not over until we reach our destination," Dumar reminded him. "That was very good, by the way," he added a minute later. "Perhaps you have a future in covert operations?"

"No, thanks," Jerrot replied without hesitation.

* * *

"Two meters, slow it down," Captain Tuplo cautioned as he watched the flight dynamics display on the Seiiki's console.

Josh tapped the flight control stick, causing another small jet of thrust to spit out of the ship's aft-facing docking thrusters, and slowing the Seiiki's closure rate on the Asa-Cafon even further.

"One meter...and..." The ship rocked gently. "Contact," Captain Tuplo reported. "Lock it in, Marcus." He looked at Josh. "Much nicer."

"Somethin' was pulling us in," Josh insisted. "I'm sure of it. That's why we hit so hard last time."

"How could something be *pulling* us in, Josh?" the captain argued. "She's a bigger ship, sure. But she isn't *that* much bigger."

"I'm telling ya, Cap'n, it shouldn't have taken that

much thrust to slow us down. Maybe their artificial gravity plating is wonky."

"Standard gravity plating doesn't work that way, Josh, and you know it. And even if they had variable gravity plating, which they *might* have in the cargo bays, they'd need to pump more power into them to increase their pull. A *lot* more to pull on a nearby ship, which I don't think even is *possible*. And that's why they're stranded out here. They don't *have* any power."

"Regardless, Cap'n," Josh replied, standing his ground, "*something* was pulling us into her that *shouldn't* have been."

"*Docking collar shows a good seal,*" Marcus reported over the comms. "*Opening inner hatch.*"

"Same as before, people," the captain instructed. "Get them on quick, so we can get back quick. We've still got to come back for the crew and the cargo, and that cargo is going to take even longer." Captain Tuplo turned to Josh. "Keep your eyes on the sensors."

"I am."

"*Cracking the Asa-Cafon's outer hatch now.*"

––––––––––––

"I've got them divided into groups of twenty-five this time, just like you asked," the Asa-Cafon's crewman said as they cranked their hatch open.

"Thanks," Marcus replied from inside the boarding tunnel. "That'll make it easier." He turned around and started back down the boarding tunnel toward the Seiiki. "All right, let's go!" He stepped back through the hatch at the forward end of the boarding tunnel, into the remaining space at the front of the Seiiki's cargo bay. After stepping through, he turned around to face the passengers coming up the boarding tunnel. "Same as before! First twenty-five to port! Head aft around the docking apparatus and up the ladder to the catwalk. Then into the corridor. Last man in the group must close the hatch behind him before the hatch at the forward end will be opened to let you in! Let's go! Let's go!"

A small blip appeared on the sensor display.

"Whoa," Josh said, his eyes fixating on it immediately.

"What is it?" the captain asked, turning to look at the screen himself.

"I could've sworn I saw something."

"Something? What kind of something?"

"I don't know," Josh replied. "An energy spike, a flash of light, maybe?"

"Like a jump flash?"

"I dunno. Maybe. But it didn't beep."

"It might not, if the reading was weak enough. The system might think it was an anomaly, or a sensor echo," the captain explained. Captain Tuplo sighed. "But if it were a jump flash, we'd see the ship that jumped in."

"Not if it went cold just after it jumped in," Josh pointed out.

"Cold?" Captain Tuplo asked, unfamiliar with the term.

"As in, shut everything down. No emissions, no heat. Stealth mode. We used to call it *goin' cold*, back when I was flyin' recon missions in the Falcon."

"You think it's a Jung ship?" Captain Tuplo wondered, his concern growing.

"Could be," Josh replied. "But the Jung don't usually try to hide. They like to come in all showy and shit, like they ain't afraid of nothin'. Stealth ain't exactly their style."

"Could be pirates," the captain suggested. "They tend to come out when things get chaotic. Play it back."

Josh pressed the replay button, causing the sensors to display the previous momentary contact reading on the screen.

"Enlarge and enhance," the captain instructed.

The image quadrupled in size, then became clearer, taking on an outline that was quite familiar to Josh.

"Fuck, that's a Jung gunship, Cap'n," Josh said.

"Are you sure?"

"Trust me, Cap'n. I've seen enough of them to know."

"How long do we have?" the captain asked, turning back to his consoles to prepare for a quick departure.

"From that distance? If they're trying to sneak up on us, then maybe ten minutes, assuming they've already detected us. If they *ain't* trying to sneak up... Way less."

"Marcus?" Captain Tuplo called over his comm-set. "How much longer until we're full up?"

"*Second group is starting up the ladders now, Cap'n. Ten minutes, maybe?*"

"We don't have ten minutes," the captain replied.

"*Don't tell me...*"

"Just be ready to cut us loose on a moment's notice."

"*And if there's still people in the tunnel?*"

"Then you get them the hell..."

A brilliant blue-white flash of light suddenly filled the Seiiki's cockpit, causing both Captain Tuplo and Josh to instinctively raise their hands in front of their faces to protect themselves from the blinding light.

———————

"Holy..." Dalen exclaimed, startled by the sudden flash of light spilling out through the main passenger compartment hatch and filling the starboard corridor where he was directing passengers. "Was that a..."

"*Get everyone in their seats!*" the captain instructed urgently over the comm-sets. "*We've got company!*"

"Oh fuck, oh fuck, oh fuck. Let's go! Let's go!" he yelled at the passengers in a panicked voice.

———————

Sensor alarms and proximity warning tones blared in the cockpit.

"Jesus! They've got both of their ventral guns aimed right at us!" Captain Tuplo shouted, looking out the forward windows at the gunship looming over them.

"We gotta get outta here, Cap'n!" Josh said urgently.

"*Unknown vessel assisting fugitive ship, Asa-Cafon,*" the heavily-accented voice announced over the comms. "*Power down all engines and reactors immediately, or we will open fire. This is your only warning. You have one minute to comply.*"

"What the fuck does he mean by fugitive vessel?" Josh wondered as his fingers danced across the controls, preparing to power up the Seiiki's propulsion systems.

"I knew it! I goddamn knew it!" the captain cursed. "Didn't I tell you something was wrong?"

"What are we gonna do, Cap'n?"

"We're going to stall for time! That's what we're going to do!"

"What?"

"Marcus, get as many people as you can on board, right now! You've got two minutes!" Captain Tuplo pointed at Josh. "Plot an escape jump!"

"Cap'n! We ain't movin'!" Josh reminded him. "You gotta be movin' to jump, remember?"

"Everything is moving, Josh. Hell, we're all hurtling through space at tens of thousands of kilometers per second. Even when we're standing on the surface, the whole damn planet is hurtling through space!"

"I was thinking more along the lines of we were moving *toward* someplace we wanna be...as in, someplace *they* ain't," Josh explained, pointing at the Jung gunship floating above them, rail guns ready to tear them to shreds.

"Uh, to the unknown black and red ship hovering over us," Captain Tuplo called over the comms. "This is the Seiiki. We are on a rescue mission. We were hired by the owners of the Asa-Cafon to evacuate the passengers and bring..."

"*Thirty seconds,*" the voice warned, ignoring Captain Tuplo's response.

"I don't think stalling is gonna work, Cap'n."

———————

"Move it, move it, move it!" Marcus shouted at the Asa-Cafon's remaining passengers.

"*Close all hatches! It's time to go!*" Captain Tuplo ordered over Marcus's helmet comms.

"I've got people in the tunnel, Cap'n!" Marcus replied. "Let's go! Let's go!"

"*You've got twenty seconds to close up before we jump the hell out of here, Marcus!*" Captain Tuplo warned.

"Move your ass!" Marcus shouted as the last of

the passengers made their way through the tunnel and into the Seiiki's cargo bay.

"There's no more room in here!" someone yelled from the port side of the docking apparatus.

Marcus turned back to the boarding tunnel. "That's it, we're full up!"

"What? You can't be! What about the rest of us?" the crewman said in horror from the Asa-Cafon's boarding hatch at the other end of the tunnel.

"We'll be back for you!" Marcus promised, even though he knew it wasn't true.

"What is it? What's wrong?"

"Marcus! Get those hatches closed!" the captain ordered.

"Close those fucking hatches up there! Port and starboard! Close them now! You hear me?!" Marcus turned back toward the tunnel, as several of the Asa-Cafon's crew came charging down the boarding tunnel, determined to get aboard the Seiiki at all costs.

Oh, fuck! Marcus pulled his weapon and opened fire on the charging crewmen. His shots struck several of them in the head and chest, causing them to collapse in the middle of the tunnel in a smoldering heap. It was just enough to slow the rest of them down, and buy him enough time to close the hatch at his end of the tunnel. "Go, go, go!" he yelled over his comms as he swung the hatch closed and spun the lock. *Fuck!* he thought as he closed his eyes and turned his back to the hatch.

_____

"Time is up," Josh announced.

"Unknown black and red ship, this is the Seiiki. We just need a few..."

The ship lurched to one side suddenly. Alarms

began sounding in the Seiiki's cockpit.

"What the fuck!" Josh exclaimed as he reached for the Seiiki's flight controls.

"They're firing on us!" Captain Tuplo yelled.

Another alarm sounded.

"We've lost lock with the Asa-Ca..."

"Decompression in the cargo bay!" the captain exclaimed. He glanced out the side window, noticing that the ship was in a lateral spin, and headed for the main drive section of the Asa-Cafon. "Josh!"

"Fuck!" Josh swore, noticing the imminent collision. He grabbed the flight control stick and gave it a twist to swing them around so their aft end was facing the rapidly-approaching drive section of the Asa-Cafon, then fired the docking thrusters to push the ship downward, below the cargo ship.

"We're taking more fire!" Captain Tuplo warned.

"I'm gonna slide under her and use her as a shield!" Josh announced as the Asa-Cafon rose above their nose, replaced by the beautiful blackness of open, interstellar space. "Be ready to jump!"

There was a deafening *whoosh* of air, and Marcus instinctively reached up and pulled his helmet face shield down. There was a terrible screech of tearing metal, mixed with the screams of at least twenty people. The entire docking apparatus suddenly shot out the back of the cargo bay, taking the last of the air with it.

Everything was suddenly silent. Silent except for the sound of his own breathing. He felt himself being pulled out into space, as he frantically reached out for something to anchor himself. As he shot out the back of the Seiiki's cargo bay, he could see passengers hanging on to the railing, trying desperately to remain within the Seiiki's cargo bay, despite the fact that the cargo door was now fully open to space. Several of them lost their fight and were immediately sucked out along with Marcus, dying within seconds, their faces twisted with grotesque expressions of fear and panic.

Marcus shot away from the Seiiki's cargo bay. Then, he stopped with a violent yank at his back. The pull spun him around, so that he was facing away from the Seiiki, the suit fabric digging into his abdomen. For a brief moment, he saw the Asa-Cafon, falling away from them, Jung rail guns tearing into her hull.

Then he spun back around, and found himself headed back toward the Seiiki's cargo bay, propelled by the yanking motion of the life support umbilical connecting him to the ship. Two bodies flew directly at him. The first one was a woman, already dead, her mouth agape and her eyes exploded outward by the sudden decompression. The second one was a man. He was still alive and flailing his arms wildly. He eyes were bulging, on the verge of exploding. The man ceased his struggling as he drifted past Marcus, his eyes finally losing their battle to remain intact in the vacuum of space, their bloody spray just missing Marcus's face shield.

Marcus grabbed at his umbilical, pulling at it like a rope to draw himself back into the Seiiki's cargo bay. He could see that Josh was maneuvering the ship under the Asa-Cafon, using it as a shield against incoming Jung rail gun fire. At any moment, Josh would fire the Seiiki's main engines and jump away. If Marcus was too far away from the Seiiki when it jumped, the jump fields would sever his umbilical, and he would be left behind, floating in space, with only the oxygen left in his suit to keep him alive.

Hand over hand, Marcus continued to frantically pull himself along, as more bodies drifted past him and out of the Seiiki's cargo bay. Then the ship thrust forward, and he almost lost his grip on the umbilical. "Wait! Not yet!" he cried out over his helmet comms, as he continued pulling himself closer to the Seiiki's cargo bay. One last body, that of an attractive young woman not much older than Josh, drifted past him as he slid under the edge of the Seiiki's aft-most section.

"Jumping!" Captain Tuplo announced over the comms.

Marcus closed his eyes tightly, and prayed. There was a brilliant flash of light, causing the inside of his eyelids to illuminate a bright orange. Then it was gone.

Marcus was afraid to open his eyes. If the Seiiki was gone, and he was about to die, he didn't want to know.

"Marcus!" Captain Tuplo called over Marcus's helmet comms. *"Are you still with us?"*

Marcus opened his eyes. The Seiiki was still there, her aft end looming no more than a meter above his head. He was slowly rotating to his right, and he saw the body of the young woman that had drifted past him, severed cleanly at the abdomen by the Seiiki's jump fields, leaving her upper half back with the Asa-Cafon.

"Marcus!" the captain repeated.

"I'm here," Marcus managed to squeak out in between breaths.

"Are you all right?"

Marcus looked at the lower half of the young woman, drifting away from him. "No, I'm not. I need a drink. Hell, I need the whole fuckin' bottle!"

* * *

Josh and Captain Tuplo rushed aft along the Seiiki's port corridor, pushing their way past the disembarking passengers who were rushing in the opposite direction. They pushed their way through the forward corridor and into the aft corridor, which was still full of people trying to get out.

Finally, they came out the aft end of the corridor, onto the short catwalk at the port side, aft end of the cargo bay. Captain Tuplo stopped, grabbing the railing and twisting forward to look for Marcus. The old man was sitting on the floor of the torn up bay, his arms resting on his knees, his head hanging down.

Josh rushed past the captain, nearly dropping down to the cargo deck without touching a single rung on the ladder. "Marcus!" Josh yelled as he raced toward him. He dropped down to his knees in front of Marcus, looking at his face. His face shield was open again, now that they had landed. "You all right, old man?"

"Right enough to punch you in the mouth if you call me 'old man' again."

Josh smiled as he unlocked Marcus's helmet and pulled it up off his head.

Marcus looked up at Captain Tuplo, who was taking in the damage.

"Jesus, Marcus. What happened?"

"Rail gun fire must've hit the tunnel. Everything just went *whoosh*, right out the back and me along with it. If it weren't for my umbilical." He looked at Josh. "You were cuttin' it a bit close with that jump, weren't you, boy?"

"We knew you were inside the jump fields,"

Captain Tuplo assured him. "Barely."

Marcus sighed. "Don't suppose we're gettin' paid for this one?"

"Not likely," Captain Tuplo replied. "Paid on completion."

"Don't suppose we can go back and finish the job?" Josh asked, already knowing the answer.

"The Asa-Cafon came apart as we jumped," Marcus said. "Nothin' to go back to."

A vehicle pulled up outside, behind the Seiiki's cargo ramp. Three men, one of them older and more nicely dressed than the other two, climbed out of the vehicle.

"Did you get it?" the older man asked as he approached the bottom edge of the cargo ramp. "Did you get my cargo?"

"We're fine, Siggy. Thanks for your concern," Captain Tuplo replied coldly.

"You didn't…" Sigmund replied, as he took note of the damage to the Seiiki's cargo bay. "You did! You went for the passengers, first, didn't you?" Sigmund grabbed the sides of his head with both hands, dumbfounded at the realization. "Are you idiots or something? I *told* you that the cargo was the priority!" he ranted, waving his hands madly as he spoke. "Get the cargo, get paid. That's what I said, word for fucking word. That was the deal!" Sigmund put his hands on top of his head and turned away, momentarily at a loss for words. "I don't believe this," he finally said, turning back around to face them. "Do you know how much that cargo was worth? It was a once in a lifetime opportunity! I mean, how often does the entire cluster get invaded?! You sons of bitches! I ought to skin you all alive!"

Marcus had reached his limit, and drew his

weapon for the third time that day. Only this time, it was in anger. "You slimy little dung heap..."

The two men flanking Sigmund pulled their weapons just as quickly, both taking aim at Marcus.

"I got the ape on the left," Josh announced as he drew his weapon, switching it on as it left its holster.

"You're gonna have to shoot 'em both," Marcus muttered, his voice seething with contempt. "I'm shootin' Siggy."

"Whoa, whoa, whoa... Easy fellas! What's with all the guns?" Captain Tuplo said, his arms out as he tried to keep them from opening fire.

"You dare point a weapon at me?" Sigmund bellowed, infuriated.

"I dare to pull the fuckin' trigger, too," Marcus sneered. "You knew it weren't no easy run, you little fuck. I oughta burn you down where you stand."

"You burn me, and they burn you," Sigmund reminded Marcus.

"Worth it," Marcus replied.

Sigmund noticed the look of determination in Marcus's eyes, as well as the confidence in Josh's. "Look, I had no way of knowing that the Jung would be looking for the Asa-Cafon."

"How did *you* know the Jung were looking for her?" Captain Tuplo wondered. "I didn't say anything." He looked at Josh, as he started moving toward the back of the cargo bay. "Did you broadcast it over comms on approach when I wasn't looking?"

"No, sir," Josh replied, his weapon still aimed at the man to the left of Sigmund.

Sigmund's right hand slid slowly toward his own side arm, realizing that a gunfight was becoming more likely with each passing moment.

"I wouldn't do that if I were you," Dalen warned

from his position tucked behind the port engine nacelle.

Sigmund looked to his left, spotting Dalen and his rather large energy rifle. His eyes widened.

Captain Tuplo leaned out from the cargo hatch to see Dalen. "Now *that,* is a *big* gun," he said. "I believe one shot would make a pretty big puddle of goo out of the three of you." A smile came across Captain Tuplo's face, as he realized that they now had the upper hand. He started moving down the ramp toward Sigmund, seemingly unconcerned with the two bodyguards who still had their guns drawn. "You knew damn well the Jung were actively looking for the Asa-Cafon. *That's* why you wanted me to get her cargo off first. You *knew* time was running out." Captain Tuplo looked at the two bodyguards. "Put your toys away, fellas," he instructed, gesturing with both hands. He returned his attention to Sigmund. "What was she carrying, Siggy? What was worth more than three hundred plus lives?"

"Nothing you need concern yourself with, Tuplo."

"Oh, I disagree," the captain said, as he continued down the ramp. "You see, now they're going to be looking for *this* ship. *My* ship. Now, we're the..." He turned to call over his shoulder to Josh. "What did they call us?"

"Fugitives, Cap'n," Josh replied from the cargo bay, his gun still aimed at the three men.

"That's right," the captain continued. "Fugitives. *Now* we're fugitives, and in the eyes of the Jung, no less. So you see, Siggy, it *does* concern me. It concerns me a great deal. In fact, it concerns me *so* much, that I'm half-inclined to step aside and let my angry friend back there burn a few holes in you just to find out."

By now, Captain Tuplo was standing toe-to-toe with Sigmund, looking him right in the eyes.

"You wouldn't dare."

"Oh, I might," the captain replied. "I truly might." He stared Sigmund in the eyes for a moment, then cocked his head to one side, looking away. "Or, I might tell all those people that I brought back how *you* told me to get the *cargo* first, and not them. Might make them a bit angry, don't you think? They might be inclined to take out their aggressions on you and your two goons here." Captain Tuplo turned back to Sigmund, getting directly in his face. "So tell me, Siggy, just what was that precious cargo of yours?" He paused for a moment, waiting, then he stepped to the right. "Don't kill him with the first shot, Marcus."

Marcus raised his weapon, preparing to fire.

"ZPEDs!" Sigmund shouted. "Mini-ZPEDs. About fifty of them."

Connor turned to look at Sigmund, surprised. "You stole fifty mini-ZPEDs from the plant on Rama?"

"No way," Marcus said. "He's too fucking stupid to pull something like that off."

"I told you there was something in her that was pulling us in," Josh reminded them.

"I didn't steal them," Sigmund admitted. "I just heard about it through back channels."

"Stolen in the midst of the chaos of an invasion, no doubt," Captain Tuplo said, putting it all together. "Yes, I expect the Jung knew about the ZPED plant on Rama all along. Probably one of the reasons they took the cluster in the first place." Captain Tuplo shook his head. "And you were calling *me* stupid. Even mini-ZPEDs create their own gravity wells, Siggy. Especially if they're not shielded correctly."

"You *are* stupid, Connor," Sigmund insisted. "If you had gotten that cargo back safe, I would've hired you to get it to the buyers as well, for a far sight more than what I was paying you to retrieve it in the first place."

"If you had offered more to begin with, you might have gotten a bigger ship interested, or at least one that was willing to put the lives of the passengers second. Either way, you'd have fifty ZPEDs in your hands now instead of a big-ass gun pointed at your head."

"Gun or no gun, I'm still not paying you, Connor."

"I wasn't asking you to, Siggy. But believe me, if I was, you'd be transferring credits to my account as we speak." Captain Tuplo sighed. "I'm getting really tired of breathing the same air as you, Daschew," he said, turning away and heading back up the ramp, while staying out of Marcus and Josh's lines of fire. "You've got about a minute to get out of my sight before you start feeling the heat of these men's guns."

Sigmund Daschew and his men backed away slowly, then climbed into their vehicle. "Good luck getting another run out of Haven, Tuplo!" Sigmund warned just before he climbed into his vehicle.

Marcus lowered his gun as Sigmund and his men drove away. "You shoulda' let me burn him, Cap'n."

"Why'd you let him go without payin' us?" Josh asked.

"We didn't finish the job," the captain replied.

"But he lied to us about the risk," Josh argued.

"Doesn't matter. A deal's a deal. I told Marcus to take the job, even though I know Siggy is a lyin' piece of shit. Besides, if we forced him to pay us, we *wouldn't* get another job. On Haven, or anywhere else in this sector."

"But you heard him, Cap'n," Josh said. "He just told us we'd never get another job 'round here anyway."

"Siggy isn't as powerful as he likes to think," Captain Tuplo told them. "Something else will come along."

"Jesus!" Dalen exclaimed as he came up the ramp. "What the hell did you do to the back of the ship?"

"So, now what?" Marcus asked, as he holstered his weapon.

"You know how much it's gonna cost to fix all this?" Dalen continued.

"Well, right now Siggy *is* making good on his promise, and telling everyone in port not to hire us. And they won't, at least for a while."

"Not that there were many runs to begin with," Marcus added.

"True. But there likely would've been a few, eventually. Ones we could've underbid in order to get people to ignore Siggy." Connor sighed. "It's going to take some time to patch this up."

"And credits," Dalen added. "At the very least, I'm gonna need some scrap to weld in to reinforce this ramp. I'm gonna have to reweld the deck plates, straighten the collar on the port side…"

"We don't have much left in the way of credits, Cap'n," Marcus reminded him.

"And every day we spend in port, even this cheap-ass port, is costing us." The captain thought for a moment. "We need someplace to park for a while. Someplace away from town. Someplace that doesn't cost anything."

"Most of the land around here is owned by molo farmers and the like. None would be too favorable to us squattin' on it for a few days."

"Days?" Dalen said. "Did you look at this?"

"I know a place, Cap'n," Josh said.

Both the captain and Marcus looked at Josh, surprised.

"It's a bit far, a few hours by ground, I think. But it's abandoned."

"Are you sure?" the captain asked.

"Well, I'm not *completely* sure. But I know the owner, and I know *she* ain't using it. Not for going on nine years now. That much I *am* sure of. I'm also sure she wouldn't mind us using it for a while."

Marcus realized the place Josh was talking about, and didn't appear to like the idea, shooting a disapproving glance Josh's way.

"Very well. That's where we'll go," the captain decided.

"I don't know, Cap'n," Marcus objected. "Maybe you should let me drive out and give it the once-over, make sure it's okay."

"That'll take too long," the captain objected. "If we're not out of here in a few hours, I'm going to have to pay for another day in this dust pit."

"All right," Marcus said. "And then what? Even if we fix all this, we don't have the propellant or the supplies to get very far. And the long night will be comin' soon enough."

"We'll figure something out, Marcus. Besides, this planet is covered with molo, so at least we won't starve. Hell, we can load up with the stuff...pack our pantry with it. And if I remember correctly, the long night brings storms along with it, which means water. So I expect we can hold out a good long while, if we have to."

"And if the Jung come?" Josh asked.

"In that case, we'll have no choice," the captain

admitted. "We'll take our chances and jump away—full of molo and water—and we'll keep jumping until we find someplace else to ply our trade. But hopefully, something better will come along before it gets to that. In the meantime, we'll be molo farmers." Captain Tuplo patted Marcus on the shoulder as he turned and headed back down the ramp to check out the exterior of his ship.

"Great," Marcus said dryly. "Just what I've always wanted." He looked at Josh. "You had to go and open your big yap, didn't ya?"

"What?"

"*Cap'n, I know a place!*" Marcus said, mocking Josh.

CHAPTER NINE

Commander Kaplan glanced back down at her data pad before speaking again. "The latest word from command logistics is that the Dorsay should be jumping out to resupply us in about twelve hours."

"What's the delay?" Cameron asked, her eyes still on the view screen at her desk.

"I guess they're just trying to get her fully loaded before she departs."

"I'd rather they just get us the basics, like more jump missiles, right now, and then bring the rest later."

"Agreed, but I suspect that they're pretty busy there. The Cape Town is already back in Earth orbit, and they're busting their behinds to get her fully armed."

Cameron finally looked up from her view screen and at her XO sitting on the other side of the desk. "The Cape Town isn't going to defend Earth all by herself." Cameron looked back at her view screen. "Especially not with Stettner in command," she added flatly.

"Stettner's a good man, Cam."

"He may be a good man, Lara, but you and I both know he's hardly qualified to command the fleet's first Protector-class ship."

"Let's not go down that road, again," Lara said, rolling her eyes in disgust.

"I loathe politics." Cameron pushed her view screen aside, rubbing her tired eyes. "How are things going, crew-wise? Are you getting everyone cross-trained?"

"We're working on it. We've been concentrating

on the critical areas first, like cross-training damage control teams to also act as medical rescue, and having the bridge staff teach each other their jobs, so they can act as relief for short breaks. We've even got a pretty good rotation schedule set up, so that no one is required to act as temp-relief during their off-duty time more than twice per day, and everyone gets at least one day per week when they will *not* be asked to act as relief while off-duty. That, and the fact that most extra shifts involve working somewhere other than their normal duty stations, should help. I'm also making sure we stock the food dispensers with more of their favorites, just to help keep morale up while we're all working extra shifts."

Cameron smiled. "Best way to a man's heart, huh?"

"Hey, a woman's heart, too," Lara replied. "I need my comfort food as much as the next guy."

The intercom panel built into the captain's desk beeped. Cameron reached for it. "Yes?"

"Just received a message from Cobra Three One Seven via jump comm-drone, sir," the comm officer reported. *"They detected a red-shifted trail in sector alpha foxtrot, grid two seven five one, elevation two eight three below the solar ecliptic. Lieutenant Commander Kono agrees it may be a Jung FTL trail."*

Commander Kaplan's brow furrowed. "That's less than a light year from Sol's heliopause."

Cameron switched channels on the intercom. "Helm, Captain. I want to investigate that possible contact. Plot a jump. I'm on my way."

"Helm, aye."

"How does your rotation schedule handle this?" Cameron asked as she rose to exit.

"By throwing it out the window and starting over,"

the commander replied simply as she also stood to leave.

Cameron walked out from behind her desk and headed straight for the hatch from her ready room to the bridge, with her XO falling in line behind her as she passed.

"Captain on the bridge!" the Aurora's port entrance guard announced as the captain stepped out of her ready room.

Cameron went directly to her command chair at the center of the Aurora's bridge. Her XO, Commander Kaplan, went directly to the sensor station to the left of the command chair and peered over the shoulder of Lieutenant Commander Kono, to see the sensor readings transmitted by the Cobra gunship that had reported the detection.

"Jump to sector alpha foxtrot, grid two seven five one, elevation two eight three below the solar ecliptic, plotted and ready, Captain," the navigator, Ensign Bickle, reported.

"Lieutenant Dinev, put us on the jump line," Cameron ordered, as she took her seat in the command chair.

"Changing course, aye," the helmsman answered.

Commander Kaplan turned away from the sensor station to face the captain. "I concur with the lieutenant commander's analysis, Captain. It looks an awful lot like a Jung FTL signature."

"There is something peculiar about it, though," the sensor officer added.

"Peculiar, how?" Cameron inquired.

"It's not what we're used to seeing. The gamma radiation levels from the trail are much higher than normal," Lieutenant Commander Kono explained.

"Don't the mass-cancelling fields on the older

Jung ships give off a lot more gamma radiation?" Cameron commented.

"Yes, sir," the lieutenant commander replied. "But the levels in the sensor reading from Cobra Three One Seven are indicative of the much older, Toran-Ot-class frigates."

"So, the Jung are using old frigates," Cameron said. "That isn't unusual."

"Only the trail is too large to be a frigate, sir," the lieutenant commander replied. "Its size suggests something at least as big as a heavy cruiser, or even one of their first generation battleships."

"No one has spotted one of *those* in *years*," the commander commented.

"A Jung ship is a Jung ship, Commander," Cameron stated matter-of-factly. "Especially when it's deep in Alliance space."

"On course and speed for jump, Captain," the helmsman reported.

"Recommend general quarters before we jump, Captain," the XO suggested.

"Good idea, Commander," Cameron agreed. "If it is a Jung battleship, even an old one, I'd much rather have our shields up and our weapons hot when we find out for sure." Cameron turned to her communications officer. "Mister deBanco, set general quarters."

* * *

The Seiiki cruised along lazily, five hundred meters above the dusty surface of Haven. Below them, vast expanses of the fungus-like plant known as *molo*, broken by the occasional farmyard, slid beneath them as they cruised away from Haven's only spaceport, toward the abandoned farm that would serve as their temporary home.

"This place is even more depressing outside of the city," Dalen commented.

"I didn't think that was possible," Neli added, agreeing with Dalen.

"It is," Marcus grumbled. "Trust me."

Captain Tuplo turned and looked over his shoulder at the three of them, standing behind him and Josh.

"We're about five minutes out, Cap'n," Josh announced, glancing at the navigation display. "We should probably drop down low now, so the spaceport can't track us."

"All right," Captain Tuplo replied hesitantly. "Just don't buzz anyone's home. We don't need them calling in a complaint."

"There's a dried-out riverbed to the east. It's pretty deep, and it's wide enough for us to fly down low. That should keep anyone nearby from getting a good look at us. We should be able to pop up and slide over to the Redmond place without being spotted. Like I said, it's pretty remote."

"If it's such a big river, why is it dried out?"

"All the rivers dry up between the long nights," Marcus explained. "They fill back up with all the rainstorms that the long nights bring. That's why you see so many water towers and tanks all over the place. Everyone fills up while the rivers are full, so they can get by when they dry up."

"Very well," Captain Tuplo said. "Take us down to the riverbed, Josh."

"You got it."

Josh adjusted the Seiiki's flight controls, causing the ship to drop its nose slightly and descend toward the surface. Half a minute later, they were in the riverbed, the shoreline rushing by above them on either side.

Josh twisted the flight control stick back and forth, rolling the ship from port to starboard, as he snaked it through the winding, dried-up riverbed. Now and again, puddles of water not yet evaporated by the searing heat of Haven were blown in all directions as the Seiiki streaked over them, disturbing the calm waters.

"Damn! I haven't had this much fun flyin' in a long time," Josh declared joyfully.

"Feel free to slow it down a bit, Josh," the captain replied, his eyes wide. "If you're so inclined, that is."

"Don't worry, Captain," Marcus assured him. "If there's *one* thing the boy can do, it's fly."

"Damn, Josh! Go!" Dalen cried out, enjoying himself just as much as the pilot.

"Don't forget, we aren't in the best condition right now, Josh," the captain reminded him.

"Ain't nothin' wrong with her maneuvering systems, Cap'n," Dalen insisted, almost feeling insulted. "And we're running as light as possible right now, so she's got lift to spare."

"I was speaking about myself," the captain replied tensely, squinting as if he were afraid to watch the walls rushing past them.

The Seiiki pulled around a sharp bend in the riverbed. Ahead of them, a massive outcropping jutted out from the right side of the riverbed, cutting the bed by more than half its width.

"Oh, shit! Pull up!" Captain Tuplo warned.

"Low bridge!" Josh yelled, almost giggling with delight. He rolled the Seiiki forty-five degrees to the right, as he fired the starboard translation thruster, sending the angled ship skidding to port. "Hang on!" The ship's starboard engine nacelle dipped just under the rocky outcropping, barely skimming the large puddle of water that had yet to evaporate due to the shade provided by the rocks above.

"Jesus!" Neli exclaimed, closing her eyes for a moment.

Captain Tuplo started breathing again. He looked at the navigation display. "Destination is coming up to port."

"Fun's over, I guess," Josh replied with disappointment, as he pulled back on the flight control stick and added additional power to the Seiiki's lift thrusters.

The ship jumped up out of the riverbed, much to the relief of everyone but Josh. Additional jets of translation thrust sent the Seiiki sliding to port, passing over fields of wild molo that seemed like it hadn't been cultivated for many years.

Captain Tuplo gazed out the port windows as the ship slipped along only four meters above the surface. "Uh, Josh?"

"No worries, Cap'n. Ain't nothin' out here."

"Where's this place at?" the captain wondered, still trying to spot the abandoned farm from the side windows.

Josh glanced at the navigation display again. "Should be right......about..."

A large, oval, depression suddenly came into view to port. The massive sinkhole had steep, nearly vertical sides, with vehicle paths carved into either end. As the Seiiki slid in over the middle of the southern end of the depression, they could see more detail below. There was a building that could've once been a residence, but had been blown open by an explosion and was never repaired. Behind it was a long building constructed of the same mud bricks used for most of the structures on Haven. Along either side of the sinkhole, what looked to be storage spaces, equipment garages, and workshops, were all built into the depression's steep sides.

"...here!" Josh finished. "Welcome to the Redmond molo farm."

"That's not a farm, it's a dump!" Neli exclaimed.

"I didn't say it was pretty," Josh reminded her. "I said it was abandoned."

"And for damned good reason, Josh," Neli argued.

"I don't know," Captain Tuplo said, intrigued by the possibilities.

Neli's eyes widened. "Cap'n, you can't seriously be considering that we stay here. Look at it! The place looks like a war was fought here...and they lost! Hell, half the house is destroyed, and that looks like the wreckage of some kind of ship over there."

"Hey, maybe we can salvage something from her," Dalen suggested hopefully.

"That's what I was thinking," Captain Tuplo agreed.

"From that?" Neli couldn't believe what she was hearing.

"There's a bunkhouse on the back side of the main house over there, Cap'n," Josh said. "All this didn't touch it, if I remember correctly."

"You were here when all *this* happened?" Neli rolled her eyes. "Why am I not surprised?"

"We're burnin' propellant just hoverin' here, Cap'n," Marcus reminded him. "We come all this way... Might as well set her down and take a look around."

Captain Tuplo leaned forward, scanning the area for a good spot to land. He looked up at the sky for a moment, then back down to the left. "Think you can put her down over there?" he asked Josh, pointing to the left. "In between that wreckage and the sinkhole wall?"

"Sure, but why?" Josh wondered. "There's tons of room over to starboard."

"It'll cut down the sensor angle from above. We're pretty high up in latitude here. Between the ridge and all that wreckage, we might go unnoticed from ships in standard orbit. Especially if we drag some of that wreckage around our ship. It'll confuse the hell out of any sensors that can get an angle on us."

"You got it, Cap'n."

"You're really thinkin' of camping out here, aren't you?" Neli said, disappointed.

"I'm not committing to any particular course of action just yet, Neli," Captain Tuplo replied, annoyed by Neli's complaints. "But if we *do* decide to stay, it would be *stupid* to waste more propellant reparking the ship, now wouldn't it?"

* * *

"Jump complete," the Aurora's navigator announced, as the blue-white flash from their jump dissipated.

"Starting sensor sweep along estimated course trajectory based on target's last known course and speed," Lieutenant Commander Kono reported from the sensor station.

"Commander Kaplan is in combat," the comm officer updated.

"Threat board is clear," Lieutenant Commander Vidmar reported from the tactical station.

"New message coming in from Cobra Three One Seven," Ensign deBanco added. "They've had no more contacts since the last momentary detection they previously reported. They want to know if they should move the search grid further along the possible target's estimated trajectory."

"Tell them to stay on their current search grid," Cameron instructed from her command chair. "We'll continue the search along that trajectory."

"Yes, sir."

"Helm, turn us onto a parallel course with the target's estimated trajectory," the captain continued. "Mister Bickle, prepare to jump us ahead one light hour."

"Altering course to parallel the target," Lieutenant Dinev acknowledged.

"Loading a one-light-hour jump."

Cameron turned slowly to her left. "Anything?" she asked her sensor officer.

"Nothing yet, sir. But I'm only searching a narrow corridor along the contact's last trajectory. I can widen the beam, but it will be less sensitive."

"Negative," Cameron replied.

"Course change complete," the helmsman reported.

"Jump loaded and ready."

"Jump us ahead, one light hour, Mister Bickle."

"Jumping ahead, one light hour, in three...... two......one......"

The jump flash translated through the Aurora's semi-spherical main view screen that wrapped around the forward portion of her bridge, momentarily bathing them in a subdued, blue-white light.

"Jump complete," the navigator finished.

"Hold course and speed, Lieutenant," Cameron ordered.

"Holding course and speed, aye."

Cameron sat confidently, watching the main view screen as if she knew what was about to happen. Even now, after all these years, she could still remember how Nathan always complained that the panoramic view offered by the Aurora's wraparound view screen served no real purpose in most situations, other than to impress visitors, and to remind them all that they were constantly hurtling through the most inhospitable environment to the human species. Such were the abstract observations of her long-lost friend, the man who, despite the fact that he had no more training or experience than she did when command had been thrust upon him, had ended up showing her exactly what it meant to be a leader.

"I'm picking up something," Lieutenant Commander Kono announced tentatively. "Red-shifted..."

Cameron turned her head toward the lieutenant commander in anticipation.

"Gamma radiation... Same course and speed..." She turned toward Cameron. "That's gotta be a Jung ship in FTL, Captain."

"Position relative?"

"About three light minutes ahead of us, Captain," the lieutenant commander replied, studying her sensor readings again. "Four light minutes to port, and two down relative. However, it may be more than one trail. The trace keeps changing shape. It may be multiple targets flying in close FTL formation."

Cameron took a deep breath and sighed. "Mister Bickle," she began as she turned forward again. "Plot an intercept course and prepare a jump. I want to put us no more than one thousand kilometers astern and to the side of that contact. I want a good solid reading before we put the entire Earth on alert."

"Yes, sir," the young ensign replied.

"Captain?" Lieutenant Commander Kono began, turning back around to face Cameron. "How did you know?"

"If you *want* someone to see you, you stand right where you'd expect them to look," Cameron replied.

* * *

The Seiiki's damaged cargo ramp smacked the ground harder than usual, kicking up a cloud of dust.

"I'll check the ramp hydraulics," Dalen promised the captain.

"Good idea." Captain Tuplo and his crew stood at the top of the cargo ramp, waiting for the dust to settle. "Josh, you know where the bunkhouse is, so you and Neli go and check it out. See what kind of shape it's in."

"Why?" Neli wondered. "It's not like we're gonna sleep there. We do have cabins on board."

"Humor me, Neli," the captain asked, not wanting to explain his reasoning.

"I can check it out by myself, Cap'n."

"I'd like Neli's opinion on it as well, if you don't mind. After all, if *she* thinks it can be made livable, then I don't have to worry about the rest of you whining if we end up having to shack up there to save power and water."

Josh sighed, then headed down the cargo ramp.

"I wasn't whining," Neli mumbled as she followed Josh down the ramp.

"Want me to start on those hydraulics?" Dalen suggested, starting down the ramp.

"That can wait," the captain replied. "I want you to take a look around that wreckage, Dalen. See if there's anything we might be able to salvage for use, or maybe even for resale."

"But it's probably been sitting there for ten years, Cap'n. It's all rusted and shit."

Captain Tuplo turned and looked at Dalen, a scowl on his face. "Why are you arguing with me? Are you under the mistaken impression that I'm having a good day? That I'm in a jovial, forgiving-type of mood, or something?"

"I'm goin', I'm goin'," Dalen replied, throwing his hands up in defensive resignation.

"Thank you." Captain Tuplo took a deep breath and sighed. He turned and looked at Marcus. "Why are you just standing there, Taggart?"

"You ain't given me nothin' to do, yet."

"Oh, yeah," the captain realized. "You search the buildings along that side; I'll search the ones along this side."

Marcus nodded, but didn't move down the ramp.

"You got something on your mind?" the captain asked.

"We goin' into the salvage business?"

"If that's what it takes to fill our tanks, then, yes. Is that a problem?"

"No, sir," Marcus replied quickly, as he headed down the ramp.

Captain Tuplo paused a moment, then started down the ramp himself. At the bottom of the ramp, he stopped and looked around. "Jesus, she's right," he sighed. "It does look like a war was fought here."

* * *

"Industry brings jobs; jobs create revenue; revenue grows the economy..."

It was the same thing the president's economic advisor had been spouting day in and day out, ever since he took office three years ago.

"We still have two million people living in camps..."

Mister Tankersly's tune hadn't improved much either. The only thing that changed was the number of millions he quoted as still being stuck in the camps.

"And jobs will get them out of the camps..."

Just once, he wanted to get these two in a room and have them discuss something without arguing.

"It hasn't in seven years..."

"Mister Tankersly," the president said wearily, tiring of their bickering, "you know as well as the rest of us that the number of people still living in the refugee camps has dropped significantly in recent years. And you also know that it happened *because* jobs were created, and those people in the camps were able to rejoin mainstream society."

"Jobs also bring pride, self-respect..."

"I'm not arguing against jobs, Mister President. I'm arguing against the percentage of our fabricators that are being tasked with helping to rebuild private industry, *instead* of building *more* public housing that would *not* require a job in order for a family to move into them."

"And continue to perpetuate a nanny state? How does that help us get back on our feet?" the president's economic advisor challenged.

"We already are! Don't you get it? We have to stop *helping* big industry get established. They already are! And they have employee shortages because we've helped them create technical positions without creating the training infrastructure to provide them with skilled technical labor."

"By that logic, we should start building more training institutions, not housing."

"And how well do you think someone learns when they're living in a tent, sharing restrooms with hundreds, and standing in line for hours to be fed?" Mister Tankersly turned to the president, pleading. "Mister President, please, we *must* provide better housing, *and* provide more job training for those people still trapped in the refugee camps. You *must* allocate a greater percentage of our fabrication infrastructure to *those* projects, and less to helping big industry."

"The idea has always been to rebuild our defensive capabilities first," President Scott reminded Mister Tankersly. "Doing that required rebuilding our industrial capacity, which the Jung bombed into the Stone Age eight years ago. We all knew it would be a challenge, and we all knew that it would mean many of our citizens would be spending years in the camps."

"Mister President..."

The president held up his hand, cutting Mister Tankersly off before he got carried away again. "However, perhaps eight years is enough. I'm not saying I'm willing to start building free houses and giving them away, as that would only serve to suppress the economic growth that we've all sacrificed so much to help grow. I *will*, however, suggest to the GFC that we refocus our global fabrication efforts to favor the improvement of living conditions in the camps, as well as getting people trained to fill those skilled positions you claim are vacant, Mister Tankersly. However, I warn you, the GFC is unlikely to commit the percentages *you* are recommending."

On the other side of the room, a red light began flashing beneath the large view screen on the wall opposite the president's desk. It was accompanied by an alert tone that demanded attention. Within seconds, the president's daughter and personal aide, Miri, and the president's security advisor both entered the room abruptly.

"Mister President," his security advisor began, dispensing with any of the customary pleasantries. "We'll need to clear the room."

"Gentlemen," the president said, standing and heading toward his desk. "If you'll excuse us."

The president continued to his desk as his guests departed. He took his seat behind it, and waited as his security advisor and his daughter came to stand behind and on either side of him. Once the door had closed, the view screen came to life, revealing Admiral Galiardi, sitting at his station in the Alliance Command Center deep inside Port Terra, in orbit high above the Earth.

"Admiral," the president greeted. He knew that the nature of the admiral's call did not require the usual pleasantries.

"*Mister President. The Aurora has detected a Jung battle group less than one light year beyond Sol's heliopause.*"

"How many ships are we talking about?"

"*Based on the number and size of their FTL trails, we estimate eight ships. Possibly two battleships or heavy cruisers, at least two light cruisers, with the rest being frigates, or large gunships. It is difficult to get exact readings as they are flying in surprisingly tight formations, especially considering they are traveling at FTL speeds. We believe they are doing so to conceal their numbers. The Aurora had to jump close-in behind them to differentiate and confirm multiple targets.*"

"Any theories as to how they have managed to get so deep into Alliance space *without* being detected?" the president asked accusingly, hinting at his displeasure.

"*There are only two logical explanations,*" the

admiral said. *"Either the Jung have developed some new type of stealth technology, or they have jump drives."*

"Any evidence to support one or the other?" the president asked.

"Frankly, Mister President, at this juncture, it is immaterial. Our priority at this point is to prevent this group from getting within striking distance of Earth which, if they are still using linear FTL, will be in approximately nineteen days."

"Recommendations?"

"First, we should put all our surface JKKV launchers on full alert. If they can get within a light year of us without being detected, they could already have ships in closer. Second, we need to move the Jar-Benakh and the Tanna to Sol. We need to send them, along with the Cape Town and the Aurora, to intercept the approaching battle group."

"That will leave Tau Ceti unprotected," the president pointed out.

"Both ships can jump back to Tau Ceti at a moment's notice," the admiral replied.

"Nevertheless, the Cetians will not like it."

"They'll like it a lot less if Alliance Command, and possibly Earth itself, are destroyed, because it's a pretty safe bet that if the Jung destroy us, Tau Ceti is next."

"And your intentions upon intercept?" the president inquired, already knowing the answer.

"Destroy them, sir. Without warning or mercy, after which I would recommend we launch a full KKV strike against all primary Jung worlds, including Nor-Patri."

"Muted," the president's security advisor said, as he pressed the remote. "Mister President, I agree that we should stop the incoming battle group. However, completely destroying them is not only unnecessary, but also sends a dangerous message to the Jung... as does a full KKV strike against their homeworld."

"The message it sends, is that we will not tolerate such blatant trespasses into our territories," the president replied with determination.

"Couldn't we send a warning message, first?" Miri suggested. "Cross this line, and all hell will break loose?"

"We already did, and they already crossed it," the president replied.

"Warning the battle group before firing on them will cause our ships to lose the element of surprise," the president's security advisor warned. "You'll be putting three of our biggest assets at unnecessary additional risk."

"Additional, maybe, but hardly unnecessary," Miri argued.

"At the very least, I would strongly advise *against* the KKV strike, sir. Especially against their homeworld. I don't have to remind you what happened the last time we did so."

President Scott shot a disdainful look at his advisor. "No, you do not."

"It is unlikely that this is a full strike on our system. If it were, they would be sending dozens of ships, including battle platforms."

"Then you still believe the Jung are testing us? Our detection capabilities? Our response patterns?"

"It's the only logical explanation."

"Logical? We have dozens of jump-enabled, kinetic kill vehicles, each of them capable of destroying an entire world, pointed at their worlds, and you think *testing* us is a logical act?" Miri couldn't believe what she was hearing. "How many ships have the Jung lost doing such testing? Do you really believe they would sacrifice so many men, just to *test* us?"

"Yes, I do," the president's security advisor replied without hesitation, and with complete conviction.

"Unmute," the president ordered. "Sorry for the delay, Admiral. Put our forces on alert. Move whatever ships you need into position. I will deal with the Cetians. However, I am *not* ready to authorize any KKV strikes at this time... Not yet. Also, I require that our forces warn the Jung battle group that if they do not stand down and surrender, not only will they be destroyed, we will also launch a full KKV strike on Nor-Patri, and the rest of the Jung primary worlds. Is that understood, Admiral?"

"*Mister President,*" the admiral began to object.

"Those are my orders, Admiral. Update me with any changes." The president nodded at his security advisor, who ended the call.

"That man is determined to get us back into a full-blown shooting war," the president's security advisor said.

"When you're a hammer, Mister Lovecchio," the president sighed.

* * *

Admiral Galiardi ripped off his comm-set and tossed it onto the table in frustration.

"He does realize the amount of risk he is asking those ships to take, doesn't he?" Commander Macklay wondered.

"He does," the admiral replied bitterly, his frustration obvious in his voice. "And if he doesn't, Lovecchio damn sure does." The admiral sighed. "I swear, that man is going to get us all killed. At the very least, he's going to cost us a few ships, ships that we can ill afford to lose."

"Then just send one to deliver the message," the commander suggested.

Admiral Galiardi looked at the commander.

"The president only told you to warn the Jung before firing on them. He didn't say to do it with *all* the ships."

* * *

Marcus and Neli bounced along the dirt road, a trail of dust wafting behind them. The old, open, flatbed hauler shook and rattled, sounding like it was about to fall apart at any moment.

"Are you sure this thing is gonna make it there and back?" Neli wondered nervously.

"These old haulers never die," Marcus insisted. "You just gotta take care of them."

"That's why I'm worried," Neli replied, as she bounced up and down in her seat. "This thing has been sitting for God *knows* how long."

"Her reactor's not even half used up, so we'll be fine. Besides, I know these things like the back of my hand. If something breaks, I can fix it."

Marcus swerved to miss a hole in the road, causing Neli to nearly fall out of the vehicle.

"I still don't know why we're wasting time driving into town!" she cried out, clinging desperately to the side of the open cab. "We've only left port a few hours ago. Does Connor really think anything will have changed since then?"

"Would you rather be helpin' them drag wreckage over to help hide the ship?" Marcus asked.

"We shouldn't be *hiding* her at all! We shouldn't even *be* here! Especially if the Jung are looking for us. We should be jumping toward the outer rim, and beyond."

Marcus shook his head. "The captain's right,

Neli. Jumping out into the unknown with limited resources is just asking for disaster."

"And staying here isn't?" Neli replied, frustrated. "Why the hell do you trust Connor so much?"

"Cuz it's his ship."

"Come on, Marcus. Haven't you ever wanted to just tell Tuplo to shove it, and take the Seiiki for yourself?"

Marcus shot a disapproving look Neli's way. "I'm gonna pretend you didn't say that."

"Oh, don't go all *loyal crewman* on me, Marcus. I know you've got a dishonorable streak in you. That's what I like about you."

"I'm not kidding, Neli."

"You're honestly going to sit there and tell me that the thought of mutiny has never crossed your mind? Not even once?"

"Never."

"Well, I don't believe you. Nobody's that stupid, *or* that loyal. One of these days, you're going to find yourself agreeing with me..."

Marcus slammed on the brakes, the vehicle screeched to a stop, nearly sending Neli face first into the dashboard.

"What the hell!" Neli exclaimed.

Marcus sat still, staring straight ahead. "You've got three choices, woman," he began in a low, menacing tone. "You can shut up, and never talk this way again; you can get out of the vehicle and never cross my path again..." Marcus turned to look at her. "Or I can burn you where you sit."

"What the hell is your problem?" Neli demanded, not taking his threat seriously.

"I ain't the one with the problem; you are. Choose."

"You can't be serious..."

"Crew is family, Neli. Either you're with us, or against us..."

"Marcus, baby," Neli cooed, "I'm only looking out for you..."

"I said choose," Marcus demanded, his right hand moving down toward his side arm. He looked her dead in the eyes. "I ain't askin' again."

Neli studied him a moment, wondering if he meant what he said. Finally she backed down. "I'm sorry, Marcus. I won't speak of it again."

"Promise?"

"I promise."

Marcus squinted, unsure if he could trust her. "I'm gonna hold you to that promise," he finally replied. "And I'll likely not give you the luxury of a warnin', should you go back on your word, Nel."

"I swear, you'll never have to, Marcus."

"The captain is a good man, you know."

"I know," Neli agreed, not wanting to escalate the situation any further.

"You just don't know him like Josh and I do."

"I suppose not," Neli replied. "Can we just pretend I never brought it up, Marcus?"

"I can pretend," he responded, as he started the vehicle moving again. "But I ain't forgettin'. Best you remember that."

* * *

Doran helped his wife out of the wine barrel, while he was still drenched in the foul-smelling, burgundy fluid.

"I look like a sun-dried garant," she said in despair, looking at her wrinkled, maroon hands.

"It will wash off, I promise you," Dumar's daughter said, as she helped the woman out of the barrel. "Although, it may take some effort, I'm afraid."

"Everyone! We have cabins ready for you all!" Rorik announced from the roadway behind the truck. "And hot showers, soap, scrub brushes... Oh, and dry clothing and hot food, as well. Please, if you'll all just follow me."

Dumar checked baby Ailsa, who was still asleep in her mother's arms. "She is still sleeping," he assured Lael. "She will be fine." Dumar closed his eyes a moment. It had pained him greatly to put the infant and her mother through such an ordeal. "I am sorry, but there was no other way."

"I know," Lael replied, almost too exhausted to speak. She placed her free hand on Dumar's arm to comfort the old man. "Better that she does not remember such horrors. I only wish I could have slept through it, as well."

"My daughter, Kyla, will help you," Dumar assured her. "She has babies of her own, and clean clothing for both you and your child." Dumar looked at the sleeping infant again. "What is her name?"

"Ailsa," Lael replied.

Dumar looked at the child for a moment, then turned to his daughter. "Kyla, help her."

Kyla moved closer and reached out for the baby. "Give her to me," she offered. "I will hold her for you, while you climb down."

Lael looked at Kyla, unsure if she could be trusted with the one thing that meant more to her than her own life. She then looked at Dumar, the man who had risked so much to smuggle them all out of Aitkenna. The old man nodded his encouragement, and Lael gave in, handing her baby to Kyla. "Thank you," she said, as she started to climb down from the back of the truck.

Doran embraced his wife as he helped her down

out of the back of the truck. "Go, get cleaned up," he whispered. "I will join you shortly." He looked beyond her, at their own, nearly grown children, who were already heading toward the cabins on the far side of the courtyard.

"Everyone, stay under the tree canopies at all times. It will keep you hidden from the surveillance satellites," Dumar instructed the group. Now that everyone was out of the barrels and on the ground, Dumar jumped down out of the back of the truck, joining Doran, Yanni, Michi, and Tori, who were all waiting for him.

"Travon, we must talk," Doran said.

"Yes, yes. All in due time," Dumar promised, gesturing toward the cabins. "But first, we must get you cleaned up. If the Jung were to show up unannounced, your coloring would likely raise suspicion."

"No, this cannot wait."

"What is it?" Dumar asked, noticing the determination on Doran's face.

"I could not risk communicating this over the public nets," Doran began, "not even in code. In all the chaos, we were forced to leave something behind. Something of immeasurable value... In the Ranni labs."

"What are you talking about?"

"Something of great importance, Travon. Something that could even change the course of humanity."

Travon was beginning to suspect that the ordeal was causing his old friend to overdramatize things a bit, but decided to humor him for the moment. "Sounds like something we should not let fall into Jung hands, then."

"That is an understatement."

"Then we shall find a way to destroy it, before the Jung learn of its existence," he assured him. "Do not worry, my friend." Dumar placed his hand on Doran's shoulder. "Now, let's get you cleaned up, and get some hot food into you."

"We cannot allow it to be destroyed," Doran insisted, pushing Travon's hand aside, irritated that the admiral was not taking him seriously. "Nor can we let it fall into Jung hands. We must go back for it."

"Doran," the admiral began, looking at him with sympathetic eyes. "Sooner or later, you're going to have to tell me what this *something* is."

Doran looked at the ground for a moment, then at doctors Sato and Megel. "Is it not enough that *I* am telling you that it is important?"

"Normally, yes. But these are abnormal times, Doran."

Doran again looked at the ground, as if he were ashamed to look the admiral in the eyes. "I would be putting your life at great risk, Travon."

"More risk than smuggling you out of an enemy-held city, only a day after its capture?" Travon wondered.

Doran looked at Michi and Tori again.

Travon exchanged a glance with Yanni, who looked as confused as he did.

"Don't look at me," Yanni replied. "I don't know what the hell they're talking about. I was in data technology. They're in bio-med."

"He will learn the truth, sooner or later," Doctor Megel said.

"We were conducting a research project," Doctor Sato blurted out.

"Michi," Doctor Megel scolded.

"He deserves to be told the truth, Tori." She looked at Doran.

"What *kind* of project?" Travon asked, becoming curious.

"Cloning," Michi replied.

Travon raised his brow suspiciously. "Cloning is not permitted by Corinairan law. In fact, most Corinairans, if not all, consider it immoral."

"We are not Corinairan," Michi replied.

"I see." Dumar thought for a moment. Then it hit him. "You two are from Nifelm, aren't you?"

"We are," Michi replied.

A terrible thought crossed Travon's mind. "And what, exactly, were you cloning?"

"Not what," Doran corrected, "whom."

"*Whom*, then?" Travon inquired, growing impatient, while at the same time, fearing the answer. At first, no one spoke up. Instead Michi, Tori, and Doran all looked at each other.

Finally, Doran answered. "Nathan Scott."

Travon took a step backwards in shock. "My God..." The implications of their actions hit him, causing him to nearly stumble. He leaned against the back of the truck, needing something to steady himself. "Do you realize the risk you are taking?"

"Admiral..." Doran pleaded.

"And you, Doran. You violated a direct order..."

"I did not," Doran argued. "I was never given such an order. Not by you, or anyone else."

"Don't give me that crap," Travon said. "You knew damn well... If the Jung discover that Nathan is alive..."

"We could not let him die, Travon..."

"He *knew* what he was doing when he sacrificed

himself, Doran! We all knew! He knew, and he was *willing...*" Travon turned away in anger. "Damn it!" He spun back around, as a realization hit him. "It was Nash, wasn't it? That brash young woman! And no doubt Telles had a hand in it. Ghatazhak logic, my ass!"

"Nathan was set up, Travon! When you gave him that mission, you knew *damn* well that he would likely not return! That *all* of them would likely not return!"

"I had no way of knowing..."

"Is that what you tell yourself?" Doran replied, cutting Travon off mid-sentence. "Is that how you sleep at night? Bacca walked him right into a trap, and you saw it coming! At the very least, you suspected it! That's why you went to see Captain Scott the night before! Look me in the eye and tell me I'm wrong!"

"It was not my call!" Travon shouted at the top of his lungs, pain in his voice as he recalled the memories that had been buried so deeply in his mind for more than seven years. "It was his, and his alone!" Travon turned away again for a moment, in obvious anguish, then turned back to look at Doran. "Don't you see? Nathan suspected that it was a trap as well, but he *knew* he had to go. He *knew* it was his destiny to save the Earth...to save us all."

Doran moved a step closer to his old friend, and commander, putting his hand on the admiral's shoulder. "That's why we did it, Travon. Because it *is* his destiny to save us all."

Travon laughed mockingly. "If you start calling him Na-Tan again, I swear..."

"Na-Tan, destiny, fate... Call him whatever you like," Doran said. "You knew it *then*, and you *know* it now." Doran shook his head. "None of us would be alive were it not for him. This very world we stand on... It would be no more than a scorched, lifeless rock, were it not for him. We could not leave him behind, just as *he* would not leave us. Not then, not now...not ever."

Dumar sighed. "We will likely die trying to save him, Doran."

"I am willing to take that chance, as are the others. The question is, are you?"

Dumar looked at Doran and the others, then gazed off into the distance beyond them. The forest, the lake, and the mountains beyond. He had known war, pain, and suffering for more than two hundred years. But for the last five of those years, he had known peace, which was something he had never expected to experience in his lifetime. And now, it was all about to end.

"Is this clone even alive?" Travon wondered, looking for an excuse to drop the plan.

"The body is fully matured, and ready to receive Captain Scott's consciousness *and* memories."

"You can do that?" Travon questioned, finding it difficult to believe. "Just flip a switch, and bring him back to life?"

"In a manner of speaking, yes," Doctor Megel replied.

"And that will work? We will have Nathan back?"

"We *believe* that *this* time, it will."

"This time?" Travon looked at Doran.

Doran took a deep breath and sighed. "It is...... complicated."

* * *

The combat jump shuttle swooped in low over the Lawrence Spaceport, coming to a hover on the apron in front of the Ghatazhak facility on the far side of the field. As it descended the last few meters to the surface, its side door slid open, and Jessica jumped the last meter to the ground, unwilling to wait for the ship to land.

Jessica jogged across the tarmac toward the office at the far end of the hangar, and burst through the doors. "When were you going to tell us?" she demanded, heading straight for Deliza.

Deliza's eyes popped open at the sight of Jessica, walking toward her with anger in her eyes. "I was afraid that..."

"When!"

"I only wanted to..."

"I could have told you as well, Jess," Loki interrupted, stepping between Jessica and Deliza. "But I didn't... And for the same reasons. My wife and daughter are on that planet, as well."

Jessica looked at Loki with the same anger, despite the fact that she had a much deeper bond with him than with Deliza. She had once died on his lap, in his arms, staring desperately into his eyes as the air had left her lungs. "We're talking about *Nathan*, Loki. *Nathan!*"

"I know..."

"He sacrificed *everything*, so that we could live. You, your wife, your baby... Hell, your whole fucking world! And this is how you repay him?"

"It's my fault, Jessica!" Deliza insisted, not wanting Loki to take the blame. "I told him not to say anything. He wanted to tell you, but I made him promise not to. I begged him to wait, and to let me tell you...when the time was right."

"And when was that going to be?" Jessica demanded.

"After we got them back safely," Deliza replied, ashamed.

"What made you think we couldn't do both?" General Telles inquired.

"I was afraid you would put Nathan first," Deliza admitted. "I knew that recovering his clone, and all the equipment needed to care for it, would be much more complicated, and that it would delay any rescue. I couldn't take that chance."

General Telles tipped his head in acknowledgment. "A logical assumption."

"Oh, shut up," Jessica snapped, scowling.

Telles pointed at himself. "General," then gestured to Jessica, "lieutenant. Try to remember that. And while you're at it, try to calm down and think clearly. Remember your training."

Jessica turned away as she wrestled to keep her emotions under control.

"Training?" Loki asked the general in a hushed voice.

"She joined the Ghatazhak four years ago," General Telles explained. "She has been in training ever since."

"Really? How's she doing?"

"There is still room for improvement," the general replied politely.

Jessica glared at them both.

"*Much* room," the general added.

Jessica turned to Deliza, still angry, but now trying to get it under control. "You were supposed to move him off-world, to someplace safe."

"We didn't have the funds," Deliza explained. "Do you know how much it costs to run that lab...even *on* Corinair? It would cost ten times as much if we moved off-world."

"More like a hundred times," Loki corrected.

Deliza looked at him.

"I saw my wife's estimates when she was crunching the numbers for you," he admitted.

"I trusted you, Deliza."

"I know, and I failed you."

"We could have helped."

"Jess, they are *so* close. Michi and Tori, they really think this one is the one. Had we moved him off-world, they would have been set back years."

"During which time, the Jung would likely expand their hold in the Pentaurus sector, and he would still be at risk of discovery," General Telles pointed out. "So, her failure to move him off-world *may* turn out to be what saves him."

Jessica turned and looked at her friend. By accepting her into the Ghatazhak, General Lucius Telles had saved her from her own self-destructive behavior, and given her a new lease on life. He had been her friend, and mentor, for the last seven years, and her commanding officer for the last four of those years. The only other man she trusted as much as him had died seven years ago, in front of her very eyes. And now, his clone, his only chance at resurrection, was trapped beneath the surface of a city overrun by the very enemy he had died trying to protect them from.

But how?

"How are we going to get him out of there?" Jessica asked the general, her anger turning to despair.

"It will not be easy," General Telles admitted, "but there is a way."

Jessica realized what the general was getting at. "You think..."

"Perhaps, it is finally time."

CHAPTER TEN

President Scott stood at his office window, staring out at the lights of Winnipeg, the North American Union's capital, and the Unified Nations of Earth, which President Scott also ruled over. Behind him, technicians scrambled to prepare for an unscheduled presidential announcement, one that he dreaded making.

As he gazed out the window at the sparkling lights of the city, he thought back to his childhood. Evenings spent sitting on his father's knee, staring out a similar window, in a similar office, over a similar city. It had been so long ago... Nearly eight decades now. His father had often spoken about how rapidly things had changed since the discovery of the Data Ark. How the people of Earth, after eight centuries of struggling to repopulate and rebuild following the interstellar devastation of the bio-digital plague, had gone from propeller-driven aircraft to faster-than-light starships, in only a century.

Wouldn't his father be surprised? Now, after only a decade, they had gone beyond FTL ships, and could now instantaneously jump vast distances. The Data Ark had opened up the newly reborn Earth to advanced technologies, and those technologies had opened up the galaxy to them.

Unfortunately, the cost of such advances had been great, almost more than what his world, and the core worlds of Earth, could stand. Had it not been for the sacrifice of his youngest child, who had surrendered himself to their enemy in exchange for the very cease-fire that was now being broken, most likely their fledgling alliance would not have survived the last seven years.

But now the Jung had broken their agreement, and Dayton Scott wanted nothing more than to avenge the loss of his eldest son, Eli, the loss of his wife, Marlene, and especially that of his youngest son, Nathan. It had stayed in the back of his mind for the last seven years, but he had been forced to suppress that feeling, for the good of his people... his world... For all the worlds of the Alliance. Even now, he wanted nothing more than to authorize the KKV strike that Admiral Galiardi had strongly recommended, but he could not. He would not be the one to escalate the tensions between them. If the Jung wanted a war, the Alliance would give it to them, and in ways the Jung could not imagine. But they needed time. It was *always* about *time*.

Gray armored vehicles emblazoned with the markings of Alliance Marines left their staging positions and began to roll through the streets of Winnipeg, their lights flashing. One by one, they turned onto Embassy Row, and accelerated quickly toward the Jung embassy at the far end of the boulevard.

"We're ready for you, Mister President," the broadcast director said.

President Scott turned and walked back across the office, stepping behind the podium placed in front of the logos of both the NAU and the UNE. He watched his daughter, Miri, who had remained at his side since the death of her mother, despite the needs of her own two children. Without her, he did not know how he would've led the Earth out of the ashes of the Jung occupation which had nearly destroyed their world eight years ago.

"Teams are in place outside the Jung embassy," the president's security advisor informed him. "They will go on the cue line in your speech."

The president nodded his understanding.

"Five seconds, Mister President," the director informed him.

———————

"If anyone beyond the embassy gates raises a weapon, you are to cut him down," Sergeant Major Saladan instructed the troops in the back of the first armored vehicle. "We will tolerate no resistance. If you are not sure, you fire. Is that understood?"

"Aye, sir!" the troops answered in unison.

"*One minute,*" the controller's voice announced over the sergeant major's helmet comms.

"Weapons hot!" the sergeant major ordered.

"Is it true, Biorgi?" the sergeant next to him asked. "Are we going to war?"

———————

The president stared straight ahead at the camera, waiting until the status light turned green. "People of Earth. It is with great sadness that I speak to you tonight. One hour ago, a comm-drone arrived from the Pentaurus cluster, carrying a fateful message. The Jung Empire has invaded the worlds of the Pentaurus cluster. Defenses of both the Takaran and Darvano systems have been destroyed, and the Jung now control the entire cluster. Twelve systems, two of which were still members of the Sol-Pentaurus Alliance, a total of twenty-three inhabited worlds, are now controlled by the Jung. Even worse, the Jung forces that captured those systems did so using jump-drive technology. We do not know how the Jung acquired this technology, but such acquisition represents a dire threat to both freedom, and to humanity itself."

The armored vehicles pulled to a stop outside the Jung embassy. Two at the front gates, two at each side gate, and two at the back gates. Squads of twelve deftly jumped out of the vehicles as they rolled to a stop. Alliance marines clad in light gray combat armor and armed with heavy energy weapons, dispersed in perfect order and took up firing positions as planned.

"This is a threat that cannot be ignored, and ignore it, we shall not. We shall meet force with force, in every way at our disposal. We will visit such destruction upon the Jung Empire that they will beg us, not for a cease-fire, but for unconditional surrender. Only then shall we cease hostilities. Only then shall we show mercy. Only then...shall we have lasting peace."

Lights all around the Jung embassy compound snapped on, illuminating the perimeter. At the same time, in the embassy itself, as well as within its walls, all the lights went dark. Jung security personnel, dressed in black combat armor trimmed with red piping, armed with their own heavy energy weapons, deployed to predetermined defensive positions about the compound, gates, and walls of their embassy.

"As of this moment, we are once again in a state of war with the Jung Empire. As I speak to you this night, a Jung battle group hurtles toward us. Our ships are positioned to intercept the enemy, and intercept them they shall. They shall destroy them without mercy, and the same fate shall meet any and all ships that enter Alliance space. We will send a warning to the Jung, demanding the immediate withdrawal of all their forces currently in Alliance space, whether they are in the Sol or the Pentaurus sectors. Should the Jung Empire fail to heed our warning, we shall annihilate all of their forces, wherever they may be, inside or outside Alliance space. If necessary, we will rain death upon their worlds, and upon their people. They shall know the same horrors they have inflicted upon us, and upon the worlds of our allies."

"Jung forces! You are hereby ordered, by the President of the North American Union and the Unified Nations of Earth, to surrender yourselves peacefully," Sergeant Major Saladan announced over the link between his helmet comms, and the loudspeakers on the armored vehicles. "If you fail to do so, you shall be met with deadly force! You have one minute to comply!"

"It brings us no joy to order our forces to attack. It brings us no joy to bring death and destruction onto the Jung people. The only solace we will find is when the Jung finally realize once and for all, that humanity will not be subjugated by them, or any other aggressor." The president looked into the camera for a long moment. "Good night, and good luck to us all."

A single flash of bright red light, followed by a bolt of red plasma energy, slammed into the armor of one of the Alliance vehicles and started the exchange. Immediately, the streets lit up with the reds and oranges of energy weapons fire from both sides, as the Jung defended their only sovereign territory on the planet. Seconds after it started, jump ships flashed in the night sky directly overhead, after which blazes of white light appeared within the walls of the embassy compound. The exchange of weapons fire suddenly became one-sided. Four Alliance marines, two on each side, a shooter, and a demolitions tech, ran up to either side of the main gate, quickly placing their charges and then retreating to cover. A moment later, the charges blew. Another jump flash, followed by several more detonation flashes inside the embassy compound followed, after which the marines outside the embassy walls charged in through the now-open gates. More weapons fire followed, mostly from Alliance weapons.

Minutes after it had begun, the first ground conflict of the war ended.

* * *

Captain Tuplo poked his way through the dusty, bug-infested workshop at the back end of the sinkhole compound. Of all the buildings dug into the sides of the sinkhole walls, this one was by far the largest. Its doors had been deceptively small, as was its external exposure. It seemed as if the builders had sought to fool anyone looking upon it from the outside as to its true internal dimensions. For what reason, Connor could not determine. He suspected that it had been some sort of machine, or equipment repair bay, given the many parts lying about, some of which seemed familiar.

Another thing he had noticed was that the entire wall was actually a door, designed to slide into a slot carved out of the wall of the sinkhole. The result would be a bay large enough to house anything from a small shuttle to a standard Takaran fighter, perhaps even a bit larger. He wondered what had once been housed in here, and what had happened to it, whatever it had been.

Neli's original assessment had been more correct than he imagined. He had already found several bodies, long decayed over the years, and mostly eaten by the small animals and insects native to Haven. But there had been enough left of their uniforms to recognize. They were of the old Ta'Akar Empire, more specifically, the regime of Caius Ta'Akar, the son of a great king who had risen to power by assassinating both his father and older brother. He had been defeated by the Karuzari, along with the help of the mythical Na-Tan that Josh so often liked to boast about having served under.

Connor did not believe in legends. Perhaps, if his memories of his life before the crash had been intact, he might feel otherwise. But being forced to live with only the memories of what had occurred since waking up in that hospital on Corinair, five years ago, had forced him to become a realist. *Or had it?* He really didn't know; he could've been a realist before the crash as well.

"Cap'n!" Josh called from the partially opened door. "You in here?"

"Yeah! Back here!" the captain replied, as he sifted through the dusty, old parts lying on the workbench.

Josh walked over to the captain.

"What was this building used for?"

"It had a Falcon in it," Josh replied, a hint of pride in his voice.

"A what?"

"Oh, jeez, I can't even remember the real name for it. F something. An old Takaran deep-space FTL interceptor. The guy who lived here once flew them in the Palee militia. Him and his daughter fixed it up together. My friend Loki and I flew it for a number of years, from the deck of the Aurora."

"Under Na-Tan, I suppose?" the captain said dryly.

"Captain Scott, yeah. He was a great man. A natural leader, someone you didn't want to let down. You're a lot like him, you know."

"Me?" Connor laughed. "Doubtful."

"No, seriously. You kept your cool pretty well outside of Rama. And during that stand-off with Siggy? Actually, we've been in a few scraps over the years together, Cap'n. You always seemed to handle them just fine."

"None of those were anything like what you guys went through back then," Connor said dismissively. "And I am *nothing* like Captain Scott. And I'm certainly no legend."

"Captain Scott didn't think he was a legend either," Josh said. He looked around at the empty building. "You know, I rescued Captain Scott and the others from this place. Me and Loki, in a fucking harvester, no less. Swooped down and picked them up, in the middle of a battle. Even took a sniper's head off by flyin' low and ramming him. It was ugly."

"I imagine so," Connor replied. He never knew exactly how much to believe of what Josh told him. He knew that the young pilot had indeed flown in combat in both the liberation of Takara, and back against the Jung in the Sol sector. However, some of his tales seemed a bit unrealistic to him. Some seemed downright impossible. One thing was for sure, though, the young man had a natural knack for flying, and Connor envied him for it.

"That's how I know about this place. The guy who owned it is dead now."

"Who was he?"

Josh laughed. "You wouldn't believe me if I told you. His daughter is still alive, and still holds the deed on this place, such as it is." Josh looked around again. "Yup, this is pretty much where Captain Scott's role as Na-Tan started. So, you might say that *I* was the savior of a savior."

Connor looked at Josh with one eyebrow raised. "Seriously?"

"Just a play on words, Cap'n."

"Josh, you don't *really* believe Captain Scott was Na-Tan, do you?"

"Well, like I said, I know *he* didn't believe so," Josh said. "As for me, I suppose I don't rightly know." Josh smiled. "Maybe someday I'll find out, one way or another."

Connor watched Josh walk away, perplexed by his words. Finally, a chuckle came out of him. "Na-Tan," he laughed, tossing the part in his hand back on the workbench. "Takes all kinds, I guess."

* * *

"All spreaders are away," Lieutenant Commander Vidmar reported from the Aurora's tactical station. "Thirty seconds until they reach their jump points."

"Very well," Cameron replied from her command chair.

"Jump to intercept point, plotted and ready," her navigator announced.

"Jump flashes," Lieutenant Commander Kono reported from the sensor station. "Two comm-drones, to port and starboard."

"Incoming messages," Ensign deBanco reported from the comm station. "The Jar-Benakh and the

299

Tanna both report that they are in position and ready to attack on your order, Captain, as is the Cape Town, directly astern."

"Very well," Cameron replied.

"Spreaders are jumping," the tactical officer reported.

Cameron watched the semi-spherical main view screen, as twenty small flashes of blue-white light appeared simultaneously, directly ahead of them. By the time the light from those flashes had reached them, the missiles had already come out of their jump and were spreading their payloads of anti-FTL mines in precise patterns across the path of the incoming Jung battle group. Once detonated, their energy would destabilize the mass-canceling fields that enabled the enemy ships to travel faster than light. They would become targets, and remain that way for several minutes, until they could reinitialize their emitters and escape into FTL again.

Those few minutes would be more than enough time for the Aurora and the rest of her battle group to destroy the trespassers. However, the fact that they were required to issue a warning, *and* give the enemy one full minute to show signs of compliance with that warning, meant they would have half that time. It would be close.

"Twenty seconds to detonation," Lieutenant Commander Vidmar reported.

"Stand by for intercept jump," Cameron ordered.

Luckily, the enemy battle group was still nineteen days away from being able to launch an attack on Earth. If they were unable to destroy all the ships this time, they would have a chance in the next attack. Although the Aurora's supply of jump missiles was still limited until she could rendezvous with the supply ship, both the Jar-Benakh and the Cape Town were fully stocked. Between them, they had enough anti-FTL mines to knock ten battle groups out of FTL.

Cameron only hoped they would not be needed.

"Anti-FTL mines should be detonating...... Now," the tactical officer announced.

Cameron glanced at the mission time display. She needed to give the anti-FTL mines enough time to do their job before jumping to the intercept point, or the energy from those countless antimatter detonations would severely disrupt the Aurora's targeting systems. When she jumped her ship into the path of the incoming battle group, she wanted to have immediate target locks on every enemy ship.

She glanced at the time again. In a few seconds, she would either be ending a war before it began, or committing the Alliance to an all-out war against the Jung, a war that would likely cost billions of lives. At times like this, she wondered why she ever wanted to be the captain of a warship.

Another glance at the time display. "Jump us to the intercept point, Mister Bickle," she ordered calmly.

"Jumping to intercept point in three......two...... one......jumping."

The blue-white jump flash washed over the bridge, momentarily canceling out the red trim lighting that reminded the Aurora's crew that they were at general quarters.

"Jump complete."

"Multiple contacts," Lieutenant Commander Kono reported. "Four of them!"

"What?" Cameron replied, her head snapping to the left.

"I only have four contacts!" the lieutenant commander repeated. "One battleship, and three frigates!"

"Broadcast the warning message, fully translated, and on all known frequencies," Cameron ordered. "Prepare to launch multiple jump comm-drones. Notify command that we have four ships unaccounted for!"

"Targets are firing missiles!" the sensor officer warned.

"Did you send the warning message?" Cameron snapped.

"Twenty-eight missiles inbound! Thirty seconds to impact!"

"Yes, sir!" Ensign deBanco replied. "But it didn't even have time to reach them yet!"

"Point-defenses activated," the tactical officer reported. "Targeting the incoming missiles."

"Lieutenant! One by one! Left to right, high to low!" Cameron instructed. "Tactical! Fire as she puts our tubes on the targets. Full power triplets on all tubes!"

"Coming onto first target now!" Lieutenant Dinev reported from the helm.

"Firing on all tubes! Full power triplets!"

"Get those comm-drones launched! I want the other ships warned as well!" Cameron directed as the bridge filled with the red-orange light of her departing plasma torpedoes. "They need to be on the lookout for those other four ships!"

"Adjusting course to next target," the helmsman announced.

"First drone is on its way to command!" the comm officer assured his captain. "Three more are being launched now!"

"Direct hits on frigate one!" Lieutenant Commander Kono reported. "Her forward shields are gone! She's turning away!"

Cameron glanced at the tactical display on the auxiliary display screen to the left of her navigator, taking note of the direction to which the first frigate was fleeing. "Get our port plasma turrets on that target, Lieutenant Commander, before she gets her good shields to us."

"Already on it," the tactical officer replied.

"Tubes on target two, another frigate!" Lieutenant Dinev reported.

"Firing all tubes!" the tactical officer announced. "Port plasma turrets are locked on the first frigate and are firing!"

"The battleship is targeting us with her big guns!" Lieutenant Commander Kono warned.

"Put a round of jump missiles on that battleship, Mister Vidmar," Cameron ordered as the bridge continued to flash with the red-orange light of her plasma weapons. "Nukes across the board. Let's give her something to think about."

"Loading jump nukes, aye!"

"First wave of enemy missiles has been destroyed!" Lieutenant Commander Kono reported.

"All comm-drones are away!"

"Changing course to the third frigate," the helmsman reported.

"Frigate one has taken more hits!" Lieutenant Commander Kono said from the sensor station. "She's lost all shields!"

"Keep pounding her," Cameron urged.

"Aye, sir!"

"Tubes on the third target!"

"Firing all tubes!" the tactical officer reported.

"Launching jump missiles!"

Cameron caught the view of her jump missiles streaking ahead of them and disappearing in flashes of blue-white light.

"Missiles away!"

"We're down to five kilometers, and closing fast," Ensign Bickle warned.

"Noted," Cameron replied.

"Missile impacts!" Lieutenant Commander Kono reported. "Direct hits on the battleship's forward shields. They're down fifty percent! And frigate one is coming apart! Frigate two is diving! She's trying to get below us!"

"Ventral guns on frigate two!"

"Ventral guns, aye!" the tactical officer replied. "Torpedo locks on the third frigate! Firing all tubes!"

"Four kilometers!" the navigator warned, as the bridge filled with red-orange flashes again.

"Helm! Get our tubes on that battleship," Cameron ordered, "and be ready to pitch down."

"Turning into the battleship now," Lieutenant Dinev replied.

"Escape jump is ready," Ensign Bickle added. "Three kilometers."

The Aurora's shields flashed repeatedly, as explosive rounds from the battleship's massive rail guns slammed into them.

"Taking heavy fire on our forward shields!" the sensor officer reported.

"Forward shield strength is dropping," the tactical officer warned. "Down to eighty percent!"

"Tubes are coming onto the battleship now!" the helmsman announced.

"Frigate two is spinning up her mass-canceling fields!" the sensor officer warned. "She's preparing to go to FTL!"

"All tubes locked onto the battleship!" Lieutenant Commander Vidmar reported from the tactical station. "Firing on all tubes!"

"Two kilometers!" the navigator warned, his voice tensing as the distance shrank between their ship and the approaching battleship.

"One spreader! Out the tube, no jump!" Cameron instructed. "Have her spit her load as soon as she clears our bow!"

The bridge flashed red-orange repeatedly, as twenty-four plasma torpedoes left the Aurora's tubes, streaking toward the onrushing battleship.

"Launching a spreader!"

"Launch another comm-drone; to the Cape Town! Tell her to jump in and target the battleship with everything she's got! Come out of her jump firing!"

"One kilometer!"

"Direct hits!" Lieutenant Commander Kono reported. "Her forward shields are down to twenty percent!"

"Spreader is away!" the tactical officer shouted. "She's clear of the bow, deploying antimatter mines!"

"Comm-drone away!" the comm officer announced.

"Pitch us down now!" Cameron ordered.

"Frigate two has gone to FTL!"

"Pitching down, aye!"

"Mines are out!" the tactical officer announced.

"Frigate three is also spinning up for FTL!"

"Clear jump line!" the navigator reported.

"Detonate the mines!" Cameron ordered. "Execute escape jump on my mark!"

"Detonating mines!"

"Jump!"

The blue-white jump flash lit up the interior of

the Aurora's bridge, as she slipped away, jumping to safety a full light minute behind the enemy battleship. A sudden calm came over the bridge now that they were momentarily out of harm's way.

"Bring us hard about, and prepare to jump back to the targets," Cameron instructed.

"Coming about, aye," Lieutenant Dinev acknowledged.

"I don't remember *that* little trick in the tactical manual," Lieutenant Commander Vidmar commented.

Cameron smiled, remembering the last time the Aurora had jumped away from an antimatter explosion. It was on the Aurora's second jump ever, and Cameron had been a young ensign fresh out of the academy, serving as the ship's navigator. The energy from the antimatter explosion had thrown them nearly a thousand light years, and put them in the middle of a battle between peoples they hadn't even known existed. It was a turning point in the history of humanity, one that had led to the very Alliance in which they now served.

"Turn complete," Lieutenant Dinev reported.

"Prepare a jump," Cameron began. "Put us astern of the targets, five up, five out, and five behind."

"Five by five by five, aye," the navigator replied.

"Be ready on all weapons," Cameron instructed. "And have another spread of jump missiles ready with nukes, just in case."

"Aye, sir," the tactical officer replied.

Cameron turned toward her sensor officer. "You didn't happen to pick up any trace of those other four ships during all that, did you?"

"No, sir, sorry."

"Jump plotted and ready," the navigator reported.

"All weapons ready, and jump nukes loaded," Lieutenant Commander Vidmar added.

"Execute your jump," Cameron ordered.

"Jumping in three......two......one......jumping."

The jump flash washed over the bridge.

"Jump complete."

Cameron looked toward her sensor officer again.

"No targets!" Lieutenant Commander Kono reported. "Just a lot of debris...and the Cape Town!"

"With a big smile on her face, no doubt," Cameron said.

"Incoming message from the Cape Town, Captain," Ensign deBanco reported from the comm station. "The battleship has been destroyed. And the second frigate. The third frigate escaped into FTL. Also, command reports new contacts on the opposite side of the Sol system. The Jar-Benakh and the Tanna are moving to intercept."

"Are we to join them?" Cameron wondered.

"No, sir," the ensign replied. "We're ordered to locate and destroy frigate three. The Cape Town is being ordered back to Earth for now."

"Very well," Cameron replied. "Stand down from general quarters. Lieutenant Commander Kono, plot that frigate's course based on her last course and speed."

"She was maneuvering when we jumped away, sir," the lieutenant commander warned her.

"Give it your best guess, Lieutenant Commander," Cameron replied. "We've got to start somewhere."

* * *

"*Mister President, with all due respect, we have multiple sightings all around the outer boundaries of our system. If this is not a clear act of aggression from the Jung, then please, tell me what is?*"

Admiral Galiardi begged from the view screen in the President's office.

"You're talking about a strike against *civilian* populations, Admiral," President Scott reminded him. "You don't think that has the potential to escalate the situation even further?"

"*Mister President,*" the admiral began calmly, "*the Jung have invaded the Pentaurus cluster, one of our allies, and using jump technology, no less. Possession of jump technology explains why we were unable to detect them before they penetrated so deeply into our territory. If they do possess jump technology, then they could appear anywhere, at any moment. Outside our system, or deep within it. If they were to suddenly appear in orbit over the Earth, they could unleash enough ordnance to destroy all life on the surface before we would be able to stop them, as our defenses are primarily designed to attack targets that are much further away.*"

"But if the Jung have jump drive technology, why are they running around this sector using traditional, linear FTL systems?" Mister Lovecchio, the president's security advisor, challenged.

"*I believe the Jung did not expect us to become aware of their invasion of the Pentaurus cluster so quickly,*" Admiral Galiardi explained. "*According to the data sent by General Telles, the Jung's capture of the Pentaurus cluster was swift and sure. Had it not been for the Ranni jump comm-drone, we would still be unaware of the situation in the cluster, and that the Jung possessed jump drive technology. They are using linear FTL in our presence, but are using jump drives to penetrate deep into our territory.*"

"That's ludicrous!" Mister Lovecchio protested. "That would mean they purposefully sacrificed their ships and crews, when use of their jump drives during battle would have prevented it! Besides, why wouldn't they just jump all their ships in and strike?"

"*Because they are testing us,*" the admiral responded. "*They are calling our bluff!*"

"But we aren't bluffing," President Scott reminded the admiral. "We have the super JKKVs, and we can fire them at any time."

"*The Jung obviously have reason to believe otherwise,*" the admiral argued. "*Otherwise, I doubt they would be engaging us in such a way.*"

"And you believe that we need to show them that we are *not* bluffing," the president surmised.

"*Precisely.*"

"Isn't it also possible that the Jung are just trying to keep us busy so that we won't send ships to the Pentaurus sector?" Mister Lovecchio postulated.

"*That is a possibility as well,*" the admiral agreed. "*However, the two are not mutually exclusive. Either way, the Jung need to be sent a message...and a strong one. We must launch a KKV strike, and we must launch it now, before this progresses any further.*"

President Scott sighed. "Admiral, I'm not convinced that such a strike will have the desired effect. If the Jung have jump drive technology, then there is nothing to stop the ships that are already so equipped, from immediately jumping to Sol to attack. I fear that launching such a strike *may* precipitate just such a reaction."

"*And that is exactly what the Jung would expect you to fear,*" the admiral replied. "*That is why they are testing us. If you do not retaliate in the very way that they most fear, they will continue to escalate testing our resolve. As of yet, we have not lost any ships or men. I do not know if that is due to our defensive abilities, or by Jung design, although, if they have jump drive technology, then I strongly suspect the latter. What I do know is that if we do not strike, they will continue their attacks, and those attacks will become more severe. Men will die. Ships will be lost. Ships we cannot afford to lose. And in the end, we will still have to launch a full strike. The only difference will be that the strike will be too late, and its purpose will be vengeance rather than protection, as by then, there may not be anything left to protect."*

President Scott sighed again. At eighty years old, he was still healthier than most men his age, but the burdens he had carried for the last nine years were taking their toll. For the first time in his life, he was ready to throw up his hands and walk away.

He looked at his security advisor. "Mister Lovecchio?"

Mister Lovecchio also sighed. "The admiral makes logical arguments, Mister President. I'm afraid that either way, we are once again looking at destruction on a massive scale. The question is, whose shall it be? Theirs or ours?"

The president leaned back in his chair, looking up at the ceiling as he took in a long breath, then let it out slowly. "I cannot in good conscience kill billions of innocent people just to demonstrate our resolve. I shall, however, authorize an immediate strike against all high-value Jung military assets."

"Mister President, we must also strike the infrastructure that supports those assets, or..."

"Let us first see how the Jung react to our first strike," the president said, cutting the admiral off. "If, as you suspect, the Jung do not believe we are willing and able to conduct such strikes, then this first strike should be enough to convince them otherwise. If it doesn't, then we will strike their infrastructure."

"And if that is not enough?" Mister Lovecchio wondered.

"Then God have mercy on their populations," the president said, "for they will be the only asset left to target."

* * *

"Incoming flash traffic," the communications officer announced.

Commander Tusel pressed the button on the overhead intercom. "Captain to the bridge," he called calmly. "Threat board?" he asked, after removing his finger from the intercom button.

"Threat board is clear!" the ship's tactical officer replied from the far side of the cramped compartment.

"Mister Baskin, how long until our next launch cycle?"

"Four hours, twenty-eight minutes, sir."

The communications officer handed the message pad to the commander.

"You triple authenticated this message?" the commander asked, looking at the young ensign.

The ensign's eyes were wide, and his face was pale. "Yes, sir. Triple authenticated, did it a fourth time, in fact. The message is valid, sir."

The XO looked at the young ensign. "It's okay to be scared, son. This is scary shit," he added, holding up the message pad.

"*Captain on the bridge!*"

The captain stepped up to the commander and the communications officer. "What's up, Commander?"

"Flash traffic, Captain," the commander replied, handing the message pad to the captain. "Fully authenticated."

The captain looked at the message, then at the frightened young ensign. "Take it easy, Mister Kyle. It's not the end of *our* world. It's the end of *theirs*." The captain handed the message pad back to the ensign, and looked at his XO. "Let's do what we're paid for, Commander."

"Yes, sir," the commander replied. "Mister Dormand, sound general quarters."

"General quarters, aye!"

The commander pressed the button on the overhead intercom again. "Weapons, Bridge, spin up all super JKKVs and prepare to receive targeting packages. This is not a drill." He turned to the captain. "Captain, please insert your launch card."

Captain Anderson pulled the small plastic card out of his shirt pocket and inserted it into the slot on the red box on the port bulkhead. "Commander, please insert your launch card."

Commander Tusel pulled his own launch card out, inserting it in the slot below the captain's card.

"*Bridge, Weapons. Launch cards verified. Loading targeting packages. SJKKVs will be ready to launch in five minutes.*"

"God help whoever those things are about to hit," the commander said under his breath.

"Well, at least it will be over for them quickly," the captain replied.

* * *

"I'm telling you, Cap'n, nothin' is movin'," Marcus insisted. "The Jung have the entire cluster locked down now. Not even the linear FTL ships are willing to take runs. Even worse, no one is *askin'*. No one wants to risk losing their cargo, and no passengers wanna risk being detained by the Jung. Everyone is layin' low, waitin' to see what happens next."

"But surely there are runs available *outside* the cluster?" Dalen suggested. "I mean, doesn't anybody want to get further *away* from the Jung?"

"Probably, but most people are probably waiting to see what happens," Captain Tuplo said. "Besides, if no one is flying *into* the cluster, then that means there will be more ships competing for runs *outside* of the cluster. When people *do* start migrating further out, the competition will be greater."

"But so will the demand, right?" Neli asked.

"Perhaps," the captain agreed. "But it's all a bunch of ifs, nothing solid." The captain sighed, considering their situation. "I don't see how we have any choice but to sit and wait it out, just like everyone else."

"We've got enough propellant left to get off this rock, and land somewhere else, don't we?"

"Yup," Josh replied. "Maybe even two depart and landing cycles, *if* we jump out quick and jump in low, *both* cycles."

"And if we don't, we end up stranded elsewhere."

"Then we jump to someplace that likely has runs available," Marcus suggested.

"Great solution, Taggart," Captain Tuplo agreed sarcastically. "I don't suppose you know where that somewhere is? Because if you don't, if we're not *sure* that runs will be available where we jump to, then we'll most likely be stuck there." Captain Tuplo shook his head. "No, I'm not risking it. Haven may be a dusty, shithole of a world, but such as we are, the known is better than the unknown. We stay put for now. Sooner or later, either things will start moving, and we'll pick up a run so we can get off this rock and move further out, or the Jung will start expanding their territory beyond the cluster, and we'll have no choice in the matter."

"Surprise, surprise. You're playing it safe again," Neli muttered.

"No one is forcing you to stay on, Neli," Captain Tuplo said. "If you don't want to be here, I'd be happy to have Marcus drive you back to town."

Marcus cast Neli a stern look.

"Sorry, Connor," Neli apologized.

"It's all right, Neli," the captain replied. "We're all on edge right now."

"Maybe we could jump back to Ladila," Dalen suggested. "I heard they were planning to hire ships for full-time round trips."

Captain Tuplo got up from his seat and walked over to the counter in the Seiiki's galley. "What makes you think people are going to vacation on Ladila now?"

"It's outside the cluster, ain't it?"

"No one's gonna be wastin' their money going to some overpriced resort world," Marcus told him. "Not when the Jung might invade *their* homeworld while they're gone."

"Well, let's size up the situation, shall we?" the captain said, as he poured himself a cup of tea. "Neli?"

"Food and water for a week, maybe two. But like we talked about, the long night will start next week, and that should bring plenty of rain. And if we start harvesting all the wild molo around here sooner rather than later, I can probably have enough cleaned up and cured before our regular food runs out."

"Dalen, did you find anything of value in that wreckage?"

"There might be a few things we could swap, but they're gonna take a lot of cleanin', and we ain't gonna get much for them."

"Anything we can use to fix the ship?"

"Other than scrap metal to help reinforce the cargo ramp, no."

"So," the captain summarized, "our options are bad, worse, and worse still." The captain took a sip of his tea.

"And we're about out of tea as well, Captain," Neli said. "So we'd better start reusing the leaves we've got left for as long as we can squeeze some taste out of them."

"So, we conserve everything, go on diets, drink less tea, and hope the runs start coming in before the Jung show up," the captain said.

A distant clap of thunder erupted from outside the Seiiki.

"What the hell was that?" Dalen wondered.

"Thunderstorms?"

An alarm sounded from the cockpit.

"That's the sensors," Josh realized. "That wasn't thunder," he said, jumping up from his seat. "That was someone jumpin' in, right on top of us."

Everyone ran out of the galley and headed aft. Dalen glanced upward as they passed through the main passenger compartment, just in time to see a shuttle pass over them. "We just got overflown by a shuttle!" he yelled as he followed them through the hatch and into the cargo bay.

Captain Tuplo jumped down from the landing to the cargo deck, followed by Josh and Marcus. They ran toward the back, their weapons drawn, but before they could get to the edge of the cargo ramp, a dust cloud blew up the ramp and into their faces, stopping their progress.

Captain Tuplo closed his eyes and turned his

head away to avoid the cloud of dust, cringing at the scream of the visiting shuttle's engines as it touched down outside. Within a few seconds, the engines began to wind down, and the thrust wash that was blasting them began to subside.

As the dust settled, four men in full combat armor came walking toward them.

"This don't look promisin'," Marcus grumbled.

"They look like Ghatazhak," Josh commented.

"Not the way I remember them," Marcus disagreed. "Ybaran, maybe?"

"We might wanna holster our weapons, Cap'n," Marcus suggested.

"What the hell would the Ybarans want with us?" Captain Tuplo wondered. "Or the Ghatazhak, for that matter."

"I dunno, but both are pretty quick on the trigger," Marcus replied as he put his weapon away.

Josh did the same, as did Captain Tuplo.

"We best act friendly," Marcus said, as he started cautiously down the ramp.

Captain Tuplo and Josh followed suit, the three of them walking down the ramp, side by side, with Dalen and Neli following behind.

Connor examined the four men. "They gotta be Ybaran," he said under his breath.

"Why do you say that?" Josh wondered.

"You told me all the Ghatazhak were the same size."

Josh noticed that one of the four men was noticeably smaller than the others. As the four soldiers approached, the smaller of them removed his helmet, revealing that he, in fact, was a she. "Jess!" Josh cried out, breaking into a run toward her.

Jessica opened her arms and embraced Josh. "How are you doing, Josh?"

"I'm great!" Josh replied. He looked at the soldier next to her as he removed his helmet as well. "Lucius!" he said, reaching out to shake the general's hand.

"It is good to see you again, Joshua."

Captain Tuplo looked confused, as Marcus also went down the ramp to greet them.

"Marcus," Jessica greeted, embracing him as well.

"Good to see ya, Jess." Marcus looked at the general. "General."

"Mister Taggart."

Captain Tuplo walked tentatively down the ramp, unsure of what was going on. "You *know* these people?" he asked Marcus and Josh, as he stepped off the end of the ramp.

"It's good to see you again, Nathan," Jessica said, stepping forward. "I almost didn't recognize you, with the beard and all."

Captain Tuplo looked confused. "I'm afraid you've mistaken me for someone else, ma'am. The name's Connor. Connor Tuplo."

"She's not mistaken, Captain," Marcus said.

The captain looked at Marcus. "What the hell are you talking about?"

"He's right, Captain," Josh said. "Your *real* name is Nathan. Nathan Scott."

Thank you for reading this story.
(*A review would be greatly appreciated!*)

COMING SOON

"RESCUE"
Episode 2
of
The Frontiers Saga:
Rogue Castes

Visit us online at
www.frontierssaga.com
or on Facebook

Want to be notified when
new episodes are published?
Join our mailing list!
http://www.frontierssaga.com/mailinglist/